from

ICE

to

ASHES

from

ICE

to

ASHES

JESSICA SIMON

NeWest
PRESS

COPYRIGHT©JESSICA SIMON 2009

Library and Archives Canada Cataloguing in Publication
Simon, Jessica, 1964–
      From ice to ashes / Jessica Simon.
ISBN 978-1-897126-47-9
I. Title.
PS8637.I477F76 2009   C813'.6   C2009-902345-8

Editor for the Board: Douglas Barbour
Cover and interior design: Natalie Olsen
Cover image: Natalie Olsen
Author photo: Richard Hartmier

While the Yukon Arctic Ultra is an actual race, this book is a work of fiction. Any similarities to places, people and events are purely coincidental.

NeWest Press acknowledges the support of the Canada Council for the Arts, the Alberta Foundation for the Arts and the Edmonton Arts Council for our publishing program. We also acknowledge the financial support of the Government of Canada through the Book Publishing Industry Development Program (BPIDP).

NeWest Press   #201 8540–109 Street Edmonton, Alberta T6G 1E6
780.432.9427 www.newestpress.com

No bison were harmed in the making of this book.
We are committed to protecting the environment and to the responsible use of natural resources. This book was printed on 100% post-consumer recycled paper.

1 2 3 4 5 12 11 10 09   printed and bound in Canada

PROLOGUE

Footsteps marched toward Annabeth in the electrical room. She flinched, clipped the system fault indicator and dropped her strippers. Bending down to pick them up, she saw two pairs of military-issue work boots stop at her door.

She jammed her snips in the bib pocket of her coveralls and stood erect in front of a wall of panel boxes. A wisp of hair near her temple trembled, as did her hands. She willed the quick breathing in her chest to slow.

Her supervisor, a burly master electrician accompanied by a soldier with the name "Orez" stitched over his breast pocket, said, "The master sergeant's looking for the commanding officer. Have you seen him?"

"No," Annabeth replied. Behind her petite athletic build, the severed wire swayed. Orez's line of sight changed, caught by the motion. Jitters wobbled from her legs to her brain. "I wasn't aware the lieutenant colonel was here," she said before her mouth ran dry. "He better find me working instead of talking."

"What a gal you are, Secord," said her foreman, sliding his hard hat back on his balding head. "Work six tens a week and still willing to come in on your days off to fine tune the controls. Come on, Orez. Axton's probably in the coffee room." The men turned and left the room. "I don't know where she gets it," Annabeth overheard her chief mutter as the men's unison tread carried on down the hall.

She kicked closed the door they'd left ajar, and yanked the wires out of the conduit. This was the end. After

9

working on this sub-contract at the post for six months, she'd had her fill of the Army Corps of Engineers. Armed co-workers gave her the creeps. Concentrating on the job, she turned her back on the sector's security camera and completed the remaining circuits, alone.

An hour later, satisfied that her work was seamless, she packed her tools, locked up the panel room and left. The dingy green hall lighting flickered on her way to ground level, telling her what to expect for weather above. Sure enough a storm raged over the tundra. Through a window by the exit, she saw nothing but dark flatness cut by blowing snow that drifted against the side of her car, the only vehicle on the miles-wide flood plain. She had to put her whole body into opening the door to the parking lot.

Out on the barren land, the wind ripped south in a twenty-mile-per-hour shimmy to the Alaska Range. The hood of her nylon parka pressed against her round cheeks and billowed on the lee side, catching a whistling eddy in her eardrum. With both hands she closed the faux fur ruff tight around her face, but the wind found her sleeves and rushed up to her elbows.

Hunched under the icy torment, she ran to her car, unplugged the block heater and climbed in. Crystal cold irritation in her lungs left her coughing. She pumped the gas pedal twice, stamped down on it and turned the ignition, urging the starter to catch before the battery died.

Her LeBaron had seen its day as a luxury sedan. Now the heap lurched forward on frost-flattened square tires for two miles through the double fencing around Fort Greely and into the Alaska night. At the Richardson Highway,

Annabeth turned right for the five-mile drive north to Delta Junction.

If her boss really wanted to know how she could work such hours, he need only drive a mile up the road to the rutted track on her left to the commune where she'd been raised. Their leader, a mail-order minister, had thought nothing of twelve-, fourteen- or even eighteen-hour prayer fasts when stocks were low.

Annabeth slowed the car as she passed the wooden WELCOME TO DELTA JUNCTION sign boasting the town's reputation as Alaska's Friendly Frontier. Quite the opposite had been her experience. "Wacko Jesus freak commie hippie," the God-fearing Christian army brats had called her in high school while they beat the daylights out of her. If they knew her now they'd be the ones crying home to mama.

Where the Richardson and the Alaska highways met was Bull's Eye Hunting and Sports, owned by her only friend, Evy Simpson. Evy had also felt the backlash of Delta's residents when she'd publicly announced her dissent against the Ground-based Missile Defense system being built at Fort Greely.

Annabeth zigzagged through the Junction to a broken-down farm, abandoned when the land and the climate had defeated the pioneers. Her house was a crappy trailer tossed on the property to rot. It sat under the snow, the roof almost as caved in as the barn behind it, looking like a stepped-on Crunchie bar, chocolate-brown siding flaking off orange sponge-toffee insulation. The effect continued inside with yellow spray-foam sealing all the window frames.

Annabeth dropped her toolbox under the boot rack and tossed her coat on a chair in the two steps it took to cross the kitchen to the beer in her fridge. She flicked on the living room light and clicked on the television before sinking into her ratty second-hand sofa.

Rolling ads flipped across the TV screen and Annabeth looked long and hard at the houseboat for sale in Valdez. Hopefully it wouldn't be sold before she was paid. She finished her beer, got another and opened her computer bag beside the phone on the coffee table. At the top of the hour, she dialled.

Across the border, in Canada's Yukon, a man answered. Annabeth leaned back and put her size-five feet up on the coffee table. She adjusted her camera on the low book-shelf beside her and plugged it into her laptop. "It's me," she said. "Are you sitting near your mini-cam?" In a moment, her screen flickered and she was looking at a cluttered dining table in Whitehorse's Riverdale subdivision. Cramped Arabic script crawled across a pale green topographic map.

"Change the angle, Omar," she said. "I'm looking at the table." The picture jerked around the room. A shaded lamp, the wing of an armchair and a swatch of Persian rug splashed over her screen until it settled on the face of Omar Ahmed, her smiling lover.

"That's better. What're you doing?" she asked.

"Plotting where I will stop for prayer during the Yukon Arctic Ultra." The dark curl that fell over his forehead threw a pang of lust between Annabeth's legs. He held up the Dawson 1:250 000 map, and before he lowered it, she had her coveralls off and her blouse open to her underwear.

"How do I look?" she teased.

"Yes, I would take you in my arms right now if I could."

Annabeth loved the cadence of Omar's English, even from five hundred miles away. She hung on to his every word.

"I met Markus Fanger recently," he said. "He is a volunteer on the Ultra race, an auxiliary constable with the Mounted Police."

She bolted upright and swung her legs off the couch. "A cop came to your house?"

"Yes, and thank Allah he cannot read Arabic. I was able to conceal my plans. And I asked him many questions about the trail."

"That's enough, Omar. You can't do this anymore. It won't work."

His tone darkened. "I can and it will. We have everything in place."

The honey-thick braid she flipped over her shoulder smacked the newspaper on the back of the sofa. She sulked. He lived for the risk, but she wasn't going to fight about it again tonight.

"Did you have a holiday recently? Homeland security upped the alert and I must'a had to show my pass about a million times."

"Yesterday. It was Eid-ul-Adha, the Festival of Sacrifice."

"Sounds gruesome. Tell me there aren't any virgins involved."

Omar laughed. "Do not worry. It is a time to give gifts to friends and family and, of course, the poor. You are perfectly safe."

She sensed the skin between her curved brows pinch. "That's easy for you to say. You aren't surrounded by the agents of destruction."

Creases in his face bracketed a small smile. "Tell me everything, Kleine." Annabeth loved Omar's terms of endearment. The words didn't sound as lame as they did in English.

She stretched out. "Yesterday we were in and out lugging conduit and every time, at every door, they had to check that my hair matched my face. All day. By the end of it, I was so mad I didn't look anything like my photo. God, I hate the military." She put her beer to her lips and tipped it up for a deep swallow. "And today I could'a just about died when my boss came in looking for the CO. He had a Master Sergeant Orez with him, and I'm sure it must'a looked pretty suspicious with a lead hanging there."

"Have you heard anything since?" Omar's question hardened to earnest concern.

"No. I shoved the wire into the bundle in the box. But I tell you, Omar, I've had about all I can stand." Propped up on one elbow, she shook her index finger at him. "Politics and religion have ruined my life enough. As soon as I have my money, I'm taking my little girl back from Marty and we are getting out of the North."

She saw Omar touch her face on his laptop. "It is not much longer now." Annabeth's sadness melted.

"You know, the stupid thing is my ex thinks I'm working here for the money. Which is true, but Marty doesn't understand. All I want is a future. 'What about our peace marches?' he asked. 'The no nuke rallies? The anti-war petitions?' What about our daughter, that's what I say. This way we'll have enough money for whatever Marie needs. It's called family planning, and it's more than giving birth to a new Permanent Fund Dividend cheque every year, like my folks did."

"I saw Marie, briefly, at the RunYukon time trials," Omar said, his tone eased.

Annabeth cut off her own rant. "How did she look? Is she happy?"

"She seemed so."

"Does she miss me?" She was on her feet now.

"I could not tell from the distance, but, yes, if she is like me, she does. Very much."

"We'll show them." Annabeth wiped her eyes with a throw blanket and murmured, "Mommy'll be with you real soon, baby." Focusing on the larger problem, she pulled herself together. "Did you talk to Marty? Is he going to let me bring Marie here?" Annabeth paced around her furniture.

"No, not yet. Please, sit." She did, and listened. "I did talk to him, but his lawyer advises against the visit."

"You said you'd help me get custody. If I did for you, you'd do for me, remember?"

"Yes, I remember," he said, controlled.

"Well, I've done for you and now I want my little girl. She needs me."

"But not before we are ready. In two weeks I will be at the Arctic Ultra startline. Will you be at the finish?"

"Yes." With less conviction than she'd hoped for, she added, "But this is definitely the last favour, Omar. I mean it."

Her screen went blank and her phone went dead.

ONE

Granted power to speak freely, Markus Fanger closed his hands firmly around the talking stick and addressed the court. "I am honoured that you have included me in this circle sentencing ceremony, and as thanks I offer to personally supervise Donjek Stoneman's community service."

The last time he'd held the talking stick was to return it as property stolen from the Tr'ondëk Hwëch'in First Nation. Today, for the first time, he used the influential artefact for its intended purpose, to mediate discussion —in this case, about how a community could divert a young offender. Fanger could no longer deny his place in the history of one of the Yukon's fourteen First Nations.

The talking stick, a weighty symbol of free speech, was a sculpted ivory shaft crafted generations ago from the rough fossil of a mammoth tusk. Crow, Maker of the World, stared at Fanger from the yellowed ages of tradition. On the opposing face, Wolf looked out with eyes and snout stained black between fiery-red cheekbones. Bands of minerals —red, yellow, black and white —recalled the power of the four directions. Swirls of malachite and azurite inlaid in the calcium reminded the bearer of their stewardship over the mountains and rivers.

Fanger laid the stick on the podium and took his seat. Across from him, Constable Jake Stoneman nodded to his nephew on his right. The accused turned away, but met his father Edwin's lowered head. Approaching them, the judge's robe brushed past the feet and chairs of observers along the aisle to the lectern.

Fanger kept his eye on Donjek, who twisted back and forth in his swivel chair, not bothering to hide his contempt for the judge, the man who had the power to commute his sentence from closed custody to one deemed fair by the elders.

The magistrate lifted the mace in a sure grasp. "The court accepts Mr. Fanger's generous offer." His curt nod to the stenographer confirmed the decision was recorded. "Court is adjourned."

Donjek's aunt, Donna, stood, poised and assured, and in Northern Tutchone gave the closing prayer. It was a way for Dawson City's First Nation to honour her as the chief in the neighbouring town of Pelly Crossing. Donna had experience with all levels of the law; when her husband Jake was away, she was the community's unofficial member-on-duty.

Approvals circled through the crowd as the assembly broke. Several people stuffed their feet into snowpack boots and ran out for a cigarette. Before Fanger escaped the stuffy chamber to join them, a youth worker let him know she would brief him after crossing the T's and dotting the I's on Donjek's probation order. Then she bustled over to the Stoneman family and led Donjek upstairs to her office. Fanger heard the teen's cuffs slap the floor; the kid in oversized jeans trailed behind the batik scarf that accented his probation officer's maroon blazer.

Fanger shrugged into his heavy parka and stepped out to the wide porch for a smoke. The wolverine ruff around his hood kept frost from building up on his beard and moustache. His hands felt the chill, but the low, fiery ball of sunshine on the horizon was the picture of warmth. Jake and his brother Edwin joined him.

Fanger flicked the butt of his rolled tobacco over a snowbank. "I love this time of year, having an extra hour of light at the end of the day," he said to them.

"Especially after an all-day meeting," said Jake. Seeing the men together, Fanger saw how his friend would age. Jake's stalwart frame would always be impressive, but in the future his proud bearing would be tempered with Edwin's outlook of wisdom. Fanger respected that outlook and hoped their idea for Donjek to complete his sentence on the Ultra would work to reform him.

"We came out to start the truck," Jake said as he jogged down the timber steps to his vehicle.

"Are you coming over for dinner?" Edwin asked.

"Gladly," Fanger answered, "but I don't know how long the PO's going to keep me."

"Janice? She won't take long. You probably noticed she's not one to skip meals."

"Right. Okay then, I'll be there." Fanger fished his keys out of his pocket. "My truck wasn't plugged in. I should let it warm up, too." Under the skiff of snow that blew across the parking lot, a row of footprints trailed from Fanger's truck—a pile of rust so old it said Datsun on the tailgate—to a line of nearby trees. He opened the door and empties clattered around his feet. "Das gibt's doch nicht! I don't believe this." He put his hand over his nose.

"What?" Edwin and Jake hurried over. The stench

18

of strong beer and stale cigarettes assaulted them from the cab.

"While we were inside working on Donjek's case, some idiot hosted a party in my truck." Fanger fired the cans into the box of the pickup.

From the passenger side, Jake dumped the ashtray into a coffee-rimmed paper cup. "At least they didn't set it on fire like they did to Joey Masters' truck last week." He closed the door and tossed the garbage. "When the weather warms up, you can lock your truck again without being afraid it'll freeze permanently shut."

Fanger got behind the wheel. "It's exactly this kind of constant nuisance crime — vandalism, stealing cars, ripping off the neighbours — that makes people think circle sentencing is a joke."

"Well, it sure doesn't make our job easier," Jake said.

The brakes and the gas were crusted in slush. Fanger pumped them loose, turned on the ignition and let the starter whine to life. When the motor stopped sputtering, he left it running and walked back to the band hall.

"Fifteen or more cases a week in a place the size of Dawson is too many," Fanger said. "I mean, there are only a thousand people living around here. It's obvious jail hasn't helped them."

Jake and Edwin quick-stepped to keep up with Fanger's long stride. "Keep Donny out of jail and we can prove diversion works," said Jake. "I'm trusting you to make it a success."

Fanger halted.

Edwin neared. "You are a good friend," he said. "I am not young. You will teach Donny something I can't." He took Fanger's hand in his own, which was as worked and worn as the hides he tanned. The elder's eyes misted, but it could have been the winter dryness.

Inside, Janice steered Fanger into the probation office with an imperious wave. "I understand the arrangement you and the judge worked out with the Stoneman family," she said, sitting. "And I am aware of your service as an auxiliary constable for the RCMP. But I would like to hear more about what you have planned for Donjek, Mr. Fanger."

"I need another volunteer to staff a checkpoint on the Yukon Arctic Ultra race. I think I just got one."

"And what makes you think Donjek would be an asset to the race?"

"He'll be out on the land and I need his skills."

"And what skills would those be?"

"Edwin says Donjek knows the trails from hunting, and he's volunteered at the Yukon Quest checkpoint at the campground, too."

"And you'll be taking him with you to Whitehorse for a few days, is that right?"

"Yeah, to help with the race prep."

"Well, let me remind you of our mission statement," she said. "Youth intervention must be handled very carefully." From a drawer, Janice pulled out a thick case file.

Fanger learned a whole new vocabulary in fifteen minutes. Sheaves of paper, white, yellow and pink, sat in bales on Janice's desk—narrow time sheets, offender reports, supervisor feedback, department evaluations. No young offender's life story was going unwritten, but as far as

Fanger knew, intervention meant listening rather than feeding filing cabinets.

"In case of emergency I call you, right?" he asked. "If something happens."

"What can? The terms of our insurance for youth-in-care prevent young offenders from engaging in any high-risk activity. That's as much to protect Donjek as it is us."

How could they expect to turn boys into men when puberty itself is a high-risk activity? The answer was not long coming. Donjek would be tracked like a radio-collared alpha male.

"This is a formative stage in Donjek's development, and although diversion has made great gains recently, more traditional restraints will apply." The first of many documents she gave Fanger described the security protocol. Not a mere list of do's and don't's, the handbook governing Donjek's life ran to several pages — don't consort with known offenders, remain under supervision at all times, no operating motor vehicles, respect the curfew. Violation of any and the offender would be remanded to custody.

"I realize these may seem like strict controls, but I must insist they are kept in place," Janice said.

"Except for motor vehicles. We're sledding out to the checkpoint."

"Under your personal supervision. And with a helmet."

Fanger nodded. "What if Donjek's got a problem with this?"

"That doesn't really come into it. These are the conditions of his sentence. But here's my number if anything comes up." She handed him a business card. He picked it up and, with a load of report forms and regulations under his arm, left the band office.

Thin shadows of lodgepole pines crossed the box of Fanger's truck. He shifted the folders, tossed them onto the passenger seat and drove away.

On the ice bridge he crawled across the river in second gear. At the Top of the World Highway, he ploughed through west Dawson in four-high before turning into Edwin Stoneman's driveway. Dogs barked and Jake opened the front door before Fanger had a sleeping bag spread over the warm engine.

"Right on time, Fanger. I knew Janice wouldn't keep us waiting."

In the mudroom, Fanger shucked his coat and snow-packs but kept the boot liners on as slippers. Jake led him down the hall past generations of family in black-and-white, colour and sepia. Moosemeat on the fry drew him into the kitchen. Juice dripped from the steaks that Donjek's mother, Shirley, turned in the cast pan. Donna, wearing an apron over the hand-knit sweater she had worn in court, put the last place setting on the table and pulled out a chair for her husband Jake, who poured coffee for himself and Fanger.

A plywood door at the back of the kitchen opened, and Edwin entered with Donjek. They hung their coats on pegs near the stove and sat at the table. Donjek pulled a smoke out from behind his ear. "Don't light that now," Shirley scolded him. "Dinner's ready." She used both hands to move the pan to the trivet in the centre of the table.

Edwin thanked the Creator for the day's judgments and the food in their home. Then the dishes circled the table.

No one spoke more than to ask for butter or salt while they ate in familiar quiet. The flavour of the land filled Fanger's mouth with each bite of wild meat. He soaked up the savoury juices with a piece of bannock.

After dinner Fanger conscripted himself and Donjek to do the dishes, "as soon as we've had a smoke." The youth escaped for the break through the back door. Fanger followed him and, from the kitchen porch, looked over a village of two dozen husky-cross pullers staked out in front of their dog boxes. Donjek had his back to him, facing an array of snowmobiles in the yard. A well-tuned machine or dog team was the best transportation on this side of Dawson, where the highway ended and mountain trails began.

"Working the checkpoint is different. It's work, but it's interesting," Fanger said to break the silence. "You looking forward to it?"

"You think if I was, I would'a been sentenced to it?" Donjek turned to Fanger and exhaled a long tobacco breath. "Look, I know you cooked up this culture camp idea with my dad and Uncle Jake, but don't think I don't see what you're trying to prove, Great White Saviour. You and that judge."

"I've known your judge — Ian — since you were a baby," Fanger said. "And fifteen years ago, when he started practising, you would have been sent to the young offender's facility in Whitehorse — where you probably would have graduated to adult corrections right next door." Fanger didn't bother telling Donjek that he was given this chance because of Ian's determination to win recognition for aboriginal justice in common law.

"It would be better than listening to my dad and uncle going on about how great you are. I think you're a wannabe Indian and you need a real one around, like me, to look after you."

"If that's the case, then I'll be counting on you." Fanger mashed out his cigarette and went inside. A moment later, Donjek followed. At the porcelain double sink they worked shoulder to shoulder.

Shirley spooned leaf-tea into a teapot. "You sure you fellows know what you're doing?" she asked. "Tell me what it is again." She tucked a strand of mostly salt hair, with a dash of pepper, behind her ear.

"It's a cross-country race. The contestants can either run, ski or ride a bicycle from here to Tok," Fanger replied.

"On the Trek Over the Top route. Jake told me that part." With more than a hint of nervousness, she added, "But Tok's three hundred kilometres away, and in Alaska."

"There are shorter distances, too," Fanger said. "The marathon stops at a lookout on the Top of the World Highway, and our checkpoint at Little Gold is the hundred-K finish line."

"I thought you said you'd only be out there a few days?"

"That's what makes the race extreme. From two PM on February twenty-first, participants have seventy-two hours to complete the hundred-kilometre run, and five more days for the rest of the course."

"Are you serious? That's fast." Shirley nudged her son, who was quietly drying cutlery. "What do you think, Donny? This will be the quickest you've ever had your community service done." The clatter of dry knives and forks falling into a willow basket on the table drowned out

24

his reply. Shirley shrugged her bony shoulders at Fanger. What's a mother to do?

Fanger couldn't remember if he'd driven his own mother this crazy when he was a teenager in Germany. He dried his hands and then, carrying a tray of cups, followed Shirley down the hall to the living room. Donjek stayed behind, absorbed in wiping the counters.

Shirley pointed to a steamer trunk where Fanger set the tray. She put down a pot of coffee and a freshly iced cake. Jake and Donna sat together on the sofa under the mount of Edwin's prize caribou. The hunter himself rocked in his recliner. Fanger declined Shirley's offer of her chair—the one with a crocheted afghan draped over the worn arms and back—and took the footstool beside Jake. Shirley served, elders and guests first.

"It's a good thing you decided to stay on with the race this year," Jake said as he poured coffee for his brother and Fanger. "What was that, anyway, about you quitting?"

"You heard that, nah? It's true I asked the race director to look for a replacement. The first two years were enough, but when the course was moved from the TransCanada Trail to here, I though I'd better stay. This trail is more challenging, and there're all-new volunteers." Fanger blew across the top of his cup. "The logistics alone have been a nightmare. All the marathoners and mid-distance runners have to be shuttled out by snowmobile. But we get the Americans' help on their side of the border, and their sponsorship."

Fanger pulled out a notebook and pencil from his pocket and, resting on the cut-burl end table beside his chair, wrote while they talked—a list of specific tasks and the supplies they would need. Donjek, who had slipped in to sit beside his aunt, read Fanger's notes and passed them to Donna. "You know I was sentenced to a hundred and eighty hours, not eighteen hundred," Donjek said.

"People are depending on you to do your share," Donna said, her quiet assurance emphasizing the responsibility that had landed in her nephew's lap.

Edwin rose and stood by the photos in the hall. "Our family have been members of the Royal Canadian Mounted Police for three generations, Donny. You are not going to become a career criminal."

Fanger woke in the dark the next morning and, before it lifted, he'd met with the management of the Gambler's Den hotel for a room quote and meal plans for the racers.

After breakfast he drove to Edwin's to pick up Donjek. Since last night, his conscience nagged—what did he, a childless single man, think he knew about kids? Especially kids with attitude. And now he was taking the kid to Whitehorse with him. Truly the last thing he expected to see was an eager assistant.

Donjek shot out the door and came at Fanger full speed. Shirley bustled behind her son and slapped a scarf over his shoulder. "You stay out of trouble, up there in Whitehorse. I don't want any more court dates."

The kid slammed his duffel into Fanger's chest. Fanger slammed the door shut on his ass. "No worries, Shirley. I'll keep an eye on him." He tossed the Flames bag into the box and, ignoring Donjek's complaints, climbed in. "Sorry, the porter quit." In response, Donjek tossed a paper bag to him.

"What's this?" Fanger folded the top back, and the meaty richness of game filled the truck.

"You want 'em? Keep 'em. I got to take some to my cousin, too, when we're in the city. My mom's so old-fashioned. Did you hear her saying I was going up to Whitehorse?" People his age drove down, south, to Whitehorse. Only old timers talked about going upstream. "Like I'm taking a paddlewheeler or something." He looked around Fanger's truck. "This thing's not much younger, is it?"

"Quit giving everyone a hard time. We'll have the moose links for dinner. And you'll tell Shirley you loved it." Fanger put the truck in gear. "Let's go. I want to be on the road before sun-up."

"Better hurry," Donjek said. "The sky's already light." He slumped against the door and huddled in his jacket. "Geez, it's cold in here," was his last comment before he slid his ball cap down over his eyes.

Fanger drove southbound on an empty highway. He put Lynyrd Skynyrd in the cassette player to drown out any more second thoughts about what he was getting himself into.

At Stone Boat Swamp, a pothole and the freezing air that poured over his knees jolted Fanger to attention. The blast from under the dash woke his passenger, who resumed his complaints. "What's the matter with your truck, man? It's stalling."

Fanger pulled over before the motor conked out cold —fuel gelled in the lines, pistons frozen in the cylinders. "Wait here," he said. "I'll check the cardboard out front."

Sure enough, one of the tie wraps holding the windbreak against the radiator grille had snapped, letting a ninety-kilometre sub-arctic gale super cool the engine. Fanger felt around behind the driver's seat and found a roll of duct tape lying near some candles. By the time he fixed the flattened box in place, Donjek was pretending to be asleep. Fanger drove on and let zz Top fill the silence, then George Thorogood, then Steve Earle.

A sign boasting the world's biggest cinnamon buns at Braeburn rang the dinner bell in Fanger's stomach. He slewed his truck off the highway and Donjek bobbled awake. The windsock across the road lifted its lazy tail, blinked in the glare of the sun-crusted landscape and dropped.

Ice glaciated the windowpanes, distorting the faces in the restaurant. Inside, Fanger led Donjek over the frost-heaved linoleum to a table beside a dry, cracked, upright piano. Their waitress, the Rendezvous Queen's Miss Congeniality, grabbed the coffeepot and greeted them. She sat in the empty seat beside Fanger to take their order. "How's it going setting up the new trail?" she asked.

Fanger told her the truth: a lot harder than he thought it would be. "I've had a hell of a time getting volunteers, what with events like the Quest and Rendezvous running at the same time." With every dog handler in the territory helping mushers on the Yukon Quest's thousand-mile dog sled race, and everyone else involved with the Yukon Sourdough Rendezvous, Whitehorse's annual winter festival, it was a miracle Fanger had managed to round up enough volunteers to stage the Ultra. But that was only one of the challenges. "This new course will be tougher on the racers, too." He looked at the topography outside. "The elevation gains around here are gradual. On the Top of the World there's wind and altitude to deal with. If this cold snap doesn't break, their gear will."

"It's too late to switch, eh?" Her smile made the invitation appealing. "We'll miss you guys, all the activity. It was fun last year," she said before leaving to serve a new customer.

Fanger rolled a cigarette and Donjek lit one of his own. "You sounded a lot more confident yesterday in front of my family," he said.

"If something happens, we're a hundred kilometres from Dawson and another hundred and twenty miles from Tok with no road access in between. At least here we had the highway." Fanger looked out the window. A pack of truck-stop dogs chased a coyote across the road, over the Cinnamon Bun Airstrip and into the carnivorous wilds.

"You don't have to tell me. I know what the country is like out there," Donjek said. He butted his smoke when their burgers arrived, bulging out of homemade buns — homemade because factory buns just weren't big enough. Fanger ate half and took the rest with him when they left twenty-five minutes later.

Donjek remained shaded behind his sunglasses and tuned into his Walkman for the last forty-five minutes of the drive.

At three in the afternoon, school buses clogged Whitehorse's downtown streets. Fanger caught red lights all the way to the log cabin he called home. It butted up against a two-hundred-foot clay cliff that kept the airport plateau above from landing on his roof. The city had never planned to have houses built under a landslide zone but, in 1942 when the US Army started nailing up shacks for its

Alaska Highway road-building crew, no one cared where they lived, as long as it was clad to weather and had a working stove.

Fanger scuffed a berm of snow away from the stoop and stepped inside to where his stove squatted in his chill, ten-by-twelve living room. The steel drum was the central fixture of the whole house. Snow fell from his boots as he kneeled down in front of the cold barrel and clanged open the door. He lit crumpled paper and kindling to get a flame, then added some split logs and a few full rounds to the blaze to hold the heat.

Donjek shouldered into the mudroom and dropped his stuff. The phone rang from the cushions on the sofa and Fanger shoved aside a pile of German magazines to find the receiver. It was Jenn Strider, registrar of the Yukon Arctic Ultra.

"Hey, Fanger. I'm at the Constantine," she yelled. Blaring over her voice was the hockey game broadcast from the Saddledome. "The trail guys are here and we sort of started having a meeting. Can you join us?" Fanger and Jenn had been organizing the Ultra since November, and now that the race was just weeks away, all the last minute details were coming together.

"Just a sec." Fanger held his hand over the mouthpiece to speak with Donjek, whose cousin worked as the program coordinator at the Skookum Jim Friendship Centre. Donjek could meet with him, as Shirley had asked, while Fanger met with the trail crew.

He uncovered the phone to answer. "I just got home and the house is cold, but sure, I'll be there soon." Fanger closed the stove's draft flue and latched the plate door shut.

Fanger dropped off Donjek at Skookies on Third Ave, and from there it was five minutes to the hotel that was guarded by a four-storey pine Mountie. In the tropically warm, cabana-style bar, the crowd enjoyed a taste of summer at the end of a winter day.

Jenn wasn't kidding about the meeting-in-progress. Fanger spotted her in energetic discussion with five others at a table for four. She waved to him across the full-to-capacity room just as a server arrived with fresh pints. "Here, Fanger, we ordered you a Grizzly," Jenn said, passing one to him.

Fanger sat in the only empty chair in the place, took a healthy first gulp and set down the beer to reach room temperature—it wouldn't take long under the heat lamps overhead. He spread open his coat. The arms draped to the floor.

"Registration ended yesterday and there's over forty people signed up," Jenn reported. She unfolded a foolscap sheet and handed it to Fanger. "I'm taking this to customs tomorrow. We finally got the list today." Obtaining clearance for the athletes, people from every corner of the world, had required the most limber bureaucratic gymnastics.

"At last." Fanger counted the stars beside novice runners. "Over a third of them have never been in a northern race," he said. "They have no idea what winter is."

"I know. The Canadians and Americans from Outside should manage okay. I am concerned about these entries, though." She pointed to the home countries listed beside the names of racers from Guatemala, Mexico and Spain.

"What about this one? Omar Ahmed?" Fanger asked. "He's from Morocco."

"Oh, Omar?" Jenn shrugged. "He's the only one I'm not worried about." Jenn's husband, George, snickered, and beside him, Ted, the trail crew boss, chortled. Marty, a local racer, hid his long face behind the glass he upended at his thick lips. "What's so funny?" Fanger asked Jenn. Laughter burst over them.

Ted thumped his stout chest and caught his breath. "Nothing, Fanger. Nothing. Just that you ask who this Omar is, and Jenn says she's not worried about him. That's right she's not worried. The rest of us are turned to stone waiting to see what'll happen next."

TWO

Fanger took out his tobacco and rolled a cigarette. "What do you mean, 'what'll happen next?' You make it sound like a comedy routine." Fanger curled the pouch closed and slid the ashtray closer.

Ted snorted. "Ask George here what happened when they went hunting."

"What did you have to bring that up for?" George, a familiar face on the sidelines of the Ultra, reddened to his ears. "You have such a big mouth, Ted."

The trail chief protested. "It's the best hunting story this year."

"Well, how was the guy supposed to know? I'm sure he thinks our hunting methods are heathen, too."

Fanger lit his smoke and settled in.

"Tell him," Ted said.

Marty, who sat nearest to the door, stood and mumbled, "Heard it," before hurrying toward the men's room.

George winked at his wife. He took a deep breath and a swig of his beer. "It's nothing really, but Jenn and I thought it'd be cool to take Omar out on the land. You know, a real experience, not just running through it. Keep in mind, this Ahmed is a Muslim. He's got a different culture, different traditions — it's not his fault, really. He takes his religion seriously."

"All right, George. You're culturally sensitive," Ted grumbled. "Get on with the story."

"I am. He was lamenting the lack of halal meat here. That's stuff he's permitted by Allah to eat." George waved to heaven. "We asked if he could eat wild meat and he said there was nothing against it in the Qur'an. So in October he comes out with us. We're on the land about three days before a great bull passes our camp. Would'a filled my freezer and the wall over the mantel. We track it into the next day, and when we call it out of the bush, it's a beauty. With a blanket Jenn could'a curled up and slept in the rack. I'm sure if we hadn't'a come along, that bull would'a had the time of his life in the rut." Beside George, Ted's laughing shook their table.

"So, I take up a bead on him and put a shot clean through the heart and lung. He drops right there in front of us, but before I can lower my gun, Omar starts shouting in Arabic, falls onto the animal's neck and slits its throat."

"What?" Fanger's glass hit the table hard. "You're kidding."

"No." George waved the waitress over. "Apparently immediate bloodletting and prayer is part of what makes the meat kosher. Or, well, not kosher, but you know what I mean." Fanger laughed. "He really wrecked a nice mount cutting the cape like that." That set everyone going.

"And then at dinner, he has the nerve to say he doesn't much care for moosemeat, because 'it doesn't taste anything like lamb.'" Guffaws spilled George's Grizzly. "Thanks, Ted." He wiped beer off the front of his overalls.

"I'll get you another." Ted spoke to the waitress, who was already at his elbow. Her smile made paying for the mess worth every cent.

"You're hardly being fair," Jenn said, leaping to Ahmed's defense.

"So, what makes a north African better able to withstand winter than a Spaniard?" Fanger asked. He gave her back the list, which she tucked into the pocket of her Mother Hubbard parka.

"He's been here since June training with RunYukon and the orienteers. We even got him out snowshoeing." Jenn left out the fact that Ahmed got lost where a sharpshooter punk had blown half the trail markers to splinters with a twelve gauge. Up until then, he'd been flying along the trail, improving his mid-field finishes. It cost thirty minutes of following blue flagging from a previous run to get back on course, but telling him how much faster he was in spite of the detour didn't take the sting out of having women run circles around him. He'd given Jenn a brusque "expected nothing less of myself" when she'd calculated his overall speed.

Ted argued with her assessment of the runner. "That doesn't mean he can hack it at minus twenty. I want to reduce the risk out there. The more my checkers and trail monitors know, the better prepared they'll be. Right, Jerry?"

The man, slouched in the seat across from Fanger, nodded. Jerry never had much to say, preferring to eat up all the gossip and spit out the bones later.

The waitress brought a new round and put menus in front of Fanger and the others. The sledders turned their attention to the big screen in time to cheer Calgary's goal against the Avalanche. Ted emptied half his glass and crossed his arms. Team Polaris stretched across his hard-riding shoulders.

Fanger unfolded the newsprint menu that declared the selection GOLD! GOLD! GOLD! GOLD! He read the list of appetizers running down Tappan Adney's pencil drawing of a mineshaft drifted out in winter. Around it, miners held screening sieves exactly like the punctured gold pans hanging from the ceiling of the tavern.

"What's this guy do for a living anyway that he can take off for eight months?" Fanger asked Jenn.

"He's some sort of contractor in Morocco. That's how he heard about the race; a Brit on his crew ran last year. Omar had a leave of absence, so he decided to come here and train."

"That's a long time to be away from his family."

"I guess he's been away before. He spends a lot of time in Germany."

"What for?" Fanger had left his former homeland years ago; he couldn't imagine returning, not even for love.

"Well, Omar's from Germany," Jenn replied. "Actually it's very romantic. He met his wife at a mosque in Hamburg when she was studying medicine or something. They

35

got married, but when she finished school she returned to Morocco where a job was waiting for her. Since Omar didn't have work, he followed her and has lived there ever since. It's such a bold step, so out of the ordinary in Muslim culture, or ours for that matter, when the husband follows the wife." Fanger hadn't when he'd once been faced with the same decision.

"He goes back to Germany to visit his folks often," Jenn said. Fanger would rather bring his parents to the Yukon. They'd visited once and after that they'd joined the jet set. Their last postcard was from Majorca.

The waitress arrived to take their order. Fanger wondered how much Ted was tipping her to get such attention in the packed bar. She stepped aside when Marty returned to his seat and asked for his regular. Ted and Jerry offered to split a plate of nachos with Fanger, but he declined; he'd have dinner at home with Donjek. But before then, he wanted to know what had happened while he'd been in Dawson.

George confirmed the banquet hall booking at the Constantine, and Jerry had rented a fleet of vans for shuttles. He had also finagled a fuel rebate from the local distributor. "Make sure you write their name large in the thank-you ads," Ted said. Fanger wrote "large thank you" in his notebook and showed it to the crew chief to confirm.

Jenn intervened with the speaker's list. The Trappers Association had yet to confirm, but a Quest racer was scheduled to talk about the challenges on the trail. The Alaskans were ready on their side of the trail.

"Yukon Ambulance will give the racers a quick spiel about hypothermia and how Medevac works here," Jenn said. Or rather *doesn't* work, at least not after dark, Fanger knew. There wouldn't be any air-assisted night rescues — but he'd worry about that at the emergency meeting.

"What about the checkpoints?" Ted asked Fanger. "I heard you got Donjek Stoneman helping you."

How did he know already? "Yeah we're going to the checkpoints as soon as we're done in town here. Is there a problem with that?"

"In all my years as a guard up at the jail, I never seen this voodoo justice work." He emptied his glass. "How you going to get this past the Americans? They'll never let a convicted felon across."

"Then I'll keep him on this side of the border."

"I'd hate to see this race wrecked because of social work. If the kid couldn't do the time, he shouldn't'a done the crime."

"Don't let politics keep you from speaking your mind, Ted," Fanger muttered into the glass he drained.

"Well, you trust a thief at your checkpoint?"

Fanger was saved from answering when Corporal La-Rouge entered. His parka added substance to his stature. He bumped past patrons. Those who feared the law downed their drinks and scurried out.

LaRouge plunked down a free chair on Fanger's foot and uttered a clumsy apology. Too excited to sit, he blurted out, "We've got a lead on the Boreal Blasters case." Fanger placed his second Grizzly, untouched since the waitress had brought it, in front of LaRouge. Like they were the day's only paying customers, she had a soda in Fanger's hand in a flash, and brought their food. Fanger couldn't get rid of her fast enough. He wanted to hear the rest. "Did you catch the guy?" he asked impatiently. Ted and Jerry leaned in closer, all ears.

Realizing what he'd just announced, LaRouge lowered his voice. They struggled to hear him over the din. "Not yet, but one of their staff remembered something about that day. Something important."

"Took him long enough," Jerry sighed, deflated. "Their explosives magazine was broken into five months ago."

"I know. But sometimes these things take a particular event to jog the memory. Anyway, it's fresh and we can follow up on it."

"How much did they get away with again?" Jerry asked. LaRouge recounted what had been in the newspapers. On or around the thirtieth of September, an individual had driven through the heaviest downpour of the year to break into Boreal Blasters' storage magazine on the edge of town.

The manager had followed the emergency response plan when he called the RCMP to report that the magazine's double locks had been sprung and over fifty sticks of PowerPro and seismic detonators had been removed. As none of the staff had been to the storage site in nearly two weeks, authorities found a pristine set of deep footprints made when the thirty-kilo cartons were carried away. The thief hadn't counted on the dry fall weather after the rain to preserve the evidence into a hardened mud track.

LaRouge helped himself to the plate of nachos and let his story hang. Jerry was agog. "So what'd buddy the employee remember?" he asked. Fanger watched LaRouge squirm as he tried to put the cat back in the bag.

"Well, I can't make the details public, but after he came

forward his co-workers backed him up and we were pretty much out of leads. This is concrete." LaRouge eased back from his listeners. "Anyway, I saw your vehicles outside. Thought I'd come in, see if I could steal some snacks." He stuffed a pepper-loaded chip into his mouth. "I'll let you get back to your meeting."

Jenn laughed. "This isn't a meeting. It's a coincidence. The real meeting's not until the race director arrives in a few days. By then you'll have the case solved, right?" Their laughter drew stares from the crowd in the bar, which Fanger noticed had thinned in the last ten minutes. His business was done and he checked the time. It was past six o'clock and Donjek was waiting.

Jenn slid her coat off the back of her chair when Fanger stood to leave. "We should go too, eh, George?" Her husband shifted in the chair he'd been comfortable in for two beers and put a couple of fives beside his glass.

"I should get home as well," LaRouge said. "I don't want to keep Martha's dinner waiting." Marty and the sled hands stayed behind.

The Striders talked as they walked out a pace ahead of Fanger. In the lobby he overheard Jenn say, "Did you see how angry Marty looked when Omar's name was mentioned?"

George nodded. "Yup, but it's not our concern."

"I know. I just wish I hadn't mentioned it," Jenn said. "Or got Ted started." George shrugged, opened the foyer door for his wife and followed her out into the lamp-lit night.

LaRouge was at the reception desk, and Fanger pulled the young officer aside to see if he could squeeze more cats out of the bag. LaRouge gave in. "All right. Go run your truck and we can talk in my vehicle where it's warm. I never turned it off."

Fanger called Donjek's cousin from a pay phone in the lobby to let him know he was on his way, and then he started his truck. LaRouge's RCMP Suburban was parked two slots over, and he jumped into the passenger side. "Okay, ten minutes, then I've got to go. Tell me about Boreal."

"We think we've figured out how the suspect found the magazine. The forgetful driver remembered seeing a traffic survey, or what looked like a traffic survey, in September. A guy with a clipboard and an orange safety vest was sitting in a lawn chair at the top of Two Mile Hill for most of a week."

"That's the part his co-workers can verify?" Fanger tried to recall if he had seen the lawn chair guy on the median dividing the Alaska Highway from downtown traffic.

"At least two of them. And the last time, the witness recalls seeing lawn chair guy on his way out to put together an order at the magazine. We're checking if the city or Community and Transportation Services had any surveys underway in September or October. If so, it's another dead end. But if not …"

"You've got a stranger monitoring traffic flow. You going to check the engineering firms in town? They might have had a crew up there, or the conservation society counting driver-only vehicles." The suspect had chosen a great disguise to hang around unseen in traffic. The drivers wouldn't notice; they barely paid attention to each other.

Fanger asked LaRouge how he figured lawn chair guy knew when they were going to the magazine, especially since Boreal employees drove company vehicles for private errands, too.

LaRouge smiled. "I've been thinking about that. It wouldn't be hard for him to figure out the law says explosives have to be stored outside city limits, eliminating the need to watch downtown traffic. From their shop in the industrial district, the quickest way to the highway is up Two Mile Hill. You watch the traffic for a couple of days to weed out the daily drives for breakfast, lunch and dinner. Then the first time you see a variation, you know they're going to the depot."

"It's not hard to follow a cube van with a nugget at the core of exploding hardrock on the side," Fanger said. "When they stop, you wait, watch them punch in the lock code and rob them blind, knowing you'll go undetected until the magazine is visited again. Very slick. But wouldn't they have a key lock as well? How'd he get the keys?"

LaRouge had no answer. "We're counting on the fact that since he was right out in the open, maybe someone saw him."

Then Fanger remembered the weather. "Or if he sat in his rain gear under a lean-to, maybe no one did."

LaRouge's grin dropped to straight seriousness. "Still, we might be able to identify him. A pedestrian might have stopped to say hi in the intersection. This is Whitehorse, after all." Where people stop to talk to anybody.

THREE

Fanger barrelled down Fourth and swung right to the bungalow tucked in behind the Friendship Centre. Peter

Stoneman lived in the family home; one could see how it had grown with every passing generation, from wall tent to frame to trailer to addition, all tacked on at odd angles and hemmed in by pickets squaring the property.

Fanger knocked and, through the sheers, saw Donjek swinging his arms into his jacket.

"You give Pete the care package you promised to deliver?" Fanger said as soon as the door opened.

Donjek sneered. "You had it in the truck." He darted out the door and a moment later skidded back, presenting the moosemeat. "There," he said with absolute finality, "mission accomplished."

On their way through town, they were stopped by only one red light across from the time and temperature signboard: 6:27 PM, -43° C. They could also see the cinema, empty on film society night. Grey neon struggled to shine behind the marquee. "Who'd see a movie called *Cold Mountain* in weather like this?" Fanger asked, pulling through the now green light. Donjek didn't laugh.

Ravens roosted on the streetlights outside Fanger's summer warm cabin. Donjek picked up his duffel, and Fanger scooped up a few logs from the woodpile to feed the stove.

Donjek lounged while Fanger prepared dinner: cream sausage over pasta. "This is good," Donjek said during his second helping.

"Tell Shirley. It's her moose." Fanger watched Donjek roll his eyes and finish off his plate. They tidied the table of dishes in favour of coffee and cards. Hand after hand, Donjek galloped along the crib board, happy to take Fanger for his last dime. "I quit." Fanger threw in his cards. "You skunk me again, and I won't be able to pay for gas up to Dawson."

On a cul-de-sac in Riverdale, a wakeful racer turned off his alarm two hours early. Omar Ahmed had taken stock of his outfit, his strategy was fixed and he was at the peak of performance.

Activity would soothe his spirit, he thought, pulling out his running clothes. He could field test his new thermals and prove the ten-minute drying time claimed on the product tag.

It had taken some convincing before the sporting goods clerk understood that he really did prefer the expensive synthetic underwear over wrapping himself in heavy wool or, Allah forbid, silk. Ahmed expended stores of patience to explain the Qur'an and Hadith, the collected wisdom from Mohammed himself, accepted by Allah's followers for over fourteen centuries. To disregard Hadith was equal to ignoring Muslim law. In the end he'd bought two pairs of the undergarments. At least the clerk hadn't suggested he freeze to death in cotton.

He unwrapped his thermals and dressed, layering his clothes from head to toe. During the Longest Night Relay in December, he and two others had run themselves blue on the frigid midnight leg. As men they understood the importance of wind shorts to prevent penile frostbite. Ahmed pulled the nylon boxers up to his waist. Then he booted his feet in an ensemble of socks, leggings and gaiters over quick-drying running shoes. He strapped a pair of snowshoes onto his pack. Not since he was a new recruit had he trained this hard.

43

The gate of the high fence around his condo opened to the forested green belt behind. The moon threw stronger shadows than the streetlights as his silhouette flickered through the spruce. He pounded over the cemented snow to where the trail paralleled the fish ladder, passed the turbine chute and, like a salmon, cleared the dam to the reservoir upstream. His heart was home on the steady climb up the dunes. Following the skyline drawn in black, he was the only man alive. His feet ground rabbit tracks flat and flicked tapers of coyote scat off the route he'd run in all weather.

At Miles Canyon, the night frost crackled between his soles and the rust-red basalt columns below. Inches from the thirty-foot sheer, his legs carried him along the ice-bound Yukon and into the trees. He came to a stop at a ski trail and pulled his scarf up to his brow for a moment, to steam off the frost crusted on his eyelashes. Winter stole the nimble warmth from his fingers in seconds, but it left him with enough mobility to secure his snowshoes to his feet and continue.

At Canyon City two kilometres away, he burst out of the bush and crossed the levelled town site. There he removed his Bare Claw snowshoes to cross a section of swamp moguls. At the river's edge he replaced the Claws on his boots and crossed the waterway. The moon's blue spot lit the track that spooled out behind him to the opposite shore, where he exited into the darkness of a crumbling ruin.

He jammed his pack in front of the rubble and planted his shoes upright against the retaining wall. A faded message greeted him: BUSH — STOP THE OIL WAR was spray-painted over a black stencil of US ARMY. Broken plumbing and a row of hand pumps that once served the decaying wringer washers were all that remained of the former laundry.

Inside the washhouse ravens squawked and flapped on the skewed lines of hollow water mains drooping from the ceiling. Ahmed scrabbled up a pile of cinder blocks to the roost and loosened a brick to shine his penlight into the block's central void. He pulled out a palm-sized obstruction, turned it over in his gloves, and put it in a pouch belted at his hips. The birds grumbled. One flew to the roof outside and banged its beak against the rusty chimney. The racket drove Ahmed away.

He jogged up Fox Farm Road, past a collapsed cabin and onto the Alaska Highway. Pacing himself at the top of the South Access, he looked down into the cold city covered by a veil of ice fog laced between the streets.

Exhaust coughed out of public buildings, and at each home a spit of smoke drooled from every chimney. He sprinted down the road's sweeping curves into smog hanging over the footpath by the ss Klondike. Combusted waste plumed out the mufflers of early morning traffic crossing the bridge to Riverdale. He flew past two schools and cut through the staff parking lot, breathing easier in his home quarter. At his back door, he shut out the phalanx of icy pollution that rushed in. He felt clammy in his soaked clothes, but his skin was warm as he changed and hung his new long johns outside.

A late wake-up shook Fanger and his ward out of bed and sent them straight to work, first checking the seams and corners of their wall tent. Spread out, the ten-by-twelve-foot shelter filled Fanger's living room. He'd offered to help when Donjek was clearly struggling, but the youth wouldn't bite. He didn't bite his tongue either, swearing a blue streak. Fanger spread first-aid supplies over the kitchen table, preparing for Donjek's frustration to build to a temper. Within minutes, he stopped the kid from tearing apart the crotch of the door fly. Donjek dropped the heavy ten-ounce cotton in a huff.

Fanger took a side and folded it into the centre. "Come on. I'm not doing this alone." Donjek stooped and held the cloth limp. "We wreck this and we're sleeping in a snowbank."

"Wouldn't be the first time," Donjek mumbled. Fanger was about to launch into a speech about it being just them out there when the phone rang.

It was Jenn. "I know you're really busy, but I wanted to know if you'd like to meet Omar. I'm going over to surprise him for Eid-ul-Adha."

"What?" Fanger shook his head and shrugged his shoulders, clearly not understanding.

"I was looking around on the internet and today's a Muslim holiday, the Festival of Sacrifice. Neighbours share gifts, but there's no one here to bring him anything. I thought it'd be nice to drop by. He likes Tim Hortons doughnuts."

"Okay, we'll pick up a box on the way. Be there soon." In thirty minutes they had wrestled the tent into a tight roll and crammed it into a sack, zigzagged through a drive-thru and arrived at Jenn's. Donjek filled the jump seat behind the passenger bench, and Jenn sat up front indicating the turns, left and right, to Ahmed's quiet home.

They piled out of the truck and followed Jenn single file up the short walk. "Hope he's here." Her knock on the screen door went unanswered. "I probably should have called first, but oh well."

Fanger, nearest to the street, had the best view of the property. A shadow flit across the backyard. He followed a squeaky-as-Styrofoam path over hard-trodden snow to a gate abutting a screened-in porch. On the other side, a slight man with no shoes on sat on the bottom step and looked up at the sky.

Fanger coughed. "Omar Ahmed?"

The man sprung to his neoprene-socked feet and hopped into his boots. "Yes. Do I know you?"

Jenn appeared at Fanger's side and unlatched the gate. She introduced Fanger and Donjek, who tagged along behind her.

"It is a pleasure," Ahmed welcomed them, "but I am otherwise occupied." He led Jenn to the back door, apologizing for being unprepared, hospitality being a virtue and cornerstone of his faith. "Please go in and make your friends comfortable. I will not be long."

Their host was bent to his ritual by the time they were indoors; they watched through a window in the mudroom door. "He's got his boots off again," Donjek said. "He's gonna freeze."

"What's he doing, Jenn?" Fanger looked over his shoulder to where she busied herself in the kitchen.

"Is he washing himself in snow?" she asked. Fanger nodded. "That's wudu, ritual cleansing before he starts his prayers," she said.

Fanger turned back in time to see Ahmed plunge his

47

hands through the ice crust and wash to the wrist with late-season snow that ran through his thin fingers like sugar, each granule frozen and melted and refrozen into a hard grain. Ahmed dug deeper, then filled his right hand with the gritty crystals, which he bit into and spit out — once, twice, and again. A few misshapen flakes dropped from his moustache.

"I guess he's rinsing his mouth out," said Donjek, sharing the view through the tiny pane.

Next, the Muslim closed his hand around a palmful of snow and pressed the moisture from the solid kernels. In three quick snorts he rinsed his nostrils, sending chills up Fanger's spine. "That has got to hurt," he said. But if it did, Ahmed showed no sign as he thoroughly scrubbed his face and arms to the elbows before wiping the pads of his glacier-cold fingers once across his brow, raising goosebumps on Fanger's smooth forehead. With the melt-water dripping from his fingertips, Ahmed made a single pass in and behind each ear. Then he took a final handful of snow to the nape of his neck, where his jet-black hair curled out beneath his toque.

"I know what it is to bathe in the snow," said Fanger, "and he's been out there twice as long as I would be. Has Omar been doing this every day?"

Jenn shrugged. "I guess so. He says the discipline of Islam will win him the race."

Donjek nudged Fanger and pointed out the yellowed square of Plexiglas. "He's not done yet." Ahmed had shucked his neoprene socks, and, as he had done with his hands, rinsed his feet, blanching the white skin whiter from toes to ankles. Fanger shivered as Ahmed pulled the wetsuit booties back on. At last he straightened, faced east and rolled out a blue foam sleeping pad.

Donjek was engrossed in the process, and he took Fanger's place at the window when Fanger ducked under the low doorframe into the house proper. The construction of the kitchen reminded Fanger that height advantage has its limits. He stooped into the first open chair. Several Riverdale homes had do-it-yourself renovations that defied building codes, and this was obviously one of them.

A small puddle collected near his foot, where Ahmed's snowshoes leaned against the wall. "He hasn't spared expense with his gear. These new Bare Claws aren't cheap." Fanger put his hand through one of the bindings and sawed the ridge of aluminum ice creepers across his palm. He growled and swiped at the air.

Jenn took the high-tech shoes away from him. "Nope, but they're worth it." She set the kettle to boil on the propane stove tucked into the corner. "He's a quick study on them, too. At his first meet he finished eighteenth out of about thirty. A month later, he came in with the mid-pack leaders."

Well above Jenn, the ceiling met the former outside wall, and from there it angled down at an impossible slope to graze the top of Fanger's head where he sat. "This looks like it used to be the back porch or the wood crib. I've never seen one converted into a kitchen before," he said. "I certainly don't want to be any taller here."

"Can't complain about the price, though," Jenn replied. "Just don't sit up straight."

Fanger slouched in his chair. He flipped through a book on winter survival and put it on top of another about how

49

to make a fire. "How did Ahmed manage to find a place like this?"

"Marty's friends own it. From what I heard, he introduced them and, after knowing Omar a week, they handed over the keys and left for Arizona. He's got the place to himself, rent free, for the whole winter," Jenn said. "Before that he was living in a tent at the campground." She adjusted the flame and took some cups and spoons out of the dish rack beside the sink. "Where're the doughnuts?" she asked.

Fanger got up and retrieved the box from his truck. When he returned, an unseen door closed at the back of the house.

Donjek's voice carried down the hall to the foyer, and Fanger heard the flow of questions he poured over Ahmed about the foreign ceremony. "Are you going to pray during the race, too?" Ahmed must have nodded to elicit Donjek's incredulous, "Every day?"

"Five times a day, as the Prophet has told us."

"But outside?"

"True, Allah did not mean for salat to be a punishment, and never did I imagine I would pray on snow." Ahmed crossed to the stove and cupped his hands to warm over the kettle. "However," he admitted, "if water is available for wudu, I will not use snow." Donjek and Jenn were laughing when Fanger entered. He passed the carton of doughnuts to Jenn and took a seat with good headroom.

Ahmed's choppy English hid any trace of European heritage, but when Fanger reintroduced himself in their shared language, he replied in smooth, fluid German before reverting to English in response to Jenn's, "Today is one of your holy days, isn't it?"

"Yes. I have been awake since four-thirty when my phone rang." Ahmed turned away from them, but the crowded kitchen didn't allow for much privacy. Fanger saw a fleeting frown. "My family is what I miss most."

"I thought so," said Jenn. "That's why we're here. We can sacrifice a box of Timbits together."

Ahmed thanked her and opened the carton. He put a chocolate bite in his mouth and caught the kettle on the whistle. "I shall make us some refreshments, yes?"

Donjek followed their host from the stove to the counter. "So, what would you be doing today if you were home?"

"We kill a sheep to recognize our willingness to sacrifice everything to Allah, as Ibrahim was when he offered his son to be slaughtered. Then at the mosque we pray with friends and family."

"Were those the prayers you just finished?" Donjek wasn't at all shy about his interest.

"No, that was salat al-zuhr. Our prayers follow the sun to set the rhythm of the day, yes. We pray at dawn, al-fajr, and now, at midday after the sun passes its zenith." Ahmed looked to Jenn to check his word use, continuing on her nod. "Late afternoon prayers are salat al-'asr, and at sunset we say salat al-maghrib. The last salat, al-'isha, is made before midnight."

"How does that work here?" Fanger asked. "On our shortest day, sunset's at three and late afternoon is dark."

"Indeed. I seemed very devout for several days. The half hour of returning daylight every week since is truly a gift from Allah."

Yes, they agreed in unison.

"Why did you have your boots off?" Donjek asked.

"To show the All Merciful that my intentions are clear."

"Do you pray in English?"

"I pray in Arabic, but like most Muslims the language of Islam is not my mother tongue."

"So what do you pray about?" Donjek's blunt curiosity was giving Fanger a better understanding of Ahmed's culture.

"Our text is broken into verses called rak'ah. We repeat them with gestures for salat." He opened a cupboard, pulled out glasses for each of them and started scooping sugar into them. "This you will like very much. Very sweet Moroccan tea." Fanger stopped counting after the fourth spoonful. Ahmed delegated the job to Donjek before taking a plant from the only window in the room and scissors from a drawer. Mint freshened the air with each stalk he trimmed. "Mix it with these leaves," he instructed his young guest. He dropped the fresh springs onto their mounds of sugar. When the green mush was ready, he filled each glass. Thick menthol steam forced a deep breath into Fanger's lungs.

"Soon we will be as warm as the desert sand. Come." He carried the glasses into the dining room where they could sit comfortably. "Drink," he insisted. A trail of sugar washed down Ahmed's throat. Jenn followed, then Fanger, sluicing down boiling mint water over molten glucose. They sucked in cool air through their clenched teeth.

Donjek laughed, then blew across the rim. Leaving his drink to cool on the windowsill framed by heavy blackout drapes, he turned to the adjacent wall where two scrolls of Arabic text flanked a calendar covered in tiny script. "What's on this day?" he asked, pointing at the highlighted square in the middle of those Ahmed had blocked off for the Ultra.

"That is Muharran, our new year. We must carefully calculate our holy days to match your calendar. It is written that if I miss prayers on that day, I am marked for death."

"I can see why you'd want to be exact, if those are the consequences." Fanger took a cautious sip of his tea.

"That's so cool how you've kept your culture," Donjek said. "My folks lost that at mission school. No prayers, no songs; they could only speak English in residence and the nuns were pretty strict about it."

"Our religion guides everything, even our government. We have fought hard to keep our ways."

Scenes from the nightly news flashed across Fanger's mind. On the same program, a Muslim analyst said Islam would consider adapting democracy to the tenets of the Qur'an, but that reasoned debate was prevented by constant aggression, which gave militants a powerful recruiting tool.

"Just like the terrorists in the movies," Donjek said.

Ahmed's face darkened. "No. Your media misrepresents our conflict. The idea we are blood-crazed radicals fighting everyone and each other is pure rubbish. It has nothing to do with the true Islam. Do you want to know why the terrorists always lose in the movies? It is not any superiority of the West. It is that they are not doing Allah's bidding. Yes, if they were, they would succeed."

"Okay," Jenn intervened. "Let's discuss something other than what Washington and Hollywood are doing." She pushed the box of doughnuts closer to the men. Donjek took a plain one and dunked it in his mint tea. Ahmed's excitement cooled.

Fanger took her cue. "Are you ready for next week?"

"I think so, yes. I am certain I could beat everyone in the desert, but it will be tougher on the Ultra trail. To win this I must master the North."

"Nature is not easy to subdue," Fanger said. "Most of my work with the RCMP stems from people caught unprepared for the elements."

"You are a police officer?"

"Auxiliary. I'm called in when they need extra help, or someone with special skills. Because of my background, I get lots of cases looking for missing Germans. It doesn't hurt that I also guide river trips in the summer."

"Are you competing?"

"Me? No." Fanger pointed to Donjek. "We're staffing the checkpoint at Little Gold."

"What is the trail like?" Ahmed asked, eager for inside information.

Fanger told him what he could, having been to the Canadian border station on the Top of the World when it was open during the summer. Donjek provided more details about winter in that corner of the backcountry. Fanger reached for his tea, then jumped at the sight of the time on the watch peeking out of his sleeve. "We better get going," he said to Donjek. "It's past two, and we've got tons to do."

"Me too." Jenn put the empty glasses in the kitchen sink and brought out their coats.

Fanger held out his hand to Ahmed. "Viel Glück beim Rennen," he wished him.

Ahmed's easy reply made it clear he wasn't relying on luck to win the race. "I look forward to our reunion on the trail," he said.

At Fanger's cabin their work was cut out for them. They had abandoned their tasks and left Fanger's home under the clay cliffs in a hurry. Now he opened the door for Donjek, who came in behind him with an armload of wood.

The table was covered with splints and bandages. While Donjek stoked the woodstove, Fanger packed the first-aid kits. Then he and Donjek tackled their next jobs.

In the shed leaning against the side of the cabin, Fanger dug around where he kept his chainsaw and files while Donjek gathered the hand tools they'd need. With both arms full, they trudged past the living room window. Fanger shoved the unlatched door open with his foot and stumbled out of his boots before depositing his load. Behind him, the axe fell on the floor, followed by the swede saw and the sledgehammer that slipped out of Donjek's grasp. "Sorry," he said before going out for the jerry can tagged 1:40 MIX. He placed it beside Fanger, who, wrench in hand, leaned over the newspaper-draped table and opened the chainsaw casing. Sawdust showered over his wool socks.

Donjek smirked and sorted the tools into rows. He took the sharpener from the bookshelf behind him to slough off burrs on the cutting edges, checked that the heads were secure and wrapped the handles in hockey tape. Before he was finished, Fanger was outside in the fading light tuning the chainsaw to the perfect pitch for the temperature.

The phone joined the orchestra. Fanger hit the guard

and cut the saw power. Inside, he snatched the receiver up to his bristling beard. "Yeah."

"Hey, Fanger, it's LaRouge." A baby burped over the line; the corporal was at home. Ever the model of Mountie manners, he excused his daughter. "Boreals' case is hot again. No one official did a traffic survey last fall. Lawn chair guy is definitely our suspect. I'm hoping to get a lead on his ID from Crime Stoppers."

"That's great you're making progress on your case, LaRouge, but I gotta make progress on our packing."

"Yeah, sorry. I won't keep you. Anything I can help you with?"

"Since kidnapping this young offender I got all the help I need. He's crashing around the cookware right now." Donjek took his head out of the cupboards long enough to scowl. Fanger kicked a box across the floor, hoping the racket would emphasize how busy they were. "We're going to the airport tomorrow and leaving Saturday to set up the checkpoint."

"Are we still meeting on Friday?" the officer asked.

Fanger confirmed the time and place. A baby's sudden shrieking split their ears. "Sounds like your hands are full, my friend. Mine too. Talk to you later." Fanger hung up.

Donjek had filled the box marked KITCHEN with utensils, and the counter with food. "The rest we'll get at the store. If we hurry we can still make it," Fanger said. They tore through the mall at closing, packing paper plates and plastic cutlery. The faster the day drew to an end, the faster they worked, readying their own outfits and stacking everything by the door. They fell into their beds, exhausted, and the race hadn't even started yet.

FOUR

Wind crowed down Fanger's chimney. He vigorously rubbed warmth into his nose, the only part of him exposed. Taking two breaths to prepare, he plunged onto the chill plank floor and into the nearest pair of old felts he could find. His crimped feet relaxed inside the warmth. He slopped along in the loose liners to the barrel stove, banged open the steel door and lit a quick fire. It did nothing to spark Donjek to wakefulness. Neither did the boot he hucked at the kid's feet.

"Get up."

The worm turned. "Mmphf, mmphf."

Fanger strolled outside in his long johns for an armload of wood.

"Shut the door, damnit. It's cold."

"Get up." Fanger clomped by and snow from his boots dropped onto Donjek's face.

"No one sleeps after you get up, do they?" Donjek yawned, displaying all the free fillings he received as part of the school's dental program, shook himself out of his sleeping bag and had a good morning scratch. He bumbled around the foyer and circled the kitchen.

"What are you looking for?" Fanger asked.

"The bathroom." Donjek swung through a blue screen door. "Wow. Clean can, man. Mind if I mess it up?"

"Not if you clean it up." Fanger pulled on his jeans. "Where have you been going?" he asked over the partition.

"Outside."

57

Fanger cocked his head. "We're in town. I don't have an outhouse."

"I know."

Donjek flushed and stepped out. "Just kidding. Don't go in there. Stinks." He shuffled to the table and spooned down some cereal. Several minutes snapped, crackled and popped by.

"You know we're always thinking in circles?" Donjek said.

Fanger looked up from his coffee. "Who's thinking in circles?"

"Us. First Nations. Medicine wheel, circle of life, talking circles, circle sentencing." He drew spirals in the air. "No wonder I can't tow the line with you guys. It's not a circle."

"Get dressed, smart ass. Erik's plane lands at eleven."

They tied the 737 for arrival, sliding through the terminal doors as the jet cruised along the runway.

Jenn jumped up and waved them over to the glass corridor from which the passengers fanned into the terminal. Erik welcomed Donjek as the newest volunteer before they picked up Erik's oversized baggage from the carousel.

Fanger drove to the Constantine with Donjek and the cargo while Jenn followed with Erik in her Jeep. On the way, she talked about the coming winter carnival in Whitehorse and how thin it stretched the local volunteer base, before the conversation turned to trapping. "Herman will be at our briefing in Dawson," she said. "Right now he's live trapping lynx to send to Colorado." They arrived at the hotel, where Jenn deposited Erik in Fanger's capable hands.

Inside, Erik's efficiency overwhelmed the receptionist. "Relax, Erik. Piano," Fanger said.

"Richtig," Eric replied, his dialect clipped clean for the business world. "I should appreciate the Yukon's slow pace while I can." Keys in hand, he thanked the clerk and smiled, a gesture that lit his face with youthful energy. She blushed.

Fanger and Donjek waited in the coffee shop for Erik to unpack. When he returned in jeans and a sweater, a notebook tucked under his arm, he looked more at ease. He sat across from Fanger.

"Are you staying longer for Rendezvous this time?" Fanger asked.

"Your Stadtfest?" As race director, Erik was usually too busy to take part. "After missing it two years in a row, I'd like to. What about you two?" The teen beside him hid beneath the brim of his ball cap. Both men shrugged. If Donjek didn't want to talk, he could at least listen.

A coffee and two refills later, Erik scrawled "fertig" across his notes and checked his watch. "What time is it anyway? This is still set for Frankfurt."

"Half four," Fanger replied. "My silent partner here"—he nudged Donjek to life—"and I have plenty to do." The three left together.

The next day saw a large group discussing the Ultra around a conference table in the Constantine's banquet room. Fanger introduced Erik to Corporal LaRouge, and his boss, Sergeant Felix. Donjek had taken the seat Jenn had offered, at the opposite end of the table from Ted, who represented the sledhands and sweepers. They reported excellent conditions.

Erik thanked them and stood to make a short speech. "First I'd like to say what your support means to me and what this race means to the ultra racing circuit. As some of you know, not only do I stage these events, but I also participate in them. And I've been in some poorly organized races." This had motivated him to seek out the Yukon as a venue — the satisfaction of pulling off a smooth race.

"And that is why it is my goal to make this race, your race, a premier event, bringing people from around the world here in wintertime to experience the snow and cold, the northern lights and all the unique things this place has to offer.

"What I know now, after three excellent years working together, is that we have a successful and hardworking team. Although we are on a new route, we can make this run like clockwork." Erik sat and turned to the sergeant.

Felix finger-combed both sides of his moustache and stood. His authority towered over them, extending to the tips of his fingers splayed out on the table. He explained the RCMP's role in coordinating search and rescue. He described arrangements with his counterparts in Alaska as he distributed a handout to race officials. "This page has all the contact numbers. What we need is the same from you."

Erik withdrew a sheaf of photocopies from a stack in front of him. "Here's the number of our call centre. It's staffed to pass messages between snowmobiles on the trail and collect updates from the checkpoints. That's how we're tracking the racers. Each checkpoint has a satellite phone or land line, and those numbers are also on this sheet."

"Good." Felix stuffed his copy into a folder already bulging with documents. "It's imperative that communication remain unbroken for the duration of the race. If any players are out of the loop in an emergency, it'll only hurt the victim." The sergeant sat.

"My trail is in great shape," Ted said, "but are you sure we're going through with this? I mean, right now it's damn cold. And windy." He listed his doubts about the athletes' true fitness but was cut off when Jenn's broken record skipped into its level-of-training track.

"He's raised an important point, Jenn," Felix said. "Are we prepared for multiple casualties? As you're aware, the terrain and environment prohibit nighttime evacuation."

Fanger answered. "I'm confident that with my previous experience and Donjek's bush skills, we can handle whatever arises." Donjek shrank at the mention of his name.

Felix warned them nonetheless. "You'll be out there on your own and under no circumstances should a checkpoint be unstaffed. Smooth communication is crucial."

The meeting dragged on with a round of what-ifs and ended with Ted still muttering about the problems of mass casualties.

Fanger hustled Donjek to the truck and aired his views. "I'm glad we only have to worry about our checkpoint. I'd hate to have Erik's job after the starter pistol fires. Our only concern is wilderness safety for the racers. Mostly that's keeping them fed and hydrated once they come in. After twenty minutes, food doesn't digest right."

Donjek slouched in the passenger seat, his head on his fist, propped up by his elbow on the armrest.

"What's bugging you?" Fanger asked.

"You have too much faith in me. I don't know how to look after sick people."

"No, but you can think with your head and your hands at the same time. Your uncle told me."

"Well it's your fault if someone dies on me," Donjek said to the window.

"Look, probably nothing will happen, but if it does, we're all they've got and you're all I've got." Fanger dropped the topic; no new one replaced it.

At Fanger's cabin, it was a simple process to load his snowmobile onto the back of the Datsun once they found a snow berm high enough to drive the sled onto the truck and tailgate. After that, space was tight to slide the trail-boggan beside the machine, and fit all the stoves and chimneys, tents and tools into the box.

Taking advantage of their last free evening, they walked a few blocks, ending up at Donjek's cousin's, where they watched a new martial arts film starring flocks of flying actors. After the climax and three warrior funerals, they headed home, two figures obscured in their hooded parkas braced against the winds out of the south.

The temperature warmed fifteen degrees overnight, and a line of overcast dawn greyed the black morning. Heading out of town on their way to Dawson, Fanger pointed at a signboard. "Look, it's only minus twenty-five. Yesterday's wind blew the cold snap away." Donjek grunted and nestled into a new dream from which he didn't stir until he was deposited at home to ready his sled.

Snow kernels drizzled over the Gambler's Den where Fanger went next to look for the owner, Dawson's mayor. He found him jiggling his corpulence out of his jacket and approached with his hand extended. "Excuse me, Mayor…?"

"Fanger, come in, come in. How's Ted?" They shook hands. The mayor's palm felt slippery.

"Good. You'll probably see him next week when he brings up our rental sleds. I wanted to ask if we can park them here on your lot. Just until the race starts."

"Of course, of course. At your own risk." The mayor's saccharine smile crystallized into pursed lips. "I heard you're bringing Edwin's boy, Donjek, with you."

Defensive, Fanger said, "I'm going to pick him up right away."

"Well, be careful. He's a real handful." More than a handful, Fanger figured. The way some people talked, the kid was a one-man crime wave.

On his way to the ice bridge, Fanger noticed what he hadn't earlier. Graffiti reversed the meaning of all the caution signs — DON'T slow down, DON'T keep right and DON'T stop. Who would vandalize signs at minus forty? At least, Fanger was sure, this time it couldn't have been Donjek.

When he pulled into the Stoneman's yard, his partner was leaning over the gaping engine of his sled. "It's good to go." Donjek signalled and dropped the hood. Trek Over the Top, Yukon Quest and Lost Patrol Commemorative

Ride emblems told the machine's history, races and events it had seen.

On the near side, Edwin stretched a gummy rubber closure into place. Fanger reversed up to the plough edge of the driveway and unloaded his sled with a hefty tug. It lurched down the snow pile. The skimmer was more awkward, but with steady effort, the pair hooked up and packed tight the high-sided toboggans.

"See you in a few days, Dad." Donjek closed his visor and roared away on Edwin's shouted cautions. Fanger waved and followed in a sweeping arc.

Needle-laden pine boughs slapped Fanger's helmet as he rocketed along the rutted trail. His vision fogged with his jagged breathing, and he thumbed open his faceshield a notch. His view of the serpentine way cleared in the rush of open air that smelled like the onset of snow, a bristling sting of ions charging the atmosphere.

Forty kilometres northwest of Dawson, the sawtooth landscape spread at a widening in the trail. Under heavy cloud cover was a panorama of peaks captured in the vacation photos of those who drove over the Top of the World during the summer. "We'll stay here tonight," Fanger said when Donjek slowed. He looked up where the pale disc of daylight oozed out of the sky. "Follow me."

They drove criss-cross over the pullout, their tracks making hardpack. "I'm going to park over there where the sun will come up on my machine," said Fanger. He swerved with Donjek into the shadows and cut the motor. From his jacket he pulled out a GPS and marked their position. He laid it under the faring where it would stay warm on the hood while he got out his pack.

Donjek pulled out a shovel and tamped down a square of snow. In front of that he cleared an equally large area to bare earth, dumping each shovelful into a mound. He smoothed the heap into a raised bed, which he let set while he tramped into the bush to collect spruce boughs to spread overtop.

In the meantime, Fanger unhitched the skimmers and dragged them close to camp. He unpacked the gear they'd need for the night and, seeing the fire pit cleared to dirt, gathered a tumbleweed of fire starter. On the exposed rectangle he set a handful of brittle twigs ablaze and released them in a nest of small branches. On this he laid finger-thick spruce and coaxed the fire to self-sufficiency. Then he broke up a pile of small brush before gathering enough dry wood for the night.

By the time Fanger returned, Donjek had snowmelt in a steel pot over the flames. Fanger built up the fire while Donjek cooked another scoop. They finished building their shelter together.

Over the snowbed they stretched open a tarp and Fanger bound the front to upper branches, left and right, while Donjek pegged down the rear at the base of the trees backing their lean-to. The protected corner held the fire's warmth and kept the mountain downdrafts at bay.

"That's enough work for today." Fanger dug around in the bottom of his toboggan and lifted out his food box. The snow he'd sensed earlier fell into the container in wet flakes while he rummaged inside for a pack of Landjaeger. "Help yourself," he said, passing the dried meat to Donjek.

The kid slit the vacuum seal and three links disappeared

into the tunnel where his mouth could be seen if there were more light. In the fresh blackness, their fire made a feeble flicker. Fanger lit a lantern and hung it from a near-reaching branch. It was short work then to find a small pot and measure off most of the meltwater. Fanger dumped in the contents of two noodle packs and let them simmer with an ice cube of butter.

Donjek sat on his haunches, poking sticks into the flames. "What else do they need for prep?" The ruff on his hood muffled his voice.

"This is where the marathon ends, so we'll need one more area to stage the finish. Also, there's no outhouse here, but I figure we can tie a sapling between a couple of trees so they have some place private to hang their butts."

"I guess we'll have to replace all this wood we're using too, eh?"

"It would be nice to leave the checkers with enough to start their first fire. At the same time we can bring in some poles for the tent frames." Fanger shoved the pot away from the heat, catching it from boiling over. He stirred and scooped the carbs into bowls. They devoured their dinner and scrubbed the dishes clean with ice crystals.

Hunkered down on stumps, hands full with hot choco-late and cigarettes, they relaxed in the hushed firelight. Fanger recalled camping as a boy in Germany. The village cop, the only one in the whole *Revier*, really, organized weekend outings for any kid who wanted to go. A regular Grizzly Adams and black powder marksman, he supervised them in the *Wald*, joining them in making it their own private wilderness. How Fanger and his friends

66

had squirmed through Saturday school, itching to get out on those blue-sky afternoons. Of course, by the time they were Donjek's age, the old *Wachtmeister* had retired and his influence waned, although they all remembered how to light illegal campfires at impromptu drunk fests. He'd always ended up sitting dumb at the fire then too, smoking and reflecting, just as he did now.

Donjek raised his hand to still the silence, it seemed, then directed Fanger to meet the gaze that watched them at his left side.

Moist, panting breath fogged above yellow licks of heat. Ice scritched under shifting muscles that brought the wolf's frost-bearded muzzle closer. Watcher and watched faced each other in the night. Paws encrusted with icy pendants clicked in a steady tread circling the camp. The wolf stopped a whisker away from Donjek's shoulder and bowed his head. His coat, black as mica, flashed an exit-red sheen in the rim of the firelight, and in a whisper he was gone.

The men blinked after the wolf, cleared their vision, and turned to each other. "That was the most powerful thing I've ever seen," Fanger said. He dashed the dregs of his cup into the fire. "Did you smell the oil in his fur? I've never smelled anything that rich."

"I don't think I was breathing." Donjek inhaled his cigarette. "That was one of the teachers, eh? Wolf gives man wisdom. I'm Wolf clan." He placed the butt of his tailor-made in the coals.

Fanger banked them for morning. "Well, it's taught me. I'll make sure our goods are stowed." He secured them, then spread his bedding over their spruce mattress.

Between it and his sleeping bag, he laid his coveralls and stuffed his clothes inside around his feet. Under his parka and in the bag's thick wool liner, he slept fast.

Not a trace of last night's visit could be found in the morning. Their tarp roof sagged under an inch of powder that blanketed their world. Fanger rose first and fixed breakfast. And ate it. And packed his kit. And started the chainsaw before Donjek stirred out of bed.

Late-morning sun broke through and worked them into a sweat before they rode north on the trail, stalking a broken line of snow fence for eight miles until teardrop moose tracks took over to lead them to a silver pool of overflow. The water, deep enough for a good soaker, was the surface melt from last night's snowfall lying on top of the ice. Fanger skimmed over it and sent up a light spray, but Donjek gunned it and got his boots full of water.

He stopped to change into dry socks. Fanger pulled apart the layers of Donjek's boots and put his hand inside of one. "Your liners are soaked. Here, wrap your feet in these first." He handed Donjek a couple of plastic bags and the felts. Among the odds and ends in a compartment at the rear of his machine, Fanger also had duct tape. "Use this to close the top of the bags around your legs. That should keep you dry until we get to camp.

Donjek pulled them on and tugged the felts and nylon shells overtop. "I gotta open the laces. Hope there's no more overflow. I don't have spare boots." He loosened the ones he had on.

The delay was minor and they made up the lost time with the throttle wide open on the straightaways. Fanger led them around suspicious patches of dark slush and rolled through the dips and rises before realizing Donjek was no longer behind him. He backtracked and found the youth tinkering under the hood. "What's up?" he said, lifting the visor on his helmet.

"It died on the uphill. Damned jets, they're still set for minus forty and it's running rich." With his thumbnail he scraped deposits off the spark plugs and wiped his hands on his snowpants. "I think I've got it now. Give it a pull."

Fanger yanked on the starter cord—nothing. He pulled a second and third time before it caught. "Well, it's running now," Donjek said. He dropped the hood and latched it. "I'll fix it for real at the checkpoint."

"Good idea. You lead out. I'll follow, in case you break down again." Fanger slapped his faceshield down and slithered through the trees behind him.

A hundred kilometres from home, Donjek skidded to a stop at the border station—Little Gold on the Canadian side, Poker Creek on the American. Fanger pulled up beside the government outpost and rolled his helmet forward off his head. Inside the shared building, a line of yellow tiles separated the nations; outside, it drifted to the eaves. "It'll be dark in a couple hours, so let's make ourselves comfortable." He emptied his toboggan and marked out twenty paces by twenty for the kitchen. Donjek shovelled up snow for sleeping ledges.

Fanger rode back a mile with his chainsaw to where a spur sloped down an easy grade to a stand of spruce edged by a dozen long, straight saplings. He felled and stripped them to use for the pole frame in their tent. Standing deadwood, rooted in place, he dropped and trimmed into eight-foot lengths. The loaded skimmer tracked slow and heavy back to camp.

Donjek had the tent floor cleared and knee-high ledges squared off. He bound the full-length poles together while Fanger rolled the firewood out of the trailboggan. They dragged the twelve-foot sapling bundle to the square of exposed bush floor and each of them fixed a pair of poles together at right angles with baling wire. Donjek lifted his A-frame upright and banked snow around the foot of the frame until it stood on its own. Fanger did the same on the opposing side. The longest sapling they laid in the notches, creating a ridgepole for their shelter, and lashed the intersections together. Under the frame, Fanger rolled the tent out. Donjek threaded rope through grommets along the roof, then slung the rest over the ridgepole. They hauled the canvas high and stretched the guidelines to the ground. The sidewalls they pulled left and right and tied to cross-poles they'd secured halfway up the legs of the structure.

"The airtight's over there," Fanger said, pointing to the stoves propped in the snow. "You set it up. I'll buck up the wood and get a fire going." Sundown robbed the land of heat while they worked. Donjek erected the stovepipe and wriggled it through the asbestos chimney ring. More than a shanty, their canvas castle, lit and warm, cast an air of permanence in the empty night.

Monday was slave labour. Beside the staff cabins for US customs agents, they slapped up three prefab walls around an outhouse bench and put a bucket under the hole, so

70

Fanger could have a comfortable dump. When he finished, Donjek was outside the biffy, splitting his sides laughing. "What's so funny?" Fanger asked.

"I'm sleeping in Canada and shitting in the States." The kid could barely speak. "Every time I go to the can I'm defecting." Donjek sure is Canadian, Fanger thought, and laughed.

Both of them worked on the woodpile and erected two more wall tents. After lunch Donjek broke probation repeatedly as they flattened a landing pad on the US side of the road for a helicopter to set down on.

"That looks pretty good," Fanger said at dusk. "I'll just log our coordinates for Dawson airport." He went to retrieve his GPS from the side pocket of his pack. It wasn't there. He checked again and emptied all the pockets with no luck. He dumped the main compartment and still came up empty. "Donjek, do you know where my GPS is?"

"No. What's it look like?"

"About the size of a computer mouse. You've seen it; I was using it on the trail."

"I ain't seen it, man." Donjek smoked in hasty puffs.

"You sure? I can't find it." Fanger poked around his sled and skimmer.

"Well I didn't take it." Donjek's defensiveness took Fanger by surprise.

"I'm not saying you did. But maybe it ended up with your stuff instead of mine."

"Oh, yeah, you think so? Well, fine." He snatched his Flames duffel and threw it in the snow at Fanger's feet. "You look for it. I'm going for a walk." Donjek stomped into the darkness without another word. At the top of the embankment above their camp he stopped, sat and hung his feet over the edge.

From two dozen feet above, Donjek watched Fanger right the sack and shake off the snow. Digging way down, he pulled out what Donjek knew was there. He'd wrapped the device in a towel and now, as Fanger revealed it, Donjek heard, "That little punk" echo off the hills around him. "Didn't he know I'd miss it?" Fanger added.

Well, what did Fanger think? It was careless of him to leave it under the faring. He would have lost it otherwise. "My luck if I sold it on the internet first. Some cash to party with," Donjek said.

He thought about his pals at home then, and their last party. He'd already cleaned out enough liquor cabinets for each to hold their own twenty-sixer, and gathered plenty of change for gas. It was worth it when he got his hands on that car; they always let him drive. He was the only sober one anyway. True, the Klondike Highway was their only escape route, but he'd outrun the cops before. And he was a driving ace, fast and smooth, as smooth as the oil that slicked his lane just before the crash — the one that sent them into the ditch, sent one of them to Vancouver, to the spine hospital, to the place his best friend would leave in a wheelchair.

No one could believe it when Donjek wouldn't write a letter of apology to the victim's family, but how could he? His friend's mother treated him like a murderer. How could he make her see what he really felt when he didn't understand it himself? And for sure that Great White Saviour down there didn't.

Fanger seethed while he made dinner. The red beacon from Donjek's cigarette marked his position overhead. No wonder he took off, Fanger thought, I'd break his neck if he were here. But hectoring and lecturing wouldn't help. There had to be a better way to get Donjek to realize the consequences of his actions. As it was, Fanger had plenty of time to think of what to say to the kid, who didn't come back for over an hour.

Donjek remained on his perch, remembering the accident. A throaty growl, with the disturbing intensity of the wild, rumbled low. The fine hairs on Donjek's nape rose. The wolf had crept up on him without a sound. He stood and sought an outline at the base of the trees, a husky breath, a glinting eye. No form took shape. Tired, Donjek made his way to the cookshack, wary of the powerful animal he sensed but didn't see.

"Your dinner's on the woodstove," Fanger said when the tent flap opened. He smoked, and gauged Donjek's mood. The teen ate in silence and would not meet Fanger's eye. "I found the GPS," Fanger said. "The coordinates are entered, so Search and Rescue will know exactly where the checkpoint is." He tossed the end of his cigarette into the firebox and said nothing more.

It was an early night from which they woke to a clear sky and a fresh start. After breakfast they packed camp and cached their supplies under a tarp against the Little Gold wall. They hauled out only a fraction of what they'd brought in and, outbound, covered ground fast. By two PM they were at the first checkpoint, where they had lunch to go.

Donjek led the way on the final leg, a line of light snaking down the darkening road. The monotone dusk stole the shadows and robbed them of contrast, but their speed never slacked over the kidney-punching ruts.

Two bright specks, they bounced out of the bush and curled down the road toward the Yukon River to stop at Donjek's house.

"I guess I won't see you until the race starts," Fanger said. "Stay out of trouble, Donny."

"You know me," he said at the bottom of the steps to the cabin.

"Exactly." Fanger didn't stay for coffee; it was a five-hour drive home, with plenty to do once he got there.

FIVE

The next time Fanger saw Donjek was at the Gambler's Den, where they were now milling around, waiting for the pre-race meeting to start. A melee of foreign speech buzzed over a dozen different English accents. To Fanger it sounded like any European train station, a deafening cackle. It made Donjek nervous, and he'd been glued to Fanger's side since they'd arrived.

A scene between Marty and Ahmed held Fanger's interest. Marty clenched a pair of gauntlets and shook his fist under Ahmed's nose. The Moroccan shied left, looked Fanger square in the eye, then back for round two.

Fanger could see Marty speaking but he heard not a word of the exchange, which ended when the Canadian's mouth formed a furious "No!" and Ahmed stormed across the room.

"How was the banquet?" Donjek asked. The question

jolted Fanger to attention. The racers had been wined and dined in the capital, followed by a VIP public speaking contest.

"Boring," he replied. "I thought they'd never shut up. The minister of tourism sounded like she's paying for the race out of her wallet." He nodded toward the minister's entourage. "They're getting their money's worth today, though, joining the start line circus."

The minister regaled a group of highly trained athletes with stories of a high school track meet she'd won thirty years ago. Over her shoulder, a tourism marketeer encouraged a pair of racers to bring their families next time, and the president of the wilderness watchdogs extolled the virtues of eco-tourism — an intro for his set speech about Yukon outfitters leading the industry with legislated no-trace camping. How picking up discarded Scottie blooms made up for barrels of AV gas burned flying to remote rivers, Fanger couldn't figure out.

Erik tapped a saucer with a spoon to break up the *kaffee klatsches*. Last coffees splashed into cups as everyone took their seats. Donjek stood with Fanger at the back of the room near the door. To Erik's right sat the guest speakers. Erik welcomed everyone to Dawson and turned the floor over to Yukon Ambulance.

The racers got a run down on the signs and symptoms of hypothermia, treatment and prevention. "You're all aware that in warm weather you need four litres of fluid a day, except for the Americans among you who need just about a gallon. In winter, it's more like five or six litres. It's a lot of work to force yourself to take in that much, but do your best. Hydration prevents most of the environmentals."

A Yukon Quest musher spoke next. The dog driver, an acquaintance of Fanger's, had plenty of experience with how the mind, his own in particular, plays tricks.

"At some point, between the shadows and the dark, when you're tired, hungry and have a long way to go, it's not uncommon to flip out." Nerves and courage tittered through the room. "You can believe it; I'm a shrink and it happened to me. You see things that aren't there, miss things that are, like signs, and it's really easy to get turned around. Then you bump into a competitor who tries to convince you you're going the wrong way, but you're sure they're lying, playing head games. Listen to them. The race *is* a mental challenge, there's no need to make it harder." He shuffled his notes. His audience shuffled their feet.

Herman Witzer was the final speaker. The trapper, six feet of sap-stained coveralls, stood. Faint animal scent wafted from his parka. "Yeah, so this is a model of a snare," he began. A birch limb erected on a plywood base supported a semi-circular fan of twigs. "It works like this." The racer sitting beside him craned forward in her chair. He lowered the display and held it close to her inquisitive face, baiting her to look inside where forked slivers held a loop of brass wire.

"Eww. There's a tiny rabbit hanging in there," she said. She jabbed her index finger at the narrow opening. "There."

"There is?" He tilted it a degree.

She kept an eye on the contents, swaying, wavering between disgust and pointed curiosity, until *snap* — the power snare clapped under her nose. She jumped, then laughed to the crowd's applause. Dropping his heavy arm around her narrow torso, Herman said, "You got the message, eh? Don't touch.

"A toy I made for my daughter." He showed them the trigger, fishing line pinched in his chapped fingers, and set the contraption beside another made of woven willows. "This is a box trap. Don't touch it either," he said.

"What if my foot gets caught?" came from the back of the room.

"It's not too likely. You'd be crawling around under the trees to find these. But one of these" — he yanked up a re-straining trap by its anchor chain — "is a number four lynx." It rattled against the table. "If you step on the pan" — he pointed to the iron disc from which the whole device was sprung — "the trigger" — a loose finger of metal — "will re-lease and it'll close when you step off. The world's simplest land mine."

Upright in front of him, steel ears intersected the semi-circular object. He gripped them firmly and pressed down to separate the smooth rubber-edged jaws. He tucked the trigger under a notch on the "handle" of the pan to hold open the six-inch-wide mouth. He sprang it with a rag-stuffed lightweight hiking boot. It nipped the shoe and slipped off. "Your feet are a lot bigger than lynx or coyote paws." He scratched his beard.

"There is a bigger version of the number four, for wolves, so on game trails keep your eyes open for deformities. If you trip one, you'll need two hands to press the leaf springs flat. Jam them open with a nail to get out. You'll be bruised and you'll want to guard against shock and frostbite."

Loud and appreciative applause ended the trapper's speech. Erik closed the meeting. "Happy trails," he said.

"See you at the start line." Racers shot out the door to their pulks and packs, checking and tightening their final ensembles.

The sledhands gathered outside. Cracked windscreens fronted three snowmobiles. "Ach, du Scheisse," Fanger said. "The farings are busted."

"I didn't do it," Donjek confessed. Fanger's "you're a dolt" sigh escaped.

Jerry, from Ted's crew, stopped short. "Am I glad I didn't sign for the rentals." He surveyed the damage. "I've got some hundred-mile-an-hour tape." He got out the red fibre tape and stitched the cracks. "This stuff is great, holds at speed and in the cold." He tore off the last strip and tossed the roll into his carryall.

Five snowmobiles rumbled away in formation. Racers on the street gave them friendly waves. Soon forty-seven athletes would gather under the START banner.

Skiers stretched and runners burst into sprints on the spot. A handful of cyclists spun their wheels. They were not all reedy bodies and fleece, Ahmed noticed. Stocky men and solid women, without the lard of armchair athletes, were of equal standing to this test of endurance.

Ahmed settled a padded pack belt around his small waist, raising a pair of half-inch PVC tubes to his hips. A sled-length behind him, a Kevlar toboggan inched forward. The pulk, full as a shopping cart, held all of Ahmed's worldly possessions — at least all that mattered for the next week. He cinched it tight to his sides.

Jenn had a camera to her eye and worked the orange line spray-painted on the snow. "Marty," she called, "squeeze in with everyone. Jill, you crouch down with Omar." Ahmed glanced at Marty's stiff posture and drew close to Jill for the quick snap.

A whistle sounded, shrill and amplified.

Standing on a platform, Erik towered over the crowd, megaphone in hand. "Ladies and Gentlemen, welcome to the 2004 Yukon Arctic Ultra." Spectators cheered.

"On the count of one, let the race begin!" He waved a checkered flag above the toqued contestants, identifiable only by their bibs. "Three ..." Ahmed narrowed his gaze and ground a divot into the snow. "Two ..." A bicyclist on his right wobbled on a balanced frame. A skier on his left crouched to glide. "One!" Erik's shot cracked the hush. Ahmed bolted to the river, jostling down the bank with the mountain bikes and skis.

The disciplines soon sorted into packs. On the Yukon's far side, the cyclists wheeled up the cutbank, filleting the snow. The skiers' herringbones climbed the steep shore next, and they were well ahead by the time those on foot turned the track to fishnet. In the half-light between the clouds and the hills, the only contrast was a strip of dirty snow. On the move, Ahmed fished his GPS out of his pocket and switched it on.

Over the ice bridge, the Top of the World Highway snaked off into the mountains. Ahmed had taken a late-season drive on the summer-only road, and he'd processed the photos in his mind until the images rolled out as a documentary. Now the minutiae slept under winter linen and the wide road-bed rolled over a mantel of snow.

He followed the tracks to the first trail marker, a shingle hanging from a tree. "Hey, Omar! How's it going?" He had barely enough time to wave before Jenn, the dynamo of the local circuit, zipped past him. Her lack of humility unnerved him. His beloved wife would never have been so bold. Ahead, Ahmed watched the seasoned athlete slow to talk to a rookie and give her a pat on the back that put a spring in her jog.

Ahmed adjusted his own pace to a steady trot. He'd pushed his endurance to the limit, keeping a low profile; now he was primed to blow them all off the trail, starting with a novice ahead.

"Hi, Omar," she said as he passed her.

How does she know my name? We have not even met. He dashed away.

Further on, the sun-spangled sky swelled out of the receding clouds, the snow as brilliant as the burning sand Ahmed had felt between his toes on the Mediterranean. Underfoot, the softened crystals leeched water, sliding a patch of ice under his shoes at every step.

Since the cold snap broke, the snow had turned to rot. By the time he reached the golf course two miles up, Ahmed was wet to his knees. He would have been soaked to his ears, but the dry air vacuumed the steam rising out of his clothes. It had passed through three layers of wicking to get there. He tore off his balaclava, wiped his face with it and stuffed it in a pocket along with his overmitts.

After an hour a hot spot flared, chafing under his waistband. He shifted his belt but the weight jabbed, increasing the friction. It worsened on the uphill. The incline tugged the pulk against Ahmed's steady slog. He felt the tension yanking on his lumbar for over three hundred steps before he quit counting. It seemed an infinity until he crested the slope, where he paused to clip his pedometer to the back of his belt, out of sight. Releasing the quick-clip relieved some of the pressure, and he dragged the pulk like a travois through the bush.

Higher up, the trees shrank to scrub and cowered at the foot of an army of mountains lording over the earth. In a standoff of man against massif, the strength of nature pounded against the heart in Ahmed's chest. The rock was too steep to hold snow; it swirled in wisps from the quartz-streaked peaks. Miles ahead through the ivory clouds lay the checkpoint. Below, the last driveway veered off the ploughed portion of the Top of the World Highway. The footpath ran on in the snow, absorbing the deepening day.

Skids slurred and Ahmed turned to see a couple puffing up the hill. "That was steep," the woman, number 008, said.

"Look there." Ahmed raised his hand.

"That's real steep." She drank from a thermos and handed it to her trail mate. Ahmed sucked on a plastic tube from the water pouch that hung against his chest. A dribble of water and a spitball of ice hit his tongue. Although he and the water were still warm, the uninsulated tube had frozen in the minus-fifteen air.

"Trouble with the straw?" the man asked.

"It is nothing. A little clog. I can warm it up at the checkpoint," Ahmed said.

"Want some water?" He passed the flask to Ahmed.

"That is very kind, yes. But what about yourselves?" He took a sip and returned it to number 008, a low-number marathoner.

"We've got lots," she said. "I packed an extra thermos for each of us."

Ahmed kicked himself for not having thought to bring an insulated water bottle.

"We're going to keep going," she said. "The sun drops so fast here, we want to use whatever light is left."

"Indeed."

The sky had tinted. Granite red, ochre and saffron clouds sailed across the aqua blue, reminding Ahmed of the coloured cloths streaming through his city's bazaars. He shot the bolts back where they belonged. "Well, goodbye," he said.

The couple waved and strode away, leaning into the slope for balance down the double-digit grade.

The sun brought the temperature down with it, but Ahmed would not forego his faith, regardless of how cold it was, reciting *rak'ah* stock-still on his knees in minus degrees. He prepared for *wudu* as he watched the couple. They were at the bottom of the dale and over the man-high drift before Ahmed unrolled his mat.

Under Allah's splendour, he prayed.

The rock faces encircling him chorused his chants, and these voices, echoing from his own, gave Ahmed his community in worship. The hand of Allah in the dimming sunset lit his connection to the world on which he stood.

Finished, he put away his prayer rug and took out his headlamp. Fixed over his balaclava, its dull yellow beam swam into the ocean-deep trough below. Through the blue dinner hour Ahmed's toes crunched to stubs in the cap of his shoes as he countered the slope with his bantam-weight.

His pulk pushed on, nipping at his heels and cutting into his ankles until, over a rock bump, its full weight — equal to a large collie — caught him hard behind his knees. He dropped, flailing onto his back, plastic poles slashing between his limbs. The inertia didn't stop; momentum egged gravity on, man and camp lunged down a blind chute to land in a heap at the bottom.

Ahmed rolled off his side, which tipped the sled upside down before he had a chance to slip the buckle. Unconcerned with the setback, he dusted himself off. He had kept to his schedule, and marching through the night would erase the height of land. He pressed on, oblivious to how high a climb it was, or how steep. His world was reduced to the dimly lit way a few paces ahead.

He swung his gear onto the ledge at the plough drift and hefted himself up. Around his hips he snugged down the pulk and marched.

He was often overtaken by marathoners calling out "passing left" or "on your right," but none stopped. Winter held the heat tight to itself and the mountains shushed in his ear. He'd read Jack London's *Wisdom of the Trail*, and indeed ten more degrees of frost drove through fur and flesh. Ahmed paced himself for the goal, not the glory, over the lonely stretch of land. He'd be in and out of the marathon checkpoint by eleven.

The night was not silent. Although his wool cap muffled his ears, he heard his cold, indrawn breath expelled as warm condensation. He closed his mouth to stay hydrated. Pumping blood whistled past his temples, fountained down into his heart and belly and flowed to his feet crunching over the firm crust.

Up and up his rhythm pulled ahead, evenly matched with the pulk. He swallowed, wetting his dry throat, his tongue rasping in his mouth. Ahmed held the straw from his water pouch between his teeth, softening as much of the stem as he could. He chewed lightly to loosen the sludge and sucked out slush but not much water.

He reached a short plateau and stopped to check his bearings. Paper maps were packed under the cargo net. He wouldn't need them anytime soon. The coordinates loaded in his GPS matched the topographics drawn by Yukon College cartography students.

If he were within five miles of the marathon banner he would keep marching. He pointed his headlamp down to read. His breath clouded the screen and he wiped it with his thumb. Nothing showed on the display. A couple taps returned a faint low-battery symbol. He shook his head and put the GPS in his pocket. There were extra batteries packed, but he hadn't expected these to die in less than a day. Perhaps one of the finishers would have more.

He pulled his cuffs back from his wrist, exposing a multi-function sport watch. Six hours ago he'd left Dawson, minus a half hour for breaks. He figured he was near the first checkpoint and lifted the edges of his cap, listening for the talk and laughter of people around a campfire, the tock and splinter of an axe splitting wood. What replied was the wind.

It cracked his lips. He gave in and eased the water bladder out of his shirt. The contents slopped to one side, and the bag twisted when he tried to unscrew it. The cap held fast. His second attempt tore the spout from the sack, split it open and spilled water over his chest. Ahmed poured the last trickle down his throat. There was still fuel to melt snow, if necessary, and he could thaw his reserve camelpack at the checkpoint. Out of water and unsure of his progress, he sucked a button to tame his thirst.

Ahmed glanced at the crescent moon, so bright. His eye traced a silver hairline closing the arced arms around an India ink night. His gaze followed the symbol of Islam as it climbed from the southeastern horizon. He churned on, gaining on his goal. His mind wandered on the edge of the world. After he checked in, in time for *salat al-'isha*, he would find a moment to pray.

A chill shuddered across Ahmed's back; his waterlogged shirt soaked him to the core. He stepped lively, warmth seeping from his bones. His mind raced, the trees blurred, the landscape rolled into a memory of his entire village assembled for noon prayers at the mosque.

In the sky of Paradise, a temple, a marble vision as white as his dishdasha *explodes into view. He runs, the chain stitch in his silver-shot tunic rattles and heaves. The heads of all the devout rise and follow him across their field. The* imam *looms on the distant horizon, his voice loudspeaker clear. "Now we start." The prayer leader bows with Allah's children.*

He pounds harder across the sand separating them, reaching but never nearing, hindered by the yards of ceremonial cloth that cling and bind his calves. On his knees he begs, "I ran. I ran all the way here." His voice cracks and breaks.

"The line of followers is a quarter mile long."

"Then I will pray here." Supplicating on all fours he pitches forward.

"Your intentions are known but the task is not complete."
The imam *rocks in a violent rhythm, fanning the flame that erupts over the mosque, shoots out the minarets and devours the worshippers in a lick.*

Handfuls of snow sprayed over him and showered the blaze. Exhausted and overwrought, he sprawled under the banner marked MARATHON FINISH.

SIX

Sixty kilometres up the trail, Fanger and Donjek swept into Little Gold. "Man, is it hot," Fanger said as he pulled off his helmet and wiped his sleeve over his beard. A shower of icicles fell onto his lap.

Donjek swung his leg over the saddle and stood beside his sled. "Thank God I adjusted the jets, and a couple other things, too. Runs great now, eh?"

"Yeah," Fanger said, wiping his nose and pocketing the handkerchief. He looked around their clean basic camp. Under the feet of forty racers, it would become as trampled as a rodeo ground.

A sleek white streak skittered across Fanger's skis and under his track. "An ermine—"

"A weasel, in winter colour," Donjek said. It popped out the other side and they chased its slinky gait over the snow. "Our stuff." Donjek flung the tarp off their cache against the border station wall.

The varmint held fast in a boxer's stance, his left leg ahead of his right. Stricken, its cheeks throbbed with hyperventilation; its belly pulsed a hundred times a minute—relaxed, contracted and shrieked—blasting them, the buildings and hills. It twisted its neck, head upside down, looped its body and on the run hit the snowbank.

"See that, all white," Donjek said, pointing at the tunnel left by the escape. "No black on the tail. A winter weasel."

Okay, Fanger conceded; everyone disagreed on what the furbearer was called. "I wonder what it wanted. There's no food in here." He lifted the lid of the weasel's last stand, serrated by bite marks. Nothing but stove parts. "Look over there in the chimney." Blue strips fluttered from the crimping. They lifted the pipe to eye level, dislodging a mouse that plopped onto the snow at Fanger's feet. A pile of pellets and shredded plastic slid down his front. "Shit. Mouse shit."

Donjek laughed and dropped the tube. "It won't be long until that mouse is dinner. We did the weasel a favour. It would have never clawed through this tin."

"Glad we didn't upset the balance of nature. Let's unpack." A food pail swung from each of Fanger's hands, and Donjek packed the stove into the hospitality tent. They grappled two deadweight water barrels into the shelter. The seventy litres of slush in each made heavy waves.

"We should get a fire going in here, before this freezes. You look after that, I'll bring in more wood," Fanger said.

When Fanger returned, Donjek had shoved his empty sled under the tent flap. The outhouse door made a perfect tabletop. It was strewn with drink powders, cutlery and condiments. In a thick pot at the back of the woodstove, a bucket of buffalo stew softened. Donjek hacked away at the frozen chunks of congealed meat and potatoes with a wooden spoon. Their own portion simmered beside the kettle at the front.

They ate and Donjek looked after the dishes while Fanger, looking forward to the last real sleep he'd get for the next four days, tramped the bumpy footpath to ready his bed in their tent. He was laying his foamie and sleeping bag over the spruce boughs on their snow bed when the sound of a two-stroke droned through the night air.

Ted pulled in, swathed in a blanket of cold exhaust. Fanger led him into the cookshack as Donjek exited, carrying a dishpan. His headlamp bounced from side to side before he bent to his knees at a patch of clean snow and started scrubbing their pots with cakes of ice.

Inside Ted dropped into a folding chair near the stove.

"Want do you want to drink?" Fanger asked.

"A fifth of rye. But a coffee will do." Ted skimmed a slurp off the top of the cup Fanger poured for him and settled into the toasty glow. "Isn't this cozy? Can I move in after the race?"

"Sure. By then the patio will be landscaped, too," Fanger said. "Donny's thinking of carving out a bench around our bonfire pit and maybe some tiered seating. The drift is three metres high."

"Even without it, I'm sure the racers will be happy to see you. The first one's probably going to show up around four o'clock. I passed him about thirty klicks back."

"What about the others?"

"Well, it's no surprise Jenn's with the front runners. They'll be here a bit after breakfast. About three hours behind them is the next pack. When I left the Top of the World, half were still on their way up," Ted said.

Donjek returned at the tail end of Ted's report. "How's Omar doing? The guy from Morocco."

Ted frowned. "A pair of marathoners passed him at the plough turnaround. He's in with a handful of three hundreds."

On a clipboard, Fanger penciled a comment on the checker's report. The chart would quickly fill with names and bib numbers, dates and times in and out and a fitness description for each athlete: very good, good, reasonable, poor or disqualified. From the safety procedures sheet beneath, Fanger confirmed his scheduled phone-in for eight A M. "Have you heard a weather forecast lately?" he asked.

Ted tossed his empty paper cup in the stove. "It'll stay like this tomorrow, hot as the sun days, twenty-five-below nights, but they're calling for a trough of cold air to move in after that." He looked at his watch. "I should be getting back. The checker there, Rick—you know, the guy from the Keystone Kops—is gonna need my help when the next batch arrives." The Keystone Kops and their paddywagon were a cornerstone of Rendezvous. Ted gathered up his small garments and reminded Fanger of the lead cyclist's ETA. Possessions accounted for, he took off into the night.

True to Ted's prediction, forty-five minutes after Fanger's alarm rang at three-thirty, snow crunched under tires pushed by heavy effort. Fanger turned up the lantern flame, chasing sleep from the shack, and took the kettle from the fire.

"I tell ya, that was tough." The cyclist, number 307, tipped his bike against a tree. He shuffled bowlegged to the nearest chair inside. "Do you have anything to drink?"

Fanger gave him a ready cup of hot water and showed him the drink fixings. "Want anything to eat? There's stew and rolls."

"Not stew, my stomach's a mess. I'll take a roll, though. Maybe that'll soak up some of the indigestion." He chewed lethargically and washed it down with plain hot water. "You were staffing a checkpoint last year, right?"

"Yeah," Fanger said. Beside 307's name, Steve Stone, he wrote the time, 0424, a dash and the date, 22/02. "You were in first last year, too, I recall. How's the trail?"

"Wide and clear, but way harder. Shoving the bike through all that soft melt this afternoon was a killer, and when the sun went down it turned solid, glare ice and glaciers. I don't feel sorry for the ones coming through in the heat of the day. It'll be slush over a skating rink. I'm surprised it's so much warmer here than in the Interior."

Fanger smiled, remembering the unbroken stream of chatter he listened to last year. After talking to themselves for a hundred kilometres, the racers were happy to speak to a responsive listener.

"Hey. Did you hear any news? Do we still have soldiers in the Middle East?" Steve asked.

"Uh, no. Wait. I guess so. I haven't heard anything since yesterday," Fanger said.

"Man, our president. I can't wait to vote him out of office." The Alaskan's views were very coherent for a man who'd been driving himself dizzy for fourteen hours.

Fanger shifted back to food. "You want something else? Another drink?"

"Naw, I'm going to crash for an hour or two. Or, yeah, I'll have a tea. Where should I lay out my stuff?"

"In here or out back." Fanger gave him his drink, and with the lantern led the way to the structure resting at the end of a short path. He tugged open the ties and held the flap aside. "That's Donjek Stoneman. You can sleep over here."

"Where here? On this snowbank?" He looked down at the rolled form on the sculpted bench and over to Fanger's bedding.

Fanger gave the coals a gentle stir and set fresh wood in the stove. "It's well off the ground and the tent's warm. You should be okay with your foamie."

"What foamie?"

"The one you brought with you."

The cyclist shook his head. Fanger cloaked his annoyance in the dark. "You don't have one. Well, take mine then." He pulled it out from under his trapper bag.

"Great," the American said. He went to his ride and tugged a sleeping bag out of the ice-crusted panniers hanging from his bike's frozen frame.

At the kitchen Fanger snapped the tent flaps shut behind him. The rustlings outside quickly died away and he was alone in the night. There wasn't much point trying to sleep now. Settled in with a coffee, he put his feet up on a stump in front of the stove and opened a book of Yukon stories scrounged out of the library discards. The exaggerated account of running the Nahanni before neoprene and rubber rafts soon spread over his chest, rising and falling in a pre-dawn doze. Only when it plopped onto the dirt floor did Fanger rouse.

He shook the mud off and held the dripping book by its spine. He tossed it on the toboggan table, then fiddled with his alarm clock and watched the minutes.

Not fifteen of them later, he took a pouch of tobacco out of his breast pocket and flipped it open. His fingers twirled in fluid movement, tucking away the sticky tab on the envelope, pressing the crease from a cut-corner rolling paper, the pinch and twist of a fresh cigarette. He nursed the smoke like a drunk's last bottle, but nonetheless stubbed it out too soon.

Snores from next door assured him Steve was breathing. The small hours crawled past in a constant round of coffee, stove, smoke, coffee stove smoke, coffee-stove-smoke. He'd have to include the smoke shop and Midnight Beans coffee in Ted's thank-you ad.

At the bonfire, Fanger picked up a long willow. Holding it with a fencer's grace, he thrust it into the skeletal cracks of the charred logs flickering in the wilderness. Overhead he tracked satellites on their orbits, wondering which one carried the phone signal—which one he was supposed to blame when it passed out of range.

Incessant beeping alarmed him, and he ran into the kitchen to kill his clock. At that moment Jenn's face appeared in the doorway.

"Hey, Fanger, get up and come outside. The first hundred Ks are just behind us. It's their race to the finish." She parked her pulk beside that of a competitor who'd joined her through the night.

Fanger shook his head clear and picked up the clipboard

on his way out. By the firelight he wrote 0734–22/02 in the Little Gold column beside entrants 304 and 301, Jenn's number. Then, grouped together on the trail, the three trained their headlamps on the distant pinpricks of light bouncing closer. With their sparked lighters held high like the Olympic torch, they cheered on the contestants trotting neck and neck.

"Come on, Jill! You can do it," Jenn yelled. Then, ever fair, "Catch her up, Rudi. You're nearly there." Runner 103 shot ahead, but his effort rolled off the slight incline. It was number 104, Jill Chester, who put a foot across the line first.

Seconds after Fanger wrote 0741–22/02, Rudi jogged over the line, his toboggan jerking to a stop beside the victor who was bent at the waist, panting. He dropped his traces and held out his hand. "Well won."

"Well run." Jill shook his hand and used the grip to help herself up. Congratulations from the others further bolstered them.

"Das war Arschkalt," Rudi said.

"Come inside and warm up," Fanger offered. "Everything's on the table; make yourselves at home. I gotta wake the Tour de Force."

Amazed Steve had slept through their commotion, he shook the peddler awake. "It's through seven thirty. You ready to get up?"

Steve sprung out of his sleeping bag, bleary eyes wide open. "It's what time? I'll be right out."

Fanger went back to the kitchen where Jenn ladled spoonfuls of rich buffalo meat into paper bowls. "Sure I can't get you anything, Jill?" she asked.

"I'm sure, thanks," 104 replied. Her proper British accent didn't match the dishevelled hair sticking up over her tomboy face, or the tongue stuck out the side of her mouth as she squeezed a tube of paste onto a dry roll. "Bloody thing's half frozen." A blob dropped onto the crust. "I brought these protein packs because everyone thinks I'm nuts doing these extremes on cheese sandwiches and peanut butter. Now I wish I'd stuck with my old diet."

"We have stew with no meat in it," Fanger said. "I can heat you a serving in no time."

"Aren't you a dear? That would be lovely." She bit into her appetizer. "Ultra races don't usually offer a choice of menu." When her meal was hot, Fanger passed a steaming bowl to the grateful vegetarian. "You're just wonderful, you know, you Canadians. A perfect combination of us and the Americans."

"That's why I immigrated," Fanger said.

Steve bounded into the kitchen. "Who's immigrating? Tough job at this border," the Alaskan said. "Got any of that for me?" Jenn thrust a roll in his hand and passed him a dish.

"You look like a new man," Fanger said. "Feeling better?"

"Right as rain," Steve said. He filled his bowl and dipped his bread in the broth. "I'll just finish this and head out. Even if I am starting later than I wanted, it's a nice boost knowing it'll be sunrise soon."

While everyone ate, Fanger woke Donjek next door by stirring the fire like a triangle at a mess hall. The youth mumbled, "I'll be out in a minute."

"In about fifteen minutes Jenn and three others are

going to crash in here. Just put your stuff to the side." Fanger slid his foam pad under his sleeping bag and took the liner out to air.

In the centre of camp, Jenn and 304 were emptying their pulks. The bike had been moved to lean against the outhouse wall. Its rider emerged, rinsed his hands in the snow and pulled on his gloves. "See you next year." He waved and wriggled away, gaining traction in the sharp morning frost as he peddled into the States. Fanger wrote 0825–22/02 for Steve's exit time.

He handed the clipboard to Donjek, who had shuffled outside in the pale early light. The youth rubbed warmth into his hands and made a couple of notes while Fanger briefed him. "I have to call in, so get yourself some breakfast," Fanger said, taking the compact phone with him as he wandered around the camp in search of the strongest signal.

Finally LED satellites floated across the phone's display. He dialled the Gambler's Den, but his connection floated into outer space. Fanger powered off and on, reconnected and got Erik on the first ring. As smoothly as the two-second transmission delay allowed, Fanger recited the stats.

"They were fast," Erik said. "I thought they'd take a few hours longer and we'd get some photos. Did you take any pictures?"

"Sorry, it didn't occur to me."

"Don't worry about it. Here's what happened overnight." Erik summarized the report Ted had given him at the end of his last sweep to Dawson. "Omar Ahmed came in to the Top of the World in a rough state. Ted's on his way back now and if Ahmed's strong enough to ride double on the sled, he'll bring him out this morning."

Fanger wanted more details, but chitchat on the sat phone wasn't practical. "That's tough," is all he said before continuing. "Jill and Rudi are ready to be shuttled out. They're napping now, so when should I wake them?"

Erik expected Jerry there by mid-morning. He asked that the sledder phone in when he arrived.

"Okay. I'll get a few winks then," Fanger said.

Two hours later, a snowmobile hummed through Fanger's dreams. He heard Jerry say hi, followed by Donjek's quiet, "Shhh, I'm letting him sleep."

Fanger stuck his head out of the tent and saw Donjek thumbing in his direction. Jenn was stowing her headlamp, preparing to leave. Fanger threw his parka on over his long johns and tramped in his loose boots toward them. "Hey, Jerry. How's the world of extreme racing?"

"I guess you already know Ahmed's out of the running."

"What?" Jenn abandoned her gear to join them.

"Yeah, Ted got back from your checkpoint just as Ahmed arrived, really out of it. Practically fell in the fire. I was sleeping so I don't really know all the details, except for what Ted told me." That would be everything, Fanger was sure.

"Rick and a couple of marathoners set him in a lawn chair by the stove, changed his wet things for dry and poured hot liquid into him. You should have seen how he perked up on two cups of sugar water."

Jenn's jaw dropped. "I would have never guessed Omar couldn't make it. He trained so hard. I was sure he'd be fine."

"Oh, he will be. They put him to bed and Ted's taking him out, probably now, in fact."

Jerry went to get himself a coffee. Through the cotton walls Fanger heard him repeat the adventures to Donjek. Another cyclist and a skier arrived at that moment, forcing Fanger to halt the gossip. He stuck his head into the kitchen and asked Donjek, "You look after these guys, okay? Write their times on the chart."

Jerry said something about shepherding in the stragglers when Fanger remembered Erik's message. "Give him a call," he said, pointing to a knoll. "Reception's best over there."

The fourth time the sledder lost his link, he folded the antennae into the phone and gave it back to Fanger. "Nothing's staying in range long enough to connect. I'll head back and get the news quicker that way."

"I better get going, too," Jenn said, fastening her pulk around her waist. "That's so disappointing about Omar." Suited up, she trotted away and gave them a sad wave.

As Fanger's alarm rang, forty miles away, Ahmed had woken between Rick, the checker, dozing glassy-eyed beside him, and an unfamiliar woman curled in slumber. His first thought — *Must go on, can't stop* — rattled him as he lifted his head. "What time is it?" he asked the man.

"Half past seven. I'll get you something to drink." Ahmed gulped down a healthy measure of water and wiped his face on his sleeve. His next actions left Rick dumbfounded.

Ahmed flung back his covers, yanked his clothes from where they hung under the ridgepole and pulled them on over his long johns.

"Are those even dry?" Rick asked. He was soundly ignored by the racer stuffing clothes into a mesh bag. "You'll freeze, man. Are you even fit to travel?"

Ahmed remained silent, except to swat the door aside on the way to his pulk. He opened the carabiners, shoved the cargo net aside and pulled his duffel wide open. His eyes roamed over the contents in a mental inventory that ended when he removed his spare water pack.

Rick's prayers that the sleeping racers would stir went unanswered, so he tried stalling.

"It's sixty kilometres to the next checkpoint. There's no shame in withdrawing," he suggested. "Everyone will understand. And if you're feeling better tomorrow, you can help out at one of the remotes further ahead." He followed Ahmed inside to the water cauldron and tried to entice him with food. He was momentarily rewarded when Ahmed sat down to murmur a short prayer before a bowl of lentil stew, but in a few spoonfuls it was gone.

Rick hovered in the doorway, hoping a snowmobile's two-stroke whine would approach. He couldn't keep Ahmed here against his will, and he couldn't go with him. What he wouldn't give for the Keystone Kops' paddy-wagon now. If only Jerry hadn't left on his sweep before Ted got back.

"Hey, at least wait until it's light before you go. You'll stay warmer that way," Rick said.

"No." Ahmed cinched down his possessions and checked the traces before fastening the padded belt around him. And that's when Rick got the idea to slow him with helpfulness.

"Well, if I can't make you stay, at least I can help you

get ahead." He pointed to the straw coming from Ahmed's water bladder. "Put that drinking rig inside your clothes, across your chest, around your armpit and up." As he wrestled the ribbed hose out of Ahmed's collar, a strong and steady carotid artery pulsed under Rick's fingers. The racer's quiet breathing became impatient.

"It won't work like this. Take your shirt off." Rick took his time adjusting the apparatus. "It won't freeze up anymore." He glanced up and down the deserted trail and kept his curses to himself.

Ahmed pushed past him and jogged away. The receding man even turned to wave. With serious concern, Rick penciled in Ahmed's departure in reasonable condition at 0755–22/02 and started filling in a blank incident report form. Rick couldn't believe the Moroccan's resilience, or determination, and didn't think anyone else would either.

SEVEN

"It's sunny and minus fifteen in Whitehorse, and this is Sid Crawford with the local and regional news to twelve o'clock."

LaRouge, across the street at M division, turned up the radio in the detachment's bullpen. As M Division was headquarters for the Yukon RCMP, LaRouge took advantage of extra resources for his investigation. Two members from the Major Crimes Unit sifted reports on overloaded desks.

Sergeant Felix passed the open door. "Heard anything from Little Gold?" he stopped to ask. He joined LaRouge at the window facing the broadcast booth of the radio station and the noon-hour traffic between the two buildings. The corporal shook his head and held his index finger to his lips.

"Police are asking for the public's help in identifying a suspect in the September break, enter and theft at Boreal Blasters' storage magazine. Anyone with information regarding a male individual seen working as a traffic surveyor at the intersection of the Alaska Highway and Two Mile Hill between September twentieth and October fifth is asked to call your local RCMP detachment or Crime Stoppers at one-eight-hundred-triple-two-TIPS."

"Today's the last day we're featuring this on Crime Stoppers," LaRouge said. "We drew a blank the last time it aired." A glimmer of hope lit up with his phone. "Ruth's directing the calls from reception to me." He put the receiver to his ear and pushed line one. The detachment secretary transferred the call.

Felix nodded his approval, drew his chair near the radio and lowered the volume.

"Finally in the news this lunch hour we have an update from the Yukon Arctic Ultra. Trail crews are on the lookout for Moroccan racer Omar Ahmed, who remains unaccounted for since leaving the Top of the World checkpoint. We'll have more for you in our news at five o'clock, but first the weather brought to you by Sleet and Snow Auto Detail." Felix glanced at LaRouge, whose shoulder crunched against the phone as his hand skimmed across a yellow legal pad.

The DJ rattled off the current conditions and segued back to Sid.

"In sports, runner Jill Chester took top prize in this year's Yukon Arctic Ultra. With a time of nineteen hours, forty-one minutes over one hundred kilometres, she beat men's contestant Rudi Wintermann by a one-minute margin. Yukoners still out on the trail are Jenn Strider leading the three hundred Ks, and Marty Secord on the final leg to Little Gold. Visitors racing for glory include cyclist Steve Stone approaching Chicken, and skiers Per Olafsen of Norway and Joshua Peters of Michigan."

LaRouge hung up and stood triumphant before his superior. "Success!" He tore several pages from the pad and laid them on the table in front of the sergeant. "We have a description, sir. No name for the suspect yet, but the caller, a teacher, will be here after school to help us get an idea of who we're dealing with."

"Excellent. That will give us time to arrange for a portrait artist. And run the image past Boreal." Felix returned to his office.

At three-thirty, LaRouge was called to the front desk, where Ruth introduced Yvonne Kovic, a grown woman dressed much as the students she taught, but for the wide crimson band over her hair. Her right hand trembled in LaRouge's handshake; her left clutched the leather strap slung across her chest. LaRouge led her to an interview room, which was already occupied by the police artist.

"I feel like I've been called to the principal's office." She stifled a nervous giggle.

LaRouge thanked her for her cooperation and counted on her being a trustworthy witness. She sat and collected herself while LaRouge brought her a glass of water, turned on the tape recorder on the table between them and cited the time and date.

"I'm Corporal Sean LaRouge and this is Dave Harrow." The artist wiped his hands clean of charcoal and shook Yvonne's.

"It's a pleasure to meet you," she said. "I visited your show at Captain Martin House. Very impressive."

"He's going to draw what you describe," LaRouge said. "Take your time and tell me what you remember that made you call in."

"I was thinking about it all afternoon," she started. "I could hardly teach. I hope I wasn't too hasty when I phoned you. You see, I could be wrong."

LaRouge was ready for this: witness stage fright. "We're grateful for anything you can tell us, and I assure you we'll corroborate the facts before proceeding." This calmed her.

"All right then. It must have been on my way to work when I saw him the first time. I remember thinking, what's that fool doing on the median in this weather? But then I lost the thought in traffic." She tasted the water. "The thing is, I only got a quick look at him on that day, but I saw him again at Thanksgiving."

LaRouge stilled his pen. "Tell me about that meeting."

Yvonne responded by rooting through her book bag until she found her teacher's day planner.

"It helps me think." She flipped to the first term of school. "Right, I was cleaning up the art corner. The bell was about to ring and the children were getting their coats on. I looked out the window and saw the two of them down there—he was doing that possession thing I really hate." She looked at LaRouge who obviously needed an explanation, not being *that* type of guy.

"You know, standing so he stops her from turning left, stops her from turning right and pins her up against the wall. Even if it's in fun and comes with kisses and laughter, it's such a power play, so aggressive, like being trapped." She shivered at the idea.

LaRouge nodded. "Do you know his name?"

Yvonne frowned, sorry to come up short. "I didn't meet him, really. And other than on the highway, that was the only time I saw him."

"Do you know the woman's name?"

"Oh yes, it's Annabeth Secord, Marie's mother. I saw him pull her close and whisper something in her ear. Then he put a package in her hand, a turquoise jump rope or something. She tried to give it back, but he stuffed it in her purse. I figured it was a gift for Marie, and Annabeth didn't want her daughter bought. I see that a lot in break-ups." She paused.

LaRouge made a sympathetic murmur. "Secord" had ignited a spark, the verge of a connection.

Yvonne leaned close to plead, "Please officer, be discreet with what I tell you. I don't want to cause any trouble for Marie; she's had quite a time of it this year, and only now, in February, is she adjusting."

"To what, Ms. Kovic?"

"Her parents' separation. I guess there were lots of argu-ments at home, and stress. Marie couldn't understand what was going on, only that mommy and daddy were shouting a lot, and she started to as well. Three times in one month we had to pull her out of screaming matches with classmates." She lowered her voice and shielded it behind her hand. "There were rumours in the staff room that the fellow I saw had something to do with Annabeth and Marty splitting up."

LaRouge got it at the second mention of the name. "You mean Marty Secord — who's racing in the Arctic Ultra?"

"Yeah, that's him. I tell you he hasn't had it easy either, being a single dad. That's why I couldn't put any stock in the rumours. Annabeth would be fool to trade Marty for the slimeball I saw."

"What's your mental picture of him?" LaRouge encouraged her: "Tell Dave and he'll put your verbal image on paper." The artist propped his sketchpad against his knee.

Yvonne had a good eye for detail and a long memory. Months after her brief glimpse, she could recall his height, five-foot-ten, build, thin like a dancer, and style, dashing like a swashbuckler. His close-fitting trousers, not jeans, and the heavy sweater under his bomber jacket completed the motif. His hair, she thought, was curly and dark, but he'd worn a watch cap. Fortunately it hadn't shaded his face, which she got a good look at. His eyes, dark like First Nations', were narrow, but flashed when excited, which was often during the exchange. His nose, mouth, chin, all equally sharp, sat well-proportioned on his long face, which was shadowed where his taut cheeks hollowed above his thick moustache.

Dave tore off the likeness and placed it between the cop and witness. Yvonne picked it up. "Funny how the mind colours things. Here he looks like a model, not like the creep I remember. But it's a perfect likeness."

"May I?" LaRouge studied the image. Yvonne was right;

there was a definite harmony to the features, which must have driven Marty frantic.

"So do you know who it is?" Yvonne asked with a definite co-conspirator tone that LaRouge quashed.

"We're not at liberty to say, but your impression gives us a good picture of him. You've been a great help, Ms. Kovic."

Yvonne stood then, closed her diary and put it in her satchel. LaRouge showed her out and checked that Ruth knew how to contact her if the information led to an arrest. "Oh, that's not necessary." Yvonne blushed, but the receptionist nodded; they had what they needed.

When she left, LaRouge dialled Sergeant Felix. "We've got a drawing, sir. And we should ask around the elementary school. Our informant spotted him there and the staff or students may know more."

"Good, get Avery on it," Felix said. "And track down a physical address."

LaRouge passed the orders on to Avery, a member on secondment from the Integrated Border Enforcement Team. Avery made it clear that his six-month transfer from Vancouver was to improve the security readiness at northern ports of entry, not to chase school teachers, but LaRouge had no time to listen to his colleague's complaints. He rushed out of the compound.

His arrival at the blasting shop on Industrial during the last forty-five minutes of the business day gave the staff a welcome diversion. At a glance, the forgetful salesman recognized lawn chair guy from the photocopied sketch. The manager looked next. His skin blanched paler than the paper he tugged in an angry grasp.

"That's Mead, all right," he said. "Said he was a new mine safety manager. Stiffed us for a bunch of special orders he never claimed."

LaRouge listened with interest to the complaint—Mead showered all with money and the promise of more. It looked good until it came time to settle up, and Mead was nowhere to be found. LaRouge took down the name.

"The only thing he did take was a small magazine, which luckily he paid for in cash." LaRouge asked for a copy of the sales orders. "Sure," the manager said. "It's here, with the rest of my outstanding accounts." He flipped through a pile of carbonless copies and pulled out the offending form.

"This really burns me up, you know? I'm out for the price of the goods, and if I ship them back I have to suck up the twenty-five percent restocking fee. And the freight." He gave the past-due notice to LaRouge, but neither the address nor phone number would bring him closer to a physical location; they were for a local hotel.

The manager fumed and muttered. "The losses from this robbery blew a hole in my finances, and all the leads keep fizzling out. You want to make my insurance company happy? Find this guy."

LaRouge met his stern gaze. The businessman tacked the sketch on the bulletin board behind his desk and wrote "Most Wanted" in heavy black felt across the top.

LaRouge stopped at the hotel on his way back to the station. The manager remembered the guest, but not his address; the register, however, listed a box number LaRouge could investigate. From an array of wall clocks over the reception desk, LaRouge checked the local time, displayed between Alaska and Alberta. The post office was open for ten more minutes. He thanked the clerk and ran to the nearest outlet on Main.

Using local knowledge — or, rather, knowledge of a local — added to LaRouge's rough outline of the explosives thief. Since the end of June, nothing had arrived for lawn chair guy, but until then Mead had received irregular deliveries of overseas mail from the Middle East and *Runner*, the only magazine he subscribed to.

"You know, wait here a moment." The postal worker locked the customer door and disappeared into the back room. LaRouge heard the push and shove of a desk being turned inside out. "Here it is," the clerk said. LaRouge wrote the phone number as it was read off to him. "It's a house-sit, I think, but he gave us this number to call when a parcel arrived. I guess you have your methods to find out whose house it rings at."

LaRouge declined comment, thanked his acquaintance and left. Since noon, the whole world had been on the side of justice for a change. He enjoyed it during the brisk walk to his vehicle and the short drive to the detachment.

In the bullpen he searched through the exchanges in the reverse telephone book until he found a match, giving him the homeowner's name and street address, which he brought to Felix's office. The sergeant would promptly secure a warrant.

"Until then, I'll see if the place is occupied," LaRouge said. "If it's a house-sit maybe the neighbours know when the residents are back. And I'll brief Dog Services on the way." LaRouge took the stairs that exited nearest the kennel.

At the penned yard, he found the handler exercising a young German shepherd. The dog chased a rubber bone while they discussed the case. The handler held little hope of finding traces so long after the crime, but she'd been surprised by the dogs before.

LaRouge used the last hour of his shift to cruise Mead's Riverdale neighbourhood. Pulling up at the property, he parked and made his first inquiry at the house to the right, where a television flickered in the front room.

The elderly woman who answered the door knew her neighbours but didn't expect to see them until May. "They're in Colorado or New Mexico, aren't they, dear?" she called to her husband. "One of those four corner states," she said when he failed to reply. No, she didn't really know the fellow who was looking after the place; it was so hard to see over the high fence.

From the new mother across the road, LaRouge learned the housesitter liked to go for long runs and that he was away, or at least his bedroom light hadn't been turned on for a few days. "He kept to himself," she said, apologetic that she didn't know when he'd return.

The sergeant was away from his desk, as was Avery, when LaRouge returned to the detachment. He scribbled a note for Felix and, frustrated, took his work home with him. He spent a restless night with his wife and daughter. Well after they fell asleep, LaRouge prowled the house. He checked on the baby, got her a drink before she fussed and soothed her to the sleep he was denied.

It seemed ages until the next morning when he was able to assemble with forensics at the suspect's house, official permission in hand. The corporal marched to the front door, hammered on it and announced himself. No reply. After two more unanswered attempts at entry, he motioned the locksmith forward and watched him punch the lock. The door swung open. Prints and Pix followed the dog into the house.

LaRouge started in the living room, inspecting the nooks and crannies that held the fine details of habitation. The books were definitely not typical bomber reading, unless the suspect had a curiosity about early childhood development. The dining room, void of clues, held a hungry emptiness and the kitchen's warmth had long cooled.

From upstairs LaRouge heard his name called and abandoned his examination of the back porch. Members searching the upper floors were as luckless as he. "There's nothing to indicate anyone's been here in months, Corporal," said the evidence specialist. "You're sure of your suspect's address?" LaRouge suppressed a retort about judgment and asked the technician to keep looking.

Barking from the basement redirected his attention downstairs, and a rookie hopped out of his way on the landing. "Physical evidence, sir." The youth stumbled after him. "On your right, sir. Careful on the steps."

At the bottom of a slanted flight, proud job satisfaction panted out of the police dog's jaws. The handler recalled her partner to heel and pointed to a cool, dark niche by a washing machine. "Right in here," she said. "Tracker wouldn't have found anything if this tag hadn't come off." She patted the canine as reward for cracking the case and showed LaRouge a segment of paper strapping, now sealed as evidence. He recognized it from the scene-of-the-crime photos.

"Look here," she said, "you can see part of the word 'detonator,' and an identification number. I'm sure he stored everything here."

LaRouge's grin equalled the dog's. "Those numbers are unique. If it matches Boreal's order, we've got Mead with hard evidence."

"When it matches," the handler concurred, without any doubt of a positive outcome.

At the detachment, LaRouge shared his discovery with Felix in the sergeant's office. "Distribute the name and drawing to all detachments along the highway, the bus station, bars, liquor stores, airports and gas stations. Better send a copy to immigration right away," Felix ordered.

"Speaking of which, did Avery turn up anything from the school?" LaRouge asked.

"I'll ask." Felix reached toward the phone at the same moment that Ruth's sultry tones issued from the intercom —a Mr. Hannes Bock from Germany was calling for Markus Fanger. He picked up the receiver at her command.

Felix had heard of the man whom Fanger considered his closest friend, but he had yet to meet the auxiliary's former colleague. The line buzzed alive with the background noise of the caller's office. "Sergeant Felix speaking. How may I help you?"

"This is Kommissar Bock from the Bundeskriminalamt in Wiesbaden," replied the caller in practiced textbook English. "Please, I would like to speak to Markus Fanger. He does not answer his phone."

"I'm sorry, Kommissar. Fanger is on the Top of the World Highway staffing an extreme race checkpoint."

"Yes, exactly that is the reason for my call."

"I'm Fanger's supervisor. Can you tell me what this is about?"

"Is a man named Omar Ahmed in this race?"

"Yes. But he hasn't been spotted since this morning."

Felix couldn't see Bock pale, but he did hear his mounting agitation. "Do you have his papers there?"

"I'm looking at his entry form." The sergeant moved around his desk, stretching the cord with him, and slapped open the Ultra folder. "There's nothing about the competitors' visas. What's happened?"

"Where to begin? I am working, as you say, outside the box, aber wann I heard this, it was my first thought to warn Fanger."

"Warn him of what? Is he in danger?"

"He may be," Bock said, followed by a sentence from which Felix recognized only the word "kompliziert." He gave Bock the same patience he'd given Fanger in the early days.

"I know this is complicated," the sergeant said. "Take your time."

Bock plunged in. "There are irregularities with Ahmed's passport. We will send a report to the Americans."

"The Americans?" Felix and LaRouge shared a look of surprise.

"Yes, in reply to the original request from the Office of Homeland Security. We must answer their questions before acting," he said.

"Pardon?"

"US customs sent the passport details of the Ultra contestants from Germany here for proving. The passport of Omar Ahmed has a red thread—nein—red *flag*, from an old case of the BKA."

"That's you, isn't it?"

"Yes, but I work in data processing. This comes from Staatsschutz, the sector for state security."

In the detachment phone register, the sergeant found Avery's extension. "May I put you on hold, Herr Bock? I'd like to have our immigration liaison officer hear this."

With Bock's consent, Felix switched to line two and pulled Avery away from his school inquiries. Felix exhausted the facts updating the new member of their group. Picking up the overseas line, the sergeant took a deep breath. "I'm putting you on speakerphone, Herr Bock. Corporals Avery from border enforcement and LaRouge have joined me."

The German eased more comfortably into his second language. "Many branches of police review the material. Our border police found the forgery, a passport. When someone dies, we bekom their documents. Then we cancel it. Ahmed's was not cancelled."

The date of birth and photo were faked, but the expiry date had not lapsed, a step better than a store-bought identity. Felix asked how Bock became involved.

"Staatsschutz, state security, called me for background data from our Netzwerk. The case has been sleeping many months."

The line fell silent.

"Can you give us a description of the man?" Felix wrote

while Bock spoke, slowing when LaRouge opened lawn chair guy's portrait.

"That's him." The sergeant thumped his desk in confirmation. "It's our explosives thief. Herr Bock, I'll forward a drawing of our suspect by fax. The name at the bottom right is his alias. Whatever he's planning, he can do it with a few cases of dynamite. Avery, as soon as you're finished at the school, talk to Boreal. Get an insight on practical applications, possible targets."

"I'll get on his port of entry, too," the corporal volunteered. "If we trace his route, we may pick up some idea of his plan, see if he's met anyone." He capped his heavy fountain pen, replaced it inside his jacket and smoothed his tie. "I'd also like to notify the Americans, sir."

"I'll look after it, Corporal," Felix said, and then into the phone, "Kommissar, could you give us a profile? All we know is he's from Morocco."

Bock's indecipherable aside to a co-worker was followed by the whisper of file documents. "That's his cover, one with a grain of truth. Noted in our Akten, but sadly unconfirmed, is a suspicion he trained there. But he is from Syria, not Morocco.

"One year ago was a bombing of a village outside Damascus. American-madebombs killed civilians — women, children and an eight-year-old boy." The German took a deep breath. "The boy was named Nassir Ahmed. The son."

It took no imagination to envision the father's wrath.

"Our Kollegen told us Ahmed disappeared in days, probably with the forged passport," he continued. "Staatsschutz believes he has a revenge motive."

All three Canadians guessed the target of that revenge: Alaska, protected by an unsuspecting man and boy.

Felix issued the orders. "Bock, send me everything you can. Avery, have Dawson ready the detachment snow-mobiles. LaRouge, alert Fanger."

EIGHT

Ahmed hurried on against the wind that found him in every gully. He tugged over the crests and down the shad-owed backs of the hills as the day crawled closer. Pellets of snow hurled against him. He pulled his balaclava down and his scarf up over his mouth and nose, never ceasing to put one foot in front of the other.

A pair of coppery discs glimmered in his periphery, flit left, blinked away, then reappeared closer by a leap. The snort rising from bulbous nose flaps identified the beast as a moose, not ten steps ahead. Forelegs spread, it staked its ground, antlers low. Abruptly, it grunted and shook. Ahmed didn't have time to chase wildlife back into the wild. He waved his arms and shouted—Arabic epithets about lazy camels—until it huffed and loped away.

Ahmed stormed across a dozen valleys and now, at a familiar pile of slide rubble, came to a stop in the lee of the rocks. His neon green survey tape fluttered from a stunted pine at this sheltered nook, and it marked where he'd gone off-road during his scouting trip. He quickly concealed himself and sucked long on his drinking straw. He jammed a couple of handfuls of snow into his water sack to replenish what he'd used.

Unwilling to waste time earlier searching for batteries, he got them out now and replaced the ones he drained yesterday in his GPS. Switching it on, he got out his topos while waiting for the satellites to zoom in on his location.

Oriented north, he disappeared on a game trail leading through the bush to Clinton Creek. He recalled how close to the main road his two-hundred-metre detour had seemed in fall. But hauling the strong box, grounding rods, locks and tools had seemed backbreaking then and that was with an ATV and trailer. Now he'd have to rely on brute strength to get the contents out to their final destination.

An upended birch pointed to his depot, camouflaged in the topgrowth. Ahmed stopped and, not even bothering to unhitch, dug through layers of leggings to the fly of his long johns. Holding himself between numb fingers, a shiver to his bowels chased liquid warmth into an aura beneath him. He'd have to make a conscious effort to drink more.

Regardless, he opted to sacrifice his meager reserve for *wudu* preliminary to *salat al-fajr*. Cleansed, he faced Mecca and prayed as Venus dimmed in the face of the rising sun. To date Ahmed had fulfilled Allah's wishes; even an infidel would have to admit he appeared to be blessed with the righteousness of Allah's glory. By day's end, he would be ready to honour the beginning of what he thought of as a Year of Understanding.

Finished, he turned to refill his water supply. Several steps from his cache he cleared a place for his stove. Before priming the cooker, he gave it a slight shake. Empty. He took out a bottle of fuel and struggled to open the cap.

With his overmitts and liners off, conduction from the metal canister seared his raw fingers. He fumbled the stove and splashes of white gas stung his clumsy hands. Fluid slopped over his exposed knuckles and left a chalky stain where the petroleum evaporated, flash freezing his bare skin. He crossed his arms and tucked his hands under his armpits until the painful stinging ebbed. Then he replaced his gloves and closed the topped-up chamber.

A weak flame sputtered from the vents and he pumped additional pressure into the tank, strengthening the output. He covered it with a pot of snow.

Alternating between body heat and holding his hands near the stove, he felt pins and needles pierce his fingertips. The water took forever to melt. He checked his watch, stamped his feet and, impatient, went to empty the cache.

When he released the locks and shunted the sand-filled lid to the side, the nauseating odour of nitroglycerin hurled out of the stuffy container. He let it air, recalling how sick he'd felt after handling the sticks five months ago.

Getting the product had been easier than he'd imagined, mining being a main industry in the territory and blasting being part of ore recovery. His first visit to the local supplier was meant to be a quick look at the outfit. But, once he'd introduced himself as a safety manager, new to town and wanting to upgrade the job site, the staff had become very friendly.

Over the following days, "in town on the way to camp," Ahmed had collected a wide assortment of product trinkets. As each visit resulted in higher sales orders, it took less than a week to become the Customer of the Month.

Never did the staff give away the location of their storage magazine, but during a discussion about lock boxes, he had a good idea where the keys were. The break-in was never discovered, of course. There'd been no alarms triggered, no prints, nothing removed; he'd been there only long enough to get impressions. He'd copied the keys later.

Cold and moisture didn't affect the brownish yellow PowerPro explosive, but for security Ahmed had purchased a small magazine "for the camp." When he pulled up in his rental pickup, they'd helped him load the four-hundred-fifty-pound chest and thrown in a pair of nitrile gloves with the company logo printed on the backs of them. "Don't forget where you got those," the manager had said.

Even using the quad and come-along, it had taken all afternoon to position the impervious box. Without the handheld winch, ramps and pipes to roll the chest, it would have been impossible to manoeuvre on this uneven ground. To anchor it he'd spent hours pounding grounding rods, as long as a man's thigh, through the permafrost, and then he'd taken a sledgehammer to the heads, bending each over the four corner grommets. Stick by stick, he'd placed the charges inside, each in its orange wax paper wrapper, and locked them down.

This was the first time it had been opened since that fall day. All was as he'd left it, including the non-porous gloves. He reached in for them and pulled back sharply, forgetting how long the compound held the cold, even though it was milder now than it had been weeks ago.

The capillaries in his fingers clamped shut, turning his pads and nails grey to the first knuckle. He adjusted his finger mitts and plucked out the gloves that prevented the compound from entering his pores and poisoning his blood. Soon, sixty charges lined his sled.

He set more water on to melt and pared his racing gear. The essentials he stuffed in a backpack and the rest he discarded in the box before resealing it. He spared none of his technology, and with the additional weight, his pulk was far heavier than himself. At least he hadn't had to drag it all the way from Dawson.

Pleased, he thought of Annabeth and when he'd seen her last, in October, with little Marie. Now that his plan was coming together, he wanted to confirm her readiness.

Via satellite he pictured her, the phone ringing beside her bed, her naked hand reaching up to answer … cut off when the carrier disappeared. He sent the transmission again and remembered their initially secret, and later open, calls when they'd waited for each other by a telephone … that wouldn't stay connected. He willed the phone to be as willing now as she had been for him and his cause … a cause that was being eternally thwarted by northern orbits.

Frustrated after these attempts, he dialled one last time. Success. "Happy New Year," he greeted her.

"Right. Today's Muharran," she said. "Happy New Year. Have you prayed for a long life?"

"Later, at Little Gold. I am at the cache now, yes, and everything is loaded. I worked like a dog getting this ready in fall. Now I will have to work like an ox to stay on schedule."

"Better make that charge like a bull from Pamplona. The commissioning has been rescheduled, and they've advanced the start up. I need you here a day early."

"What?" Ahmed shook the phone as if that would improve the transmission.

"Sorry, I just found out this morning. Since my part of the job — or rather, *ours* — is done, I'm helping another crew that's working round the clock. According to our foreman, the project manager brought us in on time, which goes well with 'under budget,' and they rewarded him by upping the stakes with another early completion bonus. Can we still do this?"

"Yes."

"I'll be in Tok on the twenty-fifth," she said. "Don't be late."

"If I am, do not wait." He hefted the pack onto his back and broke the sled where it had set in its tracks. He had another marathon distance to cover and he had to do it today.

He had not planned on resting at the Top of the World, or that Annabeth would take twenty-four hours off his schedule. He could use his first abort route, but not until he was across the border. By omitting all rests and shaving fifteen minutes off his combined prayer and meal stops, he could gain an edge.

Straining his mind as well as his body, he worked on the problem of avoiding Fanger's checkpoint. So far, the best he had come up with was to breeze through and take his rest after he was on the cut-off trail. He wondered if the shorter route would prove to be the fastest. He had not scouted the trails on the American side, being unwilling to present himself to immigration. On the other hand, what he thought he knew of this part of the trail had been erased by the seasons.

A long-track growled near. He froze behind the trees but lost the sound in a sudden gust. Then through the low scrub he saw a sleek snowmobile tip over a rise. The rider passed, looking neither left nor right. Another few steps and Ahmed would have been exposed. Only his lips moved, thanking Allah for his protection. Until he let out his breath, he hadn't realized he was holding it.

After last night he wanted to keep clear of sweepers and checkers, certain they would disqualify him. It was of no consequence if other racers saw him on the trail; they wouldn't hinder his untracked progress.

Time marched on and the barometer rose. For two hours the sky above him brightened, but not his spirits. Every half hour he had to stop to relieve himself. At each interval he drank, but it was obvious he wasn't replacing even a fraction of what he was losing. He tried to calculate how far he could go before running dry, but his thoughts were cluttered by annoyance at the frequent delays. He urged himself to increase his pace, stopping only three more times before midday.

He rushed through *salat al-zuhr*. Refreshed and right-minded, his vigour increased. Soon he met the first in a series of runners he would pass that afternoon. He spotted her, small and light, running out a hill on the flat terrain below. Snow feathered under her shoes with each long, steady stride. He barrelled past without a nod, not even lifting a hand from his sides where he clamped the traces tight against his waist.

In the next two kilometres he overtook three more entrants and set his sights on the pair that flitted in and out of the trees ahead. He closed the gap and sped by with a sneer of contempt at their plodding gait. By the time he knelt for *salat al-'asr*, he had forced himself ahead of the pack.

He ran hard, on empty, in gradually dropping degrees. By nightfall, within fifteen kilometres of the checkpoint, his earlier problem returned. He ran off trail to drain the fluids leeching out of his system and took the opportunity to prepare additional drinking water while saying his sunset prayers. The stove hissed and he drank off a mouthful of hot snowmelt. He shuddered as his cold bloodstream sucked the heat from his stomach.

Hungry, he stripped the wrapper off a protein bar and used his molars to snap off a frozen, brittle chunk. It defrosted as he chewed, and he managed to finish three squares before he thought his aching jaw would break. He added the collected melt to his water system. The contents sloshed warmth over his ribs and sternum.

On his way back he covered his headlamp when he heard the approach and departure of another snowmobile on the trail. Darkness obscured a depression on the game trail. His lamp might have reflected a layer of plastic wrap lying under a skiff of snow where a block had been carved out and replaced in the trail bed; the moon might have caught an unusual shadow where the double-pronged moose tracks were re-drawn after the snow had been disturbed. But in the moment he'd snapped light into dark, Ahmed overlooked the ruffled markings as he sidestepped a scrubby juniper, unaware of the quiet click before the bite. The trap cracked like an axe through a mirror, splintered in a horror film scream.

Shock took hold of Ahmed, and his blood pressure dropped deep. He felt his heart flutter, face blanche, palms tingle, legs crumple. He lay where he'd stood, and now prone, adrenalin flooded his brain. Eventually, he pushed himself to his knees. The restraint held fast, like the peregrines his son and father kept at home. He forced himself to relax, inhale and look at the damage. The iron agony clamped his pedal artery above; below, it snagged the ball of his foot. He pulled away, straining against the short anchor chain.

Sitting upright, he dug at the base, relenting when the motion tore at his shoe, curved as a sultan's slipper. Shards of winter sloughed over the throbbing extremity. Illuminating the vicious bind with his headlamp, he struggled to release it, but the cold robbed him of strength in his arms and body.

He unclipped his pulk and pushed the traces aside. In his pocket was a multi-tool with an awl that he bent open. He crouched down and examined the leaf springs. Focused on freedom, he stood, woozy and stumbling, and forced the iron tongs together with his uninjured foot and both hands. The awl, jammed through the safety notch, pinned the jaws open. His sweat-soaked brow frosted white, and pain froze on his cheeks as he lifted his foot free of the vise.

The jaws bit into stick as Ahmed retrieved his improvised safety catch and tossed the revolting contraption away. He hobbled to his pulk, sat on the load and slung off his pack. Grinding his teeth absorbed the screams when he removed his shoe to reveal the raging purple skin torn during his useless thrashing. Under the bruise, stretched tight and shiny, he felt a throbbing backpressure surge against the pinched blood vessels. He retched protein bar and bile over the snow.

Deep breaths helped him recover. He assessed the

misshapen ugliness. For the moment, his body's own pain-killers blocked sensation. There was some blood where the trap had clamshelled, but no bone ends grated against each other. He couldn't bend his toes much, swollen as they were from the constriction, but they didn't feel broken.

He swung his legs gently over the side of the pulk, balanced on his good one, dropped his socks under his bare foot and tested his weight. He hopped and wobbled to face his pulk, took out the few supplies he'd kept with him, then sat on the ground with his back against his load.

The sparse flesh along his tarsals needed the most attention. The small amount of external bleeding clotted —froze —as he examined it. From a pocket first-aid kit in his backpack he found a wad of gauze. He moistened it with spit and cleaned the leaking capillaries. He dressed, taped and wrapped the numb appendage. There wouldn't be any chance to change the bandages; this one injury had emptied the pouch. He stretched his socks over his engorged toes and bent his shoe into shape. With the laces removed, he slipped it over his foot. Duct tape held it shut.

Next he got out his extra sweater and spread it in front of him. From waistband to shoulders, he rolled up the bodice, folded in the sleeves and wrapped it around his foot. Taping the soft horseshoe in place held it from mid-calf to ankle. The garment finished in a neat fold across his toes.

It wasn't much immobilization, but after an hour of wilderness first aid, he could limp ahead. It was a struggle, with his good leg stiff from laying on the snow and his bad leg no help at all.

He disassembled the towlines of his pulk and removed the PVC tubes to tape into a makeshift crutch. It aided his balance, and he depended on it.

Relaxed at last, his circulation improved, bringing with it a resurgence of anguish. Pain like a pickaxe struck the messy soft tissue. The thin layer of muscle and bone on which he stood was usually at body temperature inside his skin. Now it burned in the frigid air. Time for physiotherapy; he had to keep moving.

Under the weight of his backpack, he tottered a few awkward steps forward and bore the flood of excruciating pain that punished him for his carelessness.

He put his pedometer on beside his watch and noted that it was past eight o'clock. When he stopped to relieve himself fifteen minutes later, he'd reached the trail edge. He longed for fresh hot packs like the ones he'd found littering his sleeping bag this morning.

By nine, on unstable footing, he'd dragged his overloaded sled two kilometres, less than half his earlier pace. He was hungry, but the sensation in his leg overpowered the one in his stomach. He was thirsty, but sweat shivered down his face and salted his lips. He was cold, but his body heat dropped out the hole in his foot. He was tired, but he dared not sleep.

Listing to the side to avoid the night's few passing racers, he staggered on. Twice he stood to rest and paused often to urinate, not deviating from the trail. Only the approach of trail sweepers motivated him to dive. Covered behind a drift he hid his pulk in snow.

Rising from one of these sudden bursts of activity, he felt oddly better, fully oriented and robust. The cold and drudgery didn't bother him anymore, but nature's excessive calling did. He had to stop for it every time. What he didn't realize in his world of glacier blue pain was that his footprints made a weaving line down the trail, and the nerve endings in his face and digits were senseless.

Morning overtook him two hours from Little Gold. In his condition it took him an additional five before he limped around the half-kilometre curve leading into the border station.

NINE

A steady stream of competitors trickled into Little Gold. Jerry ushered in a pair of frostnipped ears that soon thawed under warm towels, and a queasy stomach relieved by a pinch of baking soda in water. When Jerry returned to Dawson, the camp rested in a lull.

Fanger lazed in the sun. Forest scent baked out of the spruce at his back, and his legs stretched across the exposed earth at the base of the tree. Across his lap lay a clipboard on which he filled out Donjek's neglected paperwork. On the stump next to him, the probationer sat hunched over his time sheet.

"They want to know what I do in a day, but they don't give me enough space to say on these skinny things," the teen complained.

"At least you have the truth to draw on," Fanger replied. "Justice wants me to make up objective answers to subjective questions. Did you maintain a willing and helpful nature through the course of your duties?"

Donjek chucked a mittful of snow onto Fanger's copies.

"Hey!" He tossed down the board and raised his arms to deflect the snowballs assailing him. They had chased each other onto the trail when Fanger called a truce and pointed into the distance. "Look, someone's coming."

Donjek dropped the snow and followed Fanger's gaze.

A speck, enlarging to the form of a man, wobbled into view. He listed left then arced right, snaking toward them.

"Come on." Fanger rushed to the racer's aid, muttering, "Er tickt nicht richtig."

"It's Omar," Donjek said, supporting the injured racer. "Take his pulk off. I'll pull it in. Can you get him into the tent?"

Fanger nodded and guided the senseless man inside to a lawn chair. Crouching in front of Ahmed, he held the man's lolling head. "Omar, it's Markus Fanger. What happened?" He tried again in German and got an incomprehensible groan in response. Unzipping Ahmed's jacket exposed the athlete's damp inner layers. Salt stains traced Ahmed's form in the dark fleece.

Donjek entered and lit the gas lamp. "So much for our lull, eh?" He threw together a foamie and sleeping bag to put under Ahmed's exhausted body.

"Help me get him out of these things," Fanger instructed. "He's soaked." Ice as white as Ahmed's skin fell from his balaclava as Donjek removed it. Ahmed's deathly cold torso puckered as Fanger rolled his shirt up and along his arms, which Donjek held over his head. They blanketed his naked skin in wool and laid him on the waiting bed.

"Fanger, have you seen this?" Donjek pointed at Ahmed's foot bound in a soft cloth worn through from use. Together they cradled the injury and lifted it. Ahmed winced but didn't pull away.

"Take control of his leg. I'm going to loosen this. Gently," Fanger instructed, calming himself, Donjek and, he hoped, his casualty. The makeshift moccasin fell away. Fanger cut the duct tape binding Ahmed's shoe and held the heel as he guided the sole up and over the toes. He peeled the sock down over a crumpled dressing stuck to the swollen black appendage.

"Holy cow. That's gross," Donjek said. "Stinks."

"Hold your breath and keep still," Fanger growled. He pulled Ahmed's cuff open and followed the mottled skin to the ankle before instructing Donjek to lower the injury. "I'll need some time to work on this, but let's get him out of these wet leggings." Supporting Ahmed's lower body, they removed the clammy thermals and covered him.

Fanger asked for some hot water bottles rolled in dish-towels. "Put them at his chest and neck, and get a hat for his head."

While Donjek prevented Ahmed from losing precious heat, Fanger held his wrist, where he wrote the pulse count beside his respirations. Palpating head and body, arms, hips and legs revealed the single injury. He supported Ahmed's leg on padding over wedges of split firewood, stacked low at the thigh and rising for elevation. Then he soaked off the dirty gauze.

Compared to the healthy leg, this one was waxy, cold and a full size bigger. He examined the grooves of crushed skin on the back and ball of Ahmed's foot, two perfect arcs. "Donny, look at this. Any idea what would make these dents?"

Donjek braced himself for the sight of the mess, then measured against his hand from Ahmed's big toe to the edge of the gash. "A number ten? It would be about that wide and the jaws would pinch like that. He's lucky he ran into it this way and not the other way round, otherwise it would have closed above his ankle. Could have broken his leg."

Donjek stood and shook out the racer's thin clothes. "These smell like piss," he said, spreading the hose to dry near the stove.

"Hmm. In his condition, I'd probably wet myself, too. It must have been a hard night."

Fanger refreshed the water in his basin and clasped a lukewarm cloth around the knuckles at the base of Ahmed's toes. He wiped crusted filth from the abraded flesh until he held a clean wound, relieved to find no sign of exposed bone.

By then Donjek had retrieved the first-aid kit and was ready to assist. "Open a compress and give me a roller gauze," Fanger said. He dressed the upper wound. "And another, for below." This done, Fanger found an elastic bandage and stabilized Ahmed's foot, cautious to leave room for circulation and a place to check it. He protected the lower leg with a rigid, corrugated plastic quick splint from the kit.

"Let's get him in the other tent to rest," Fanger said, recording a second set of vitals while Donjek pulled the trailboggan up to the snowbed. They slid Ahmed, bedding and all, inside for the brief ride over the snow, at the end of which they scooped him up and, keeping his leg elevated, placed him inside to recover in warmth and comfort.

"I'll stay with him a little longer," Fanger said. "Could

you bring the race forms? I'll fill them out while everything's fresh."

"Sure," Donjek said, and exited into dusk. "Aw, shit, it's a mess out here. All our stuff's been blown around." Papers stuck to low spruce branches and the probation report near his foot was an unreadable inkblot. He turned Fanger's clipboard face up—the evaluation, good or bad, was impossible to decipher. Donjek smeared away the sticky pine needles, dug a pen out of the snow and brought it to Fanger.

"I'll clean up some," he said and left. It wasn't long before Fanger lent a hand. Donjek struggled to couple Ahmed's pulk to the skimmer hitch on his snowmobile. "I thought I'd hitch up his pulk to pull it out when we leave, but this thing weighs a ton. No wonder he was so exhausted."

"Speaking of which, I better phone in." Fanger helped hook up the load. "Get some transport at first light. He's all right for now, but I doubt he'll make it out on his own steam."

Fanger found the best reception outside and, waiting for the uplink, grumbled about the need to train more satellites over the poles. "I'd love to have the same access as people in the south, especially in an emergency," he muttered. No signal. He pressed the end button and tried again. This time a low battery tone beeped before he got a connection. "Great. Even if I do get a line, I'll have no time to say anything." He packed the useless technology in its case and brought it into the kitchen tent.

"I guess we'll wait for the next sledder. Our spare battery's almost out."

"What about Omar?" Donjek asked.

"He's stable, and I'll keep an eye on him." Donjek offered no argument or alternatives. Instead he worried his cigarette.

Fanger tapped the youth's shoulder with a pen and handed him an emergency information sheet. "I doubt you'll get your mind off this, so you might as well dwell on it. Write out everything you did, the highlights, and then go back and fill in the details." Donjek poured himself a coffee and hunched over the chore. Justice's triplicates sat in a soggy lump by the stove.

Fanger cranked up the lamp wick against the encroaching night. Their dinner—a roll munched, stew slurped and washed down with coffee—filled their stomachs as ink filled their pages. A quick check on Ahmed, his face slack in relaxed sleep, showed no change in his condition. A couple of hours later Fanger wrote the time, signed his name and stretched. "Finished. I'll try the phone again," he said, and turned it on.

Outside, crystal stars crackled in space. Satellites sashayed through the violet-green folds of the aurora's skirt, and faded into a sky as black as the phone display in Fanger's hand, dead. Damn. He clamped the dud in its case and trudged back to the tent.

The cold front nipped at his nose and cheeks and he stocked up on wood in anticipation of burning a day's worth in one night if the temperature kept dropping. He expected Donjek to take the bundle from him once inside, but the shelter was empty and their dishes gone. Fanger dumped his armload, and noticed that Ahmed's wool and fleece clothes no longer hung over the heat. He pulled on his headlamp and returned outdoors.

The firepit blazed beside their snowmobiles where a silhouette bent over Ahmed's pulk pawed through the gaping duffel. Fanger pointed his beam down and edged closer, unnoticed, his grinding footfalls muffled by the noisy search being conducted ahead. Directly behind the searcher he flicked his lamp over the scene, lifted Donjek by his shoulders to his full height and patted him down.

"Get a good haul?" He wheeled Donjek, stunned, to face him, furious.

"Wait! Wait. It's not what it looks like." The youth steadied himself.

"Convince me you're not rifling through Ahmed's stuff. You're practically wearing that duffel."

Donjek held up his hands, keeping Fanger at arm's length, but not with the arrogant defensiveness Fanger expected. "I finished writing and was going to do the dishes. Then I checked Ahmed's clothes and they were dry so I wanted to put them away." His frantic gestures and tumbling details left him panting.

"So what were you doing in the bottom of his gear?" Fanger checked his temper but not his skepticism.

"Look at this." Donjek pulled a brick-sized case up by its strap. "It's full of connectors." He opened it. "And this." He spread back the sack, revealing orange sticks with the words "Danger Explosive Strong Oxidizer" imprinted on each. "There are a lot of them."

Fanger swept his weak beam over the contents. In a flash he recognized it as the PowerPro from LaRouge's Blasters case. "Ach, du Scheisse. Ahmed is lawn chair guy."

A clear pouch caught Fanger's attention and he lifted

it out for examination. Facing him were maps annotated in Arabic. Turning the package over, he found a passport for Canada, one for the European Union and another for Syria. American twenties and hundreds stuck out from banded stacks.

As if his fingers had suddenly blistered, he dropped the plastic bag and zipped up the duffel. "Help me pack this up." They tugged at the duffel and crammed it into the pulk under the stretched cargo net. "Act natural when Ahmed wakes up. We can't let him know we've seen this."

"Cannot let me know you have seen what, Mr. Fanger?" An icy hand grasped Fanger's throat and torqued him around. The death grip dug deep into Fanger's trachea. His vision blurred. His cells gasped for air. He flailed in a fit of oxygen-deprived panic, and collapsed to his knees. Howling pain shot to his jaw as the vise tightened around his breathlessness.

Ahmed, dressed in one runner and a blanket tied as a toga over sparse underclothes, slammed Fanger's head on the ground, shaving his face with the razor-edged hard-pack. Like a wrangler he writhed, keeping clear of Fanger's kicking legs and clawing hands. Fanger's eyes bugged out of their sockets, his mouth gaped, lips stretched, tongue strained in a noiseless scream. Donjek jumped away from the wrestling pair.

"Keep your distance, young man," the assailant growled.

Was this the same guy who offered him mint tea and talked about the glory of Allah? Donjek cast about for a weapon and lunged for the paring knife in the dishpan; Ahmed's free hand snatched it away. Fanger was hauled to his knees, his jugular against the blade.

"I can slit your throat, Mr. Fanger, just as easily as the bull I have bled. Only, yes, the bull had more honour."

From the right of Fanger's muffled senses, he heard a snarl gather strength. In his dimmed periphery, a starburst of light speckled the grave blackness. A flaming streak flew past his head and singed his hair. The wrenching tug stretching his windpipe broke, at last freeing his airway. A lungful of winter brought up spit and vomit in spasms.

Fighting for control, he jumped from the charred log that smashed to hot coals near his hand. Donjek landed beside the embers under Ahmed's tactical blows. Fanger sprawled toward the stump of the steaming brand, found the edge of the knife against his knee and clutched both weapons. Swinging with one and slashing with the other, he landed a blow across Ahmed's back, dropping him into Donjek's gut punch. Oblivious to an approaching group, Fanger sunk his snowpack into Ahmed's ribs and bounced him into a heap. Ahmed rebounded like the white weasel, his left leg ahead of his right.

A cluster of headlamps gathered on the edge of the scene, and Ahmed bolted to Donjek's sled. It fired on the first pull and he darted into the boreal wilderness, half clad and half mad.

"Who was that?" a voice under a headlamp asked.

Fanger took the offered support and stumbled toward Donjek. "That's the first time my sled's ever fired up like that," the youth said, favouring his bruised side.

"Are you all right?" A lower headlamp approached.

"What? Yes. Are you?" Confused, Fanger absorbed the questions and oriented Donjek to the cookshack. Inside, he poured coffee.

The new arrivals dropped their ice-crusted laundry, revealing Marty Secord in their number. Fanger borrowed his compass and used the mirror to inspect the fingerprints embedded on either side of his Adam's apple.

"Looks pretty bad," Marty said. "It'll be hard to swallow."

"I'll say," Fanger croaked. "There's a lunatic taking a bomb to Alaska and we have no communication."

TEN

Felix emptied his office with a wave of his hand; his other grasped the phone. The unit members scattered to their desks at opposite ends of the detachment.

As Avery had suspected, when Felix reached the Americans, they were leery about acting without proof. Their interest rose when the sergeant stressed the link to the explosives theft. "Is there anyone to spare for a patrol?" he asked. Felix could guess what the chief of the understaffed force would say.

"Any of my boys not on active duty are already up there," the southern-born trooper said. "If this is true, I'll have to recall them. Get me hard evidence I can send on up to higher authorities and I'll see it gets there." He'd personally alert the volunteers along the Taylor Highway, Alaska's continuation of the Top of the World.

In the meantime, LaRouge had commandeered the nearest phone. He looked at his watch — just past seven — and checked the call-in time for Little Gold. Ten minutes to and after the even hour. No way would Fanger have the phone on, unless he was calling out, but on the chance he'd get through LaRouge punched the buttons with a typist's speed and squeezed the phone into submission. It rang twice before being cut off by the vixen of voice-mail cooing, "The customer you are seeking is currently out of the service district."

He called the Gambler's Den next, where he was invited to leave a message, which he did before redialling to demand Erik be brought to the phone, in person, thereby denying the receptionist a chance to suggest he try his room, the restaurant or bar. Impatient, he thrummed his fingers on his desk while she ran after the race organizer — and she better be running.

"It's Sean LaRouge." His intensity pre-empted Erik's greeting. "I've got some vital information about Omar Ahmed, the contestant on his way to Little Gold."

"What is it?" Erik reacted to the urgency and, with annoyance, shooed away an interruption. "Give me a moment, Corporal. I'll call you from my room where it's quieter."

LaRouge counted off the minutes, one to exit the command centre, another to take the stairs in pairs to his room and two more until his phone rang. He picked up where he'd left off, gushing information, until Erik broke in. "Are you telling me my race has been taken over by a saboteur? Surely not."

"I'm afraid so," LaRouge said. "I couldn't get through to Fanger's checkpoint. Can you keep trying? Whatever it takes, Fanger has to be warned."

"With a threat like this, of course. A snowmobiler is on his way up now. I'll pass the word when he calls in."

LaRouge reminded him of the precautions. "I don't want them to spook Ahmed. There's no telling what his reaction would be. The sledhands are not to provoke the situation. Have them report arrival and departure times, and estimated travel time. If anything unusual happens, or they're delayed, phone in."

Erik understood the magnitude of the problem. "I'm not sure this is the kind of publicity I want for my race," he said.

"I'd suggest building a reputation for cooperating with the police. We'll get you some back up immediately," LaRouge said, and then hung up.

LaRouge dialled and redialled, unsuccessfully, for the ten minutes before and after eight o'clock that Fanger was scheduled to have his phone on. He banished the worst-case scenarios — cold batteries, uncooperative satellites, bad weather — and hoped for the best, and prayed Erik would get through.

Donjek displayed his battle wounds to the astonished crowd — the best, a shiner blooming on his cheek. He held Marty's compass and probed the bruise. "I got this from his elbow," he said, "but I came back low." He snapped the compass shut and held a plastic bag of snow to his face. "My expensive new gloves are burnt to a crisp. Now I'll have to steal me a new pair."

The men laughed and marvelled that Donjek, just a cub, could joke about the incident. He told the racers what he'd discovered among Ahmed's equipment. "That's why his pulk was so heavy."

"Do you think he hauled that stuff all the way from Dawson?" Marty piped up. "His pulk didn't look overweight when we left the start line."

"Good point," Fanger said as he winced and swallowed hard. Small sips of warm water soothed his aching throat. "If I was him, I'd have cached it just before the road closed for the season." Fanger took a sheet of paper from his clipboard and passed the log sheets to number 312. "Write down your arrival times." He coughed and jotted "search for munitions dump" on the bottom third of his page. Then he wrote a brief outline of events.

Racer 312 entered her time a minute ahead of her husband's and handed the register to Marty. "Shouldn't we phone the coordinator?" she asked.

"Battery's dead," Fanger and Donjek chorused. In a column along the right margin of his page Fanger requested supplies—sled, fuel, batteries, phone and first-aid kit. The one they had was nearly empty.

"What'll you do now?" Marty asked. He filled in his arrival time and returned the forms to Fanger.

The tent surged with activity, and Fanger slid out of the bustle to the back of the snowbed. He wrote a couple of recommendations to end his brief and spoke again. "First I want to fix this"—he stretched his collar—"and then get help."

He held a slush-drenched compress over his Adam's apple and wiped blood from his beard. With the remaining four-by-four dressing, he covered his throat and tied the last bandage around his neck. He knotted the ends and tucked them in, then put his scarf over the lot.

"There's only my sled left, and one of us has to stay here," he said. "Donny, you know the trail best. Can you get this to Erik and the Dawson detachment?" Fanger tucked the brief into Donjek's sleeve pocket.

The right man for the job, Donjek's confidence surged. "I'll ride like the wind."

"You'll have the most information, so stay to help the response team," Fanger said.

"You bet. But what if Ahmed returns? I saw a case the size of a laptop in his duffel. It might have been a computer, but it could be a handgun."

"We'll have to take our chances. The way he lit out of here, it didn't look like he'd be back soon."

Marty bent over his bare foot where raw blisters had turned his heel to hamburger. "I'll stay here. I'm not limping another two hundred K on this."

"Donny, start my machine," Fanger said. "It's getting colder, so suit up warm." A man on a mission, Donjek strode out of the tent.

"No fear in him, eh?" Marty said. "Now that he's a crime fighter, for a change."

Fanger had a thermos of hot juice and food packed when Donjek strutted in with his helmet tucked under his arm. He stowed the snacks and dropped hot packs in his overmitts.

"There's three more on the trail behind us," 312 said. "Keep an eye out for them."

"I will," Donjek said. He drew his helmet on and cinched the chinstrap.

The peace sign he snapped on departure disturbed Fanger; he didn't want to consider the consequences of Ahmed's success. Fanger's trust in a safe outcome swept away on Donjek's receding tail light.

"Don't worry," Marty said. "He'll do us proud."

"Let's see that blister, Marty." Fanger welcomed the

distraction. Marty reared his foot onto an upended piece of wood. Fanger helped him clean the palm-sized patch and painted a ring of friar's balsam around the wound. The syrupy adhesive turned the healthy skin flypaper yellow and just as sticky. An astringent odour rose from the natural extract's stain, but the no-stick dressing stuck and held, sealing the wound. Fanger cut four finger-thick strips of foam from a sleeping pad, and Marty held them around the edges of the dressing. He taped the cushioning across his Achilles, down the sides of the heel and under the bottom of his foot, framing the injury site.

"Put your whole weight on it," Fanger said.

Marty pulled his sock over the padding, slid his foot into his shoe, and bounced gingerly. "Wow, no pressure at all. I'm still not walking to Tok, though." He finished his stroll at the coffee pot and helped himself. "It's a relief to scratch. I don't have to push myself anymore." He relaxed in a chair. His competitors ate slowly, and then went next door to sleep.

The Yukoners sat around the stove and warmed their ideas.

"Remember the ricin incident in Beaver Creek? When they found all that deadly poison."

"Yeah, ten times what we're allowed in the whole country for research, just sitting there unsecured," Fanger said. "In a locker at customs."

"Crazy what passes through our border. But honestly, who would expect a terrorist infiltration of Alaska on foot in the winter?"

"No one. Most certainly not the Americans." *We'll probably be blamed for letting him across,* Fanger thought as he reached for his tobacco.

"Where do you think he's headed?" Marty asked.

"I don't know. Eielson? Elmendorf? The Lower Forty-eight? Now he's in the States, he can go anywhere he wants. He might not even have an Alaskan target in mind." He held up his cigarette. "You mind?"

Marty shook his head. "Your throat's better then?"

Fanger stifled his retort and lit his smoke. "There's Delta Junction, too, on the way to Eielson."

Marty stiffened. "I doubt he'd threaten Greely." His sour tone caught Fanger's ear.

"What makes you say that?"

"Annabeth's working at Ground-based Missile Defense, for the electrical contractor."

"Ahmed knows this?"

"Knows? I swear he showed her the job posting."

Marty took a deep breath then talked about his wife's past. "She was raised in a commune, after her parents left Russian Siberia for Alaskan Siberia. Born at home, even. Used to say she was the first baby of freedom, or something like that," Marty said.

"As the oldest, the army brats at school made her answer for being Russian during the Cold War. Hence, her hatred of the military industrial complex. When it comes to that, she's all in." Marty's mouth curved in a smile of fond memory.

"That's how we met, in fact. I was in Seattle training for missionary work abroad, and there was a rally against nuclear subs at the navy yard. A handful of youth missionaries went, but I'd already committed to volunteering at a park building project. Well, a section of fence came down and the missionaries were detained by military police, along with a bunch of other demonstrators, including Annabeth. When we showed up, Annabeth was reared back, ready to plough a captain in the face. Her clothes were torn; she had a bloody lip and a black eye. I grabbed her wrist and said, 'That's not very godly behaviour.' We convinced the shore police she was one of us and then we took her to a hospital.

"The doctors told us the truth then. They'd found evidence of rape only a few hours old and that Annabeth's fetus had not survived the accompanying beatings. In a week she was physically well enough to leave the hospital, but spiritually, she needed long-term care." Annabeth had stayed at the mission training centre for about a month, and the couple married a year later.

"That's why it took me seven years to convince her to have a baby," Marty said. "When we finally did get pregnant, she was so protective of the baby I could hardly get near her." Marty's memory wasn't so fond now.

"Sometimes, when she was carrying Marie, she'd rub her belly and look at me as if I'd tricked her into this condition and that they — she and the baby — would get their revenge."

After Annabeth immigrated, she earned her electrical ticket and had steady work, while Marty enjoyed patchy employment. "An aspect of communal life I hadn't expected was Annabeth's real need for security. She's terrified of poverty." Marty had the soppy look of someone who'd been had. "When she announced Alaska was looking for trade workers, not five miles from where she grew up, I thought she was telling me about it as an item of curiosity, like, 'Hey look, their so short-handed they're recalling ex-patriots.' I was wrong. I couldn't believe she'd work for them.

"Me, I'm basically a coward. I fear for my life if the weaponry is unleashed, especially now with these new Greely missiles. Even if they do blast the threat out of the sky, we'll all be killed by the shrapnel."

"What I don't get is how Ahmed's involved," Fanger said.

"My mistake, I guess. I introduced them after meeting Ahmed at the Mayo Midnight Marathon. It wasn't very long before they were seen together, taking Marie to the pool, meeting for coffee. She said there was nothing to it, but during one of our fights about her working at Greely, she said something like, 'At least Omar supports me. He wants me to take the job.' At that point I blew my stack. 'Fine,' I said, 'if you're there and he's here, at least he can't screw with our marriage.' 'You're right,' she said, 'cause we won't be married anymore.'"

Marty suspected she'd gone straight to Ahmed's that very night. "I saw him a week later and he said she was going to Delta. At that moment I thanked my lucky stars our daughter was here. I didn't want her involved, but ten days later Annabeth started a custody battle and Ahmed's been her gallant knight ever since."

That would explain the comments Fanger had heard from Jenn and George. But Marty was kidding himself if he thought his wife was safe.

Fanger looked at the travel alarm on the table — nearly midnight. Donjek, driving the way he could, would be near the Top of the World pullout by now.

A single headlight halted at the marathon checkpoint as Donjek approached. He closed the gap and slowed his sled to a puttering idle, lifted his visor and felt a pinching grasp on his upper arm.

"What're you doing with Fanger's sled?" The words barked at him through the mouthpiece of the speaker's helmet. The visor flicked up, and the murderous tone matched the menace in Ted's eye. "You've had a fight. Fanger tried to stop you stealing his sled, right? Admit it. We've caught you joyriding." Ted had Donjek by both arms now, the desire to shake the life out of him poorly controlled.

"No. Stop! If I was joyriding do you think I'd've slowed down, let alone stop?" The young offender wrested away from his accuser.

Rick came between them. "Enough. Why are you here?"

Donjek took a couple deep breaths through his frosted balaclava. "Damn, it's cold." He reached for his thermos and Rick raised his hand to block the motion.

"Tell us what you're doing out here first."

"Omar Ahmed's some kind of terrorist. He's got three passports, tons of money, my sled, a bunch of dynamite, the works. And he's taking it into Alaska."

The jaws of the two men dropped in the face of such a bold accusation. "How'd he get your sled?" Ted fired back. "You give it to him?"

Donjek mimicked Fanger's "you're a dolt" look, astounded at how dense Ted could be. He wished for a firecracker to drop down his pants. Fat lot of good that would do. Only calm, honest persuasion would influence the men, so he tried it. "He overpowered us, grabbed a knife and almost killed Fanger. When some racers arrived, he let us go and escaped on my sled. *He* stole *my* sled."

Ted choked on his coffee. "You don't expect us to believe that, do you?"

"It's easy enough to check," Rick said. His usual slow and purposeful way seemed slower now that time was of the essence. Rick put up his hand for quiet when his call was answered.

"Thank God you phoned," Erik said. Rick heard Erik's relief as clear as their connection. "Fanger and Donjek are in danger. The racer Omar Ahmed is wanted by the RCMP for an explosives robbery, and in Germany by the federal police."

Rick's face paled and his sweat froze. "Donjek's with us. Just a minute, Erik." He lowered the phone, incredulous, and turned to his companions to say, "It's true."

Donjek stood, smug, and sauntered over to pour himself a cup of coffee. Rick put the phone back to his ear.

Ted's suspicion was not appeased. "If what you say is true, why didn't Fanger contact us?"

"Our phone died. We tried to call when Ahmed came in with his foot all messed up. We were waiting on you guys. Where were you?"

"Us?" Ted sputtered. "Well, we were … we were here, packing the camp and we were hungry. It was late, so we had dinner…."

"You were taking it easy," Donjek smirked. "Good job. Well, now we have to get to Dawson, so I hope you enjoyed your rest. Where's Jerry?"

"He had to go home, for Rendezvous." Ted's hackles rebounded. "He's got a life, you know."

"And we almost lost ours." Donjek seethed, fists ready to pound the elder sled boss, when Rick broke in.

"Donny, ride in with me. Ted, you go on and herd the last racers into Little Gold. Don't leave them unattended once they're rounded up. As soon as they cross the hundred K line, start shuttling them out to Dawson. We'll pick up their gear in the morning. Erik wants the trail cleared as fast as possible."

Leaving Ted alone to head north, Donjek jumped on Fanger's machine, revved it and took off south with Rick chasing after him. They pulled up to the Gambler's Den in time for last call, which Rick answered as soon as Donjek rushed off to find Erik.

Details spilled out of Donjek in an undammed stream of pent up anxiety and anger. Erik was at a loss to understand more than the "You have to do something" he kept repeating.

"Slow down," Erik said. He put his hand on Donjek's shoulder and led him into the command centre. There, Erik showed him to a chair, draped a blanket over him and brought a steaming coffee.

Donjek dumped three packs of sugar into the brew and stirred it, all the while continuing his garbled summary. He ended on the plea, "Here, believe this. It's a letter Fanger wrote."

Erik took the brief and read it. He excused himself for a moment to make copies at the front desk. "Please distribute these when the RCMP arrive," he asked the receptionist, and returned to the teenager. "That's some ride you made to get us this information," he said, startling the drowsy rider. "You're exhausted."

"And frozen," Donjek replied, yawning.

"I bet. It's minus forty-five at the airport," Erik said. "I know you live just across the river, but I've rented an extra room and you're welcome to stay here."

"What about Fanger? We've got to send him some help."

"Ted's on his way and the RCMP are following as soon as possible. Rest easy. You've accomplished a lot." Erik stopped when he saw the way Donjek picked at the handle of his mug, his head down, and wiped his nose. He helped the spent messenger to his room, pausing only for the key from the night clerk. Donjek pulled off his boots and, un-burdened, flopped onto the nearest bed.

When Donjek came down for breakfast the next morning, fifteen minutes after Erik knocked on his door, Corporal LaRouge and the old cop from the emergency meeting were waiting for him, as were several members of the local detachment and the race committee.

"Morning," Donjek said, sitting between Erik and the window. He ordered breakfast and met the serious gaze of Fanger's superior. Felix held Fanger's letter for all to see. "This recommends we listen to you."

Surprised to be on an equal footing, Donjek nodded. "Ahmed's got a gun, I think, as well as the other stuff listed."

"This says you saw connectors with the sticks." Felix placed the refolded note in front of Donjek. "Did you see any other devices or wiring? They would have been turquoise bundles."

"I don't think so."

"Hmm, that leaves the legwire and detonators un-

146

accounted for." Felix glanced at LaRouge and found agreement. This was the rejected gift witnessed by the school teacher. Felix wondered what tactics Ahmed had used to make Annabeth accept it.

"Think back to when you drove to Little Gold. Did you see any signs of activity leading off trail? Recently travelled maybe?"

Donjek shook his head. "No. He came in pretty messed up with a foot injury, though. He might have stepped on a wolf trap. That would be even more likely if he went off trail." His breakfast arrived. "Ahmed's foot was a stinking, disgusting mess," Donjek continued. "Fanger took really good care of him and this is the thanks he gets, a maniac crushing his airway." Donjek stabbed his egg with a corner of toast and watched the yolk bleed over his plate.

"It showed courage to defend him," Felix said as he reached past Erik to pat Donjek on the back.

"Well, none of you were around last night." Donjek looked each officer in the eye. "If I hadn't flattened that asshole with a flaming stump, we would'a had it." He rubbed his bruised eye and looked down where weeping blisters erupted from his scorched palms. "Ahmed's crazy, and such a liar. I hope he missed those prayers that mark him for death and that he burns for it. No way this is part of Allah's teachings."

Donjek hid his injury with the motion of taking up his fork, palm down, but he wasn't quick enough.

"Those burns look serious," Erik said. He insisted that Donjek get treatment at the nursing station and, mindful of the need to protect his racers, asked, "Who's still on the trail?"

"There are still three of the hundred Ks to come in, and three of the long distance runners arrived during our fight," Donjek said. "A guy Fanger knows named Marty scratched after he scared Ahmed away, and he's staying in camp."

"Marty Secord?" LaRouge asked, his interest piqued. Donjek wanted to say yes, but he couldn't be sure.

Felix delegated his force. He and LaRouge would ride directly to Little Gold. Dawson members, with some recruits from the Canadian Rangers, would comb the trail north of the marathon finish for offshoots to a possible cache. Donjek would stay with Erik.

The sergeant led the way on a detachment machine, and LaRouge rode after him under the bone-chilling sun. At noon they passed Ted riding southbound with a passenger.

"There's two more at the checkpoint," the sled boss told the sergeant.

"See Erik about your back up. This might be your last run."

"Good. I've been up and down so many times, I could run it in my sleep." He paused. "I probably was for the last two hours."

"Drive carefully," Felix cautioned as they parted.

Just past one PM, they pulled into the border station. Fanger rushed to meet them and took LaRouge's outstretched hand. Marty limped behind. "Are we happy to see you," Fanger said.

"Still alive then, eh?" Felix wiped his frosted moustache. "How's everyone else?"

"We're holding up, sir," Fanger said. "The runners who

came in with Marty left before Ted came in with his first racer. He brought the last ones in about four this morning. They're passed out in the sleeping tent."

"We met him on the trail. He's beat. Have you had any sleep?"

"Some." Fanger rued the reminder and stifled a yawn. "I was hoping to ride out directly. Marty's going to tend the camp until Ted has the racers out."

Fanger edged away from the group. Felix followed as Fanger knew he would. Sure they were out of earshot, Fanger named the likely target. "Sir, Marty's wife left him for an electrical job at Fort Greely and she's seeing Ahmed. It can't be a coincidence." Felix whistled low; this wasn't happening.

To LaRouge, Fanger said, "I see my sled's here. Were you able to bring the gear I asked for?"

"Yup." The corporal spread the items on the seat of Fanger's Arctic Cat and put two full jerry cans in the rear rack. "We'll double up on the detachment sled for the return trip."

"I'll call in my findings." Fanger strapped the phone and batteries to his backpack. He laid the first-aid kit on the riser seat and clipped it to the carrier.

"Findings?" Felix asked. "I've notified the Troopers, Fanger, and they have jurisdiction. You can't pursue Ahmed into the States."

"Just doing some trail riding, sir. Beautiful country out here. Would you look at that view?" He escorted the sergeant some paces across the border to a vista where he convinced his boss to look the other way. From a height so lofty, above valleys so peaceful, it seemed unfathomable that there were people on earth below—people who would destroy it.

ELEVEN

LaRouge and Felix made for civilization. In the opposite direction, Fanger spun snow and scree out of the border station. He drove like he was surfing with a Chevy, seat-belts not recommended.

Neither his long-track nor Donjek's trail machine were made for the summit powder ahead, and Ahmed had more than a twelve-hour headstart. But Fanger had more than twelve winters of sledding, and from what he'd seen of Ahmed's skill, it was worse than a virgin driver behind the wheel of a standard.

Fanger's own machine vibrated under him and he rode hard, unburdened by his trailboggan. His faceshield and helmet protected him from crosscut winds in the bends and speed smoothed the way over the first three miles that dropped twelve hundred feet. He swept downhill in a slalom of graceful rail slides, controlled curves he made by balancing his weight from ski to ski. Peacock sprays of snow fantailed behind him as he swooped down into Boundary, a modern roadhouse opened specially for the Ultra. In this town, population eight, gas flowing from the pumps kept food flowing to the table.

The town father rushed out and yelled for his kids to stay inside. "What's going on?" he demanded of Fanger. "You're the second guy to blow through here." Fanger explained with such authority that Boundary's leading citizen took him at his word. "Holy cow!" was the town's official response. "Gas is on me," was the municipal contribution, and "Go get him!" the local sanction.

Fanger rattled over the next dozen miles of trail, tread marks and ski grooves criss-crossed like shuntings at a train yard, the rails made not of iron but ice interspersed with stretches of naked scree, finger-long rock shards, arrow-sharp and slick as oil. At times, ruts set in a washboard of ridges brought Fanger from his seat like a steeplechaser hurdling a hazard. The clear sky frosted as he blasted away Ahmed's lead.

At irregular intervals, odd depressions in the track surface made him realize Ahmed's grip strength on the throttle lever varied, and he'd reacted to the unexpected bursts of power by alternately slamming against the hardpack or breaking the crust to sink into pockets of deep soft. Judging by the depth, he'd buried the track.

Within the hour, Fanger found the scene of an obvious upset. He pounced off the trail where a gold dredge, a floating rock sorter, loomed out of the snow frozen into the muck of its own pond.

Riding blind in a lightning bolt curve, Ahmed had met the wrecked dredge too quickly. Where it rested on its hull, he had spun out, clipped the rear of his sled and launched through the air.

A snow angel who'd fallen to earth, hard, outlined his landing. There wasn't a scratch on the dredge. In the drift Ahmed had dislodged on impact, Fanger found plastic fragments. One, a picture of a dog in harness, had snapped off Donjek's sled like peanut brittle. The rest of the Quest decal had run unfettered from the scene.

Thrown into this meat locker climate, Ahmed's brain

must have turned to ice fog, Fanger guessed. He looked between the starboard slats and inside the dredge's cavernous hold. Where ancient looting had perforated the decking above, patches of snow lay on the weathered lower deck, along with pieces of blood-frosted scree. Indentations from a three-legged camp stove pointed to Ahmed's common sense to warm up.

Fanger withdrew from the shelter. To the left were the trampings Ahmed made to free his pulk. He'd torn at the snow pile until he'd found something to latch on to, a tie-down or the cargo net, and leaned back for counterweight. Heels, thighs and buttocks left an impression at the edge of a rectangle that marked where he'd hauled the load upright. Fanger hoped Ahmed appreciated that, while he'd rested at the checkpoint, his dry clothes had been repacked. He figured Ahmed must have truly believed in Allah's ability to provide for his flock when he discovered them.

The low rumble from Fanger's idling sled changed pitch, and he waded back to it. As he reached for the throttle lever, a shot split the sharp arctic air. Fanger dove behind his sled and hit the kill switch, garrotting his motor. He strained to gauge the origin of the report before it died in the mountains.

The Northland has a silence all its own, but, with the droning wind and spattering snow grains, the echo of the report eluded him. After a moment he peeked over his seat and swept the unblemished skyline for the ugly threat. Nothing moved. He rose to a low crouch, straddled his sled, lifted the kill switch, and held down the electric start. He expected a fresh round to rip the sheen of winter; when none did, he clawed up onto the trail.

The road straightened at a meadow, where cabin chimneys brooded on snowy ridgepoles. This was Chicken, a town so named because the founders couldn't spell "ptarmigan," the wild poultry that feeds several species in the northern food chain. Fanger abandoned the town site to be pecked by the building wind.

Miles of landscape unfurled and sidehills dropped away as he sliced the distance to his target. He bounded down pancake stacks of ridges, gathered speed on the ground and popped out of the sugary powder. Over and over, he hugged his machine as it launched from Earth in weightless hang time. He tested his mettle at machete-edge drop-offs and, on the runners, dove under the peaks until the sled and trailboggan track turned into a mess of footprints.

He slowed. Ahmed had left the trail. Probably to draw a bead on me, he thought. He backtracked, stalking his prey, to some smashed scrub that tallied the number of runs Ahmed had taken to shove Donjek's sled off-trail.

Fanger humped over the splintered stumps, and within fifty metres the bush thinned. On foot he returned to the Taylor Highway and entered the start point into his GPS. He attacked Ahmed's route, parallel to the highway, and watched his headway crawl south over the display.

No matter how much manpower scoured the race trail on the closed highway, Ahmed would encounter no resistance in the negative space between the travelled lines marked on the map. Now, heavy blowing snow filled the sky. Fanger itched to call in, but he was unwilling to lose Ahmed to weather.

The terrain slowed his progress. The trail he'd left had a solid base of hardpack levelled by repeated use. The building wind shrouded the trail and the crust often crumbled. Fanger's machine moved like a hobbled horse. He stood in the saddle, using his legs as shock absorbers in the pitch and roll of his wobbly descent on the punchy route.

Hills converged to a vanishing point at a needle eye opening. Beyond that a void teased gravity. He pierced the emptiness and teetered at the lip of a gorge.

The mountain capped with the treeless Terrible Terrace rose on his right. Spindrift airbrushed the cornices suspended from the top ridge. The slope, by contrast, screamed in barren meanness. The sidehill lay torn from the shoulder of the mountain like an arm ripped from its socket.

Had Ahmed seen the terrain as Fanger did, self-preservation would have slowed his progress. Instead he had triggered an avalanche, dislodged a mountainside and tumbled down a fold of the Terrible Terrace.

Fanger was beside a creek that made up the near side of the tear. It ripped along the waterway, freeze-dried this late in the season. Ahmed's weight had come to bear on the layer of ice over thin air, and the soufflé had fallen an inch to strike the length of the creek bed. The jagged cut met the opposite side of the fault, serrating the gully into a double-edged wedge that had released and knifed down the gorge. The debris had pushed into a natural cleft at the treeline and filled it like cream in an éclair. The powder blast in the wake sprinkled dark pulpy shavings over all.

Fanger looked for tracks hinting to where Ahmed lay. The surface, chewed and littered as it was, gave no clues. The path of the run-off would have flushed Ahmed into the hanging valley and buried him. Of course, Fanger was guessing. He hadn't witnessed the event, and there weren't any signs plastered on the billboard-sized blocks scattered around the scene. The scene, as he viewed it, might not even be real, depending on the features of the land beneath the snow. If Ahmed had tried to arc across the slope, he would have had to ride on full power to stay ahead of the frozen tide. That would be an anomaly for a new rider; usually, in a clinch, they clutched the brakes.

Under the glaring white sky, Fanger scanned the rends in the fabric of the mountain's epaulet. He plotted a route and leaned into the grade to avoid sliding down. At a moderate tempo, he basted a skeletal-thin trail around the disaster. Pea-sized snowballs rolled into cannonballs released by his rig's seven hundred pounds. Overturned powder broke under his skis as he threaded the tear. He kept his eyes on the ominous overhang and his feet on the runners, ever ready to spring off his sled if necessary.

On the safe side of the danger, Fanger spotted the double imprint of a loaded toboggan being dragged over a snowmobile track. He knew the outcome and, in snow to his crotch, waded down to where Ahmed had ridden out the avalanche. In the destruction, he'd lost his pulk and dug it out. He must have worked like a gravedigger to break up the jumble. And he was still going and still dangerous.

In the west, the tail end of daylight waved goodbye on the rollercoaster of false summits to the peak of Mount Fairplay in the distance. Felix wouldn't have reached Dawson yet, so Fanger rode on.

During a short break, he wolfed a snack and coffee, also determined to enjoy a cigarette in peace. The idea was shattered by a shot. Muffled, it was the same sound he'd heard at the dredge, definitely man made. He froze and listened, but as before it was a lone report.

If Ahmed lay in wait, ready to shoot him, would he forfeit his decreasing lead to protect his back, or lengthen it by running like a demon over a frozen hell? Fanger had no idea what he would do if ambushed. He had no protection, no firearm, and as far as he knew, he was on the only route in or out. He didn't wait to find out.

Ahmed had woken in Little Gold aghast by the realization that *Muharran* had passed without his devotion.

In this climate, the polar opposite of any desert he'd known, if he were to die, it would be as a humble servant protecting Islam from its enemies. He'd envisioned the martyr's paradise awaiting him — steaming baths, furs underfoot and an end to the bone-cracking chill of Earth.

The cold had peeled layers of heat from his skin, but he'd sped on until he slammed into a sunken dredge that knocked him from his ride and into a pit. Woolly headed, after tunnelling out of the crash site, Ahmed had dug in his pulk for something, anything, to keep warm, and found clothes he didn't recall packing. Wearing these to protect himself against wind, the still-functioning part of his will to live had pulled him to his feet. He'd crawled into the hold of the hulking dredge and sat on his haunches. A blurry idea of making pocket warmers from hot rocks had swum out of his memory, and with no idea if the trick would work, he'd gathered his wits and a pile of stones, which he'd heated on his undamaged camp stove. By the time his last drop of fuel had vaporized, he was wearing a smouldering blanket as a vest from breast to navel. Confusion melted away.

He'd looked at his wrapped ankle and had to credit Fanger's first-aid skills as he rose; immobilized in the quick-splint, his injury gave him no trouble. He'd fished out his maps, and although the batteries in his headlamp were gone, he'd oriented the topographic in the glare of the high beam on his snowmobile. In right-minded clarity he had triangulated his position and set his bearing. The escape route ended at civilization, but what lay between here and there was a complete mystery.

Master of the throttle, he'd held it wide open, bent on making up lost time through the night. His sled had coughed and gasped as he made tracks to Chicken. From there he had descended into the Dennison Fork of the Fortymile River, a gauntlet of buck brush — arches of willows and poplars locked tight under frosty loads — and got a thrashing in each cluster.

Finally, he'd reached the edge of an old burn and bashed through the low scrub on the trail on his GPS. His motor had threatened to quit and complained in loud retort, but after the streak of hard luck he'd ridden so far, he didn't care. His legs were slashed with scree and his hands, although clenched around the grip warmers, were frozen bone white. By the time the overnight lows dropped to their alcohol-freezing depths, he'd neared the part of the mountain called the Terrible Terrace: a hazard Canadians talked about in excited whispers.

There was always a risk of avalanche, and he'd heard mountain skiers in the Yukon complain about sledders who chased fresh powder in the calm between storms.

But there had been no storms, and the cold nighttime air had hardened the snow into a solid crust. He disregarded the wind.

At the first open grade, Ahmed had let fly, riding smooth toward the thirteen-hundred-metre pass at Mount Fairplay. His excitement had grown as pockets of scrub flit past, leading to an opening on the horizon. At alarming speed, he'd realized too late that his horizon was indeed the end of the road. His legs had clamped the seat as his sled fired off the ledge and dropped.

He and his rig had cracked like a gunshot when they slammed into the world. And, with a *whoompf*, the world had slammed back.

A rip had opened, and before it reached the wind-blasted ridge top, Ahmed had full-throttled on the shortest vector out of the headwall of the avalanche that would come at him at a hundred miles per hour. He'd jumped the gap dividing the slab from land and cleared the gorge. Behind him, a block of solid ice had roared downhill and frozen foam shot his pulk into the air.

The mountainside had smashed around him, riding flat out, and jumble clipped his hip. He'd jerked and flexed his body to hold fast in the monster hailstorm that bounced at crazy angles to punch him in the ribs and slew him sideways. Melded to his machine in free fall, now up, now down, he'd ducked behind the windscreen to shield himself from the suffocating spray. His ski hit a rock and he'd twirled laterally then tumbled in a spider-monkey roll to the bottom of the icy sheer. Forest debris, reduced to kindling, had showered splinters into the air. Ice mites floated in the aftermath.

He'd pried his clenched fingers open and tumbled out of the winter washing machine. Yellow nausea spewed over the snow. With a handful of clean crystals he'd wiped vomit from his chin and breathed a sigh of relief that stabbed his right side. Reaching across his chest to guard his ribs, a pulsating ache had spread from his shoulder. He had welcomed the pain, a sensation shared by the living, and let the climate anaesthetize him.

When he woke, sprawled on his belly, he'd shifted in the loose fallout to glance at his watch. He didn't know what time it was when the avalanche hit, but in a few hours it would be daybreak. Before standing he'd turned his head to the chaos. Somewhere in there was his pulk. He'd gotten to his hands and knees, but the jab in his shoulder had forced him to crawl three-legged. He'd stood then, although his splint pinched his foot. The stones in his vest had scattered and he pulled the blanket tight around him.

In the weak moonlight he had charted the towering incline he'd have to mount. Falling away from his feet, snow kernels traced fine silver squiggles, like storm-driven rain on a frozen windowpane. He'd loathed the idea of descending into the bowl in the pitch dark to retrieve his gear. But there it was, the waistband hung up on a low branch at the edge of the gully, with the rest of the load buried to the traces. Thoroughly sick of digging, he'd taken a short-handled shovel into the quarry and hacked at the debris.

Friction generated by the speed of the descending slab made heat that fused the colliding snow particles into concrete. The blocks he chipped away had sheared in striations. Hoarfrost from frozen dew, corn snow and wild snow, topped by a stellar crust, had been compacted into ply. The whole load had ridden a layer of pebbly grauple underlying everything.

He'd chiselled into the hardpack and, at last, it gave up his load, free from winter's weather patterns. He'd hauled and shoved it toward his sled and coupled them. Using his machine to maintain traction and balance, he'd burrowed up the hillside. Bush and snow had plugged the air intake. The engine had gasped to draw fuel against gravity. His bones and joints tore apart when he'd shifted his weight to block any backsliding. Sputtering, he'd inched toward the lip of the slope in incremental gains until, exhausted, he'd lifted the front end onto flat land and out of the path of ruin.

Slaving against time, he'd hurried to break away. Someone would have relieved Fanger at Little Gold and brought him a sled. He'd be advancing while Ahmed lost time with every minute he'd spent grunting and shoving his load uphill.

Remounted, with the pulk in its makeshift hitch, he'd tapped the gas, too hard, and canted back as his tail light disappeared in the powder. The tilt had increased on the second try, yanked the grips out of his grasp and bumped him against the switches on his handlebars. For no reason at all the motor quit.

Ahmed had pounded the seat he straddled, and given the starter a hefty tug. Under the hood, a magneto whirred but didn't catch. He'd put his weight into the next try and the next, and succumbed to desperation and panic. Fed up with the gadgets, he'd toggled all the switches, including the flattened kill switch, jammed the ball of his thumb against the throttle and ripped on the recoil. Mechanical life backfired into the frigid air. The growl of his two-stroke was music, and he'd revved the motor high before shrieking down the sculpted planes.

At Tanana Valley State Forest the scrubland grew into stunted trees, growths of spruce and tamarack that dropped into stands of quaking aspen and paper birch. Bushwhacking is as difficult by snow machine as it is on foot, and Fanger had to dismount every few sled lengths to snowshoe ahead. He often calculated the time lost and considered dumping the machine, sure he'd be faster without it. But he remained committed to this road less travelled and prayed it would open up soon.

He figured darkness would slow the terrorist and expected to overtake him, but three hours after nightfall there had been no sign that the trail would end or get easier. Branches sparred and jabbed in a strong blow that tilted the trees. Drifts piled up at the base of the stocky trunks. In the few clearings he'd crossed, blowing snow obscured Ahmed's tread marks, and Fanger tracked him with difficulty, following the harum-scarum of directionless twists and turns. He'd delayed reporting until daybreak, when he'd hoped to have a fix on Ahmed's location. But at dawn, less than twelve miles from Tetlin Junction, he met disappointment.

Abandoned and dumped, Donjek's sled had nosedived into a shallow snow-lined grave. The front end was ploughed into a mess of branches and the tail light rose like a beacon in the air. Fanger latched on to the rear and used his weight to right the machine. He yanked on the starter, but not a shoelace of cord came out. The dry flywheel clamped fast on its shaft.

Ahmed's pulk was gone and its flat bottom erased the snowshoe prints of the man who pulled it. A foot-wide depression slid under an obliterating drift that fanned away into three sloping tongues, none of which disgorged a trace of Ahmed's passage. Nature had given him a cloak of secrecy.

Now Fanger had all the time in the world to call in. He unpacked his phone and, from inside his coveralls, removed the battery pack he'd kept warm overnight. He connected on the first attempt and Felix answered, from the moon, it seemed.

"Fanger, glad to hear from you."

"Would you still be if I told you he got away?"

"I don't know what I would have done if you'd caught him." Felix laughed, but it was no joke. He couldn't protect the auxiliary. "Where are you?"

"Off the beaten path about two kilometres from Taylor Highway. I dogged him all night and found Donny's sled, abandoned. That's where Ahmed slithered under a drift and I lost him."

"I'll give the State Troopers the location. They've had whoever they can spare on the trail, but they're in a whiteout over there."

"Me too. Any sign of the weather breaking?"

"Not for another six to twelve hours. Dawson's calm, though. What should I tell Donny about his sled?"

"I'm flagging it now. It'll have to be towed. How is he anyway?"

"Great. He's helping Erik coordinate information, bouncing between his folks and the hotel. It's hard to believe he's a young offender."

Fanger smiled. "I knew he'd step up."

"More than that. He asked Edwin to assemble the elders and briefed them on our behalf. He must have done a great job, too, because cousins and uncles, chief and council all showed up to help."

"That's resourceful." Fanger's pride was evident.

"It is."

At the Clinton Creek Road a member of the Tr'ondëk Hwëch'in First Nation searched his trapline a short distance and discovered a storage magazine bolted to the ground. "Donjek took the call an hour ago and as soon as our members are done collecting whatever evidence they find onsite, they'll work on a way to bring it back in." Felix added, "Without the Tr'ondëk Hwëch'in's help we'd still be searching."

"I hate to tell him what's happened to his sled." Fanger recounted his trek over the top. "Ahmed tripped a snowslide and I was sure he was under it until I found a track leading out. Somehow he got his sled and pulk out, but the machine must have seized when the temperature fell." Fanger spoke from experience when he added, "That's a ton of work. Once you put the effort in to self-rescue, you really appreciate having five or six guys around to help you."

"No kidding. I've been the guy on the end of the shovel plenty of times. It's amazing he got out at all," Felix said. "Whose side is God on anyway?"

Fanger shared Felix's exasperation but he didn't have time to chat. The wind was sucking the batteries dry.

"I thought he might've backtracked on me, but he's beating a path out of here as fast as he can. There must be a deadline. He didn't let up all night."

"That's determined, considering the problems he had in the minus twenties. Now it's twice that cold."

"There's another problem. Ahmed's definitely armed."

"What?" It sounded as if Felix dropped the phone.

"Two times I heard a shot, when I stopped my sled. A single round each time, although the second one didn't sound right."

"Misfire?"

"Backfire? From Donny's sled? Who knows," Fanger replied. "Anyway, I lived." *Scared the life out of me though,* he realized.

"Right. Return immediately." Felix laid down the law.

"Happy to. I'll pick up Marty on the way," Fanger said. "Any luck with the Americans?"

"Plenty. We're sharing information under Hands Across the Border. I'll add this to our brief," Felix said.

"I wish I could give you his target. He'll intercept the Alaska Highway on his current heading, but he'll be tough to pin down, cutting across country."

"And he's good at covering ground," Felix agreed. "Avery's been researching Ahmed's entry, but so far it looks like he never entered Canada, not through official ports anyway. No visa was issued and there's no record of him clearing customs. He figures Ahmed may have been smuggled in with the human trade, the way about a quarter of our refugees arrive. It would be nothing for a terrorist to book first-class passage on black market transport."

TWELVE

Felix uttered his last sentence into a buzzing phone. He hung it on the empty cradle beside the failsafe radiophone in the Gambler's Den banquet room. LaRouge and the few people in the race command centre looked up.

"We were cut off, but Fanger's on his way back with the location coordinates for Donjek's sled. The State Troopers will probably take it to their impound, and we'll need a couple of members to tow it back," Felix said.

LaRouge nodded. "I'll ask the first two back from relief. The trail crew is just bagged."

"I know. I'm on my way to the detachment now to spell someone off. It's only until the handful of competitors still out there come in safely." Felix put on his parka and shot his remote start in the general direction of his vehicle. "Ride with me," he said to LaRouge. The corporal followed his sergeant's recap out the door.

"You wouldn't believe the dumb luck our Muslim's had." Felix repeated the adventures as Fanger had related them. "Not enough to go over the Top of the World where the Terrible Terrace could drop a rider a few hundred feet, he takes the backside where a rider could drop forever."

"From the sound of it, Ahmed should have died five times this week," LaRouge said. "Hypothermia, wolf traps, avalanches; he's overcome it all. And now the Syrian super spy is at large."

Felix scowled. "If I read that phrase in the paper tomorrow, Corporal, you'll have a lot to answer for."

"Yes, sir." LaRouge busied himself with opening the sergeant's door.

When Felix noticed Erik walking toward the Gambler's Den, he stopped in the middle of the road to tell the race director they were returning to the detachment. The officers drove parallel to the river, upstream, on Front Street, past Victorian edifices in colonial posture, to Dawson's new RCMP station.

Shiny as a cadet's badge, the paint inside glistened. Felix had been given a desk and phone, and the moment he tossed his parka over the chair back, the phone rang.

"Sergeant Felix, bonjour," the sergeant answered with the standard M Division greeting. It was Orez. "Thank you for returning my call, Master Sergeant. Another member of the investigating team is here. May I put you on speakerphone?" Felix listened for the reply, pushed the line button and replaced the receiver.

LaRouge swiped his files from his paper tray and, while stating his name and rank, took a seat across from Felix.

"Whitehorse detachment said I'd reach you here. The State Troopers in Tok notified us that you suspect a threat to the security of the United States." Orez made the statement seem routine. "Is there a confirmed target?"

"Not at this time." Felix kept Fanger out of his reply. "In the past hour his last known location has been fixed, putting him a mile from the Taylor Highway. He's on foot on a course to reach Tetlin Junction, possibly tomorrow."

"The Troopers will follow up on that. Our military installations in the region have their own protocols to mitigate attack. Tell me about the terrorist."

"The thief," said Felix, although he knew the case would never be tried. Ahmed could expect a one-way flight to Guantanamo following his capture. "We've uncovered the suspect's nationality and a motive, plus some insight into his activities in Europe. We've also learned he has connections to someone in Delta Junction working at Fort Greely."

Felix told Orez what Fanger had learned from Marty. "Bloody fights and a gang bang that caused a miscarriage; that would motivate me to a new level of dedication," Felix said. "The kind that allows me to bide my time until the perfect opportunity arises."

"And Ahmed is that opportunity." Orez murmured a plea to a patron saint.

Felix summarized Fanger's encounters on the trail, Donjek's discovery of evidence, LaRouge's school teacher, Avery's illegal aliens and the BKA's background information.

LaRouge got the nod to speak. "Bock's called since and is on his way here, presumably for Rendezvous, which starts in a few days." Both he and Felix wanted this case closed before then. "I understand he's rented a snowmobile. It was dropped off here yesterday."

"We will want to talk to him," Orez said.

"I'm sure we all do." Felix gave him the call centre's extension at the Gambler's Den, ensuring he could be reached.

"About your idea that Fort Greely is the target," the master sergeant continued. "I doubt one man with fifty sticks of dynamite is going to have much of an effect on Ground-based Missile Defense. The silos are seventy-five feet deep and they withstood a seven-point-nine earthquake with an epicentre thirty miles from here. It was our first real test and the tremors rolled through the construction with barely a ripple."

"I didn't say it made sense, just that he's en route."

"True. I'll bring this to the commander." Orez gave Felix his direct phone number. "Please call when you get the sled coordinates or any fresh information, especially regarding the target."

Orez hung up as a Hercules carrying a load of lubricants scheduled for delivery to the Cold Regions Test Center rumbled overhead. Orez watched it touch down at the airfield a mile away on the new post. The pilot was on his way to Eielson Air Force Base, twenty miles this side of Fairbanks.

The vast frontier outside Orez's window reduced the army's architecture inside the double fence to the scale of GI Joe's training camp. The circa 1950 buildings surrounding him came straight out of his boyhood. He glanced down and to the right, where a jeep putted across the intersection to a gas station at the end of a row of precision tract housing he'd called home for the past three years. Built to withstand minus-fifty Celsius, each unit had the utilitarian drabness of any army installation in the Lower Forty-eight. He scratched the quarter-inch moulding framing his office window. It was closer to a half-inch thick after decades of laying on paint to ensure full value for the taxpayers' dollars.

Could one man break in? Orez phoned his superior, Mr. Thurlow, the deputy commander at Fort Greely.

"It's not enough they're breeding terrorists in the Middle East, they've got to recruit locals, too?" Thurlow fumed in his frustration. "Get the brass together. We'll meet in the conference room as soon as the commander's in."

Assembling too many hours later, at day's end, on the

third floor of the administration building, Thurlow was carrying on the same conversation with post commander, Lieutenant Colonel Axton. "Can't they see the benefits of adopting democracy? We just want to do business with a stable elected government."

Axton's government-issue bifocals had slipped down his Seneca nose to sit level with the epicanthic eyelids he had inherited from his father. He humoured his deputy with a smile from the full lips on the ebony face of his mother's heritage. "Calm down, Thurlow. You're preaching to the converted."

At that moment the room snapped to attention as Colonel Carla Lewis from Fort Richardson entered, followed by Colonel Adam Ghirrard from missile defense command. They faced the assembly, then sat at the head of the conference table, Colonel Lewis near the post colours, Colonel Ghirrard by the Stars and Stripes.

Greely's commander welcomed them. "Colonel Ghirrard is reporting to the Alaska region's new brigadier general," he said, mostly for the benefit of the civilians in the room — project manager Jeff Weatherton and Clive Kalupik, president of Yukon Flats Management Corporation. "Colonel Lewis is a specialist on our detainment policies in the War on Terror."

She sat erect in her fatigues. Her only concession to fashion was a French braid that bound her hair. "Everyone has read their briefing notes." She asked, but it was not a question. "Good." She opened her folder. "Master Sergeant Orez has been on the phone most of the day with police on both sides of the border. Report developments, Sergeant."

"As you know, Canadian authorities contacted us through the State Troopers about a suspected terrorist, Omar Ahmed, who crossed into our territory at Poker Creek on a stolen snowmobile. We have since located it in a ditch near the Taylor Highway." Orez unrolled the Tanacross topographic map he'd brought with him. "Coming from Dawson, the Dennison Fork Trail splits north of Tetlin Junction and follows the east side of Highway Five south to where it comes out, here, less than a dozen miles from Tetlin." He drew his fingers to the intersection of an easting and northing in a grid square with sparse features.

"Thank you, Master Sergeant," the garrison commander said. "Focus your search. Also, continue your liaison with the Mounted Police." She hoped the tradition of cooperation between the Troopers and Mounties extended to their colleagues in the BKA. "If possible, debrief the officer from Germany. We may glean enough information to round up accomplices," she said. "I want to hear from the rest of you. Your perspectives, what's at stake here?"

"On American soil, this guy could be anywhere," said Thurlow. "As I've said for years, the X-band radar at Eareckson Air Station is our weakest link in the defense shield. A good-sized rock aimed at the radomes would blind us. Pray he isn't riding the tide in a fishing boat off Shemya Island."

"I doubt our suspect is going to the tail end of the Aleutians in a trawler, Mr. Thurlow," Axton said.

We can't afford to ignore the possibility, thought Lewis. "What's missile defense's view, Colonel Ghirrard?" She turned to the officer in the tailored uniform beside her. Off and on Ghirrard had worked with Carla for fifteen years, been best man at her wedding even, but no one would guess from his formality.

"Indeed." He straightened his cuffs. "Mr. Thurlow is correct in that there are several GMD component installations a terrorist could access in Alaska, starting with our eyes on Shemya, but we have determined the Rock is out of reach in this case. In the fifty-mile-an-hour fog they get, he'd need the kind of tracking equipment we've got installed there just to find it. I doubt he'd get close enough without them knowing."

"'In God we trust. All others we monitor,'" Thurlow said. "That's putting a lot of faith in their motto."

"Granted. But, I think we can put them at a lower response level, as we have with Kodiak," Ghirrard said. "If that's his destination, he's taking the long route to get there. Also, it doesn't make sense to go after the dummy targets we use for system tests. The Canadians' preliminary assessment is most likely correct. Battalion has assigned additional resources to improve security of the missiles."

"Which brings us back to Fort Greely," said Axton, who paused before voicing the difficult question. "Does everyone understand how realistic the GMD is as a target?"

Thurlow couldn't control himself. "It doesn't have to be strategic, just a showpiece, a political statement. Tampering with the GMD will make America afraid. He'll sabotage our very idea of safety and freedom. We cannot afford to be defenseless for a moment. Vigilance is the only protection we have against their quick strike approach."

"Order, gentlemen," the colonel said, and she was

obeyed. "In the course of my duties, I've studied the use of propaganda and terrorist communication. A strike of this magnitude would be a powerful weapon for the fundamentalists."

Axton expected to hear their views reiterated in debrief, if there ever was one. He looked outside at the A-frame church, slab recreation complex and PX in the foreground to the squat Cold War warehouses and barracks he commanded. "It may be a small thing that brings us to our knees. If he blows the fuel depot, for example, we'd be down. Not out, mind you, but certainly down."

A timid voice spoke next. "I know this is outside my job as project manager, but I keep thinking about that guy with the hunting rifle a few years ago," Weatherton said. "You know, the one who took up target practice on the pipeline?"

Orez nodded. "They had to scramble to get the Trans-Alaska back on line." He glanced at Kalupik, who was from Yukon Flats. The facilities manager leaned into the shadow cast by the deep windowsill behind him. He'd faced enough embarrassment about his tribe's involvement in the incident.

Weatherton spoke again. "With Pump Station Nine only a mile from the missile field, blowing that up could cause a lot of grief. Or a shooter with a fifty cal could keep it shut indefinitely. I read that one spill was in the range of three quarters of a million gallons of crude. Imagine a new hole everyday."

"And the clean up," said Kalupik. "Our tribe won't let that slide," he added by way of apology; how could they know the band member would run amok? "When I was a boy this base was all new." His line of sight out the window spread from the defoliated test bed to the black spruce that grew between the toes of the distant range of peaks that rose to fifteen thousand feet. He pointed to a small river glinting in the shallow valley that paralleled the post's doglegged eastern perimeter. In the dying sun, it stood out as one of the few features on the prehistoric floodplain.

"My dad used to bag moose along Jarvis Creek, just outside that fence. There's over a half million square miles of wilderness out there and only a few roads. But if he stays on the Trans-Alaska, it'll take him to the terminal in Valdez. A few charges in the right places would take out the main transfer point for Alaska crude."

Colonel Lewis was well aware that represented fifteen to twenty percent of the nation's fuel supply. It was a number nine priority target for risk management. "I'll initiate a sweep and increase surveillance," she said.

"You might want to add the old eight-inch fuel line from Haines to Eielson to your list," Weatherton suggested. "The supply line was torn out years ago, but if our terrorist intersects the right-of-way a few miles north of Delta, he's got a straight shot to the air base."

"Eielson's our primary transfer facility for shipping components for the booster missiles. We must ensure safe passage," Colonel Lewis commented. "Alternatives are dwindling for our Syrian. He can only press forward. Hypothetically, if we don't catch him and he gets to the GMD, what are his options?"

"Well, he can't just blow up the silos," Weatherton replied, confident to speak from the familiar ground of construction. "They're sunk in a glacial moraine. The overburden is sand, studded with pockets of gravel. And they're two different designs, each with its own complex command and communications system wired through the utilidors that connect the silos to the mechanical-electrical building. It's completely separate from anything here on the old post."

Kalupik mixed in another factor. "Aside from really pissing off the president, if this guy does succeed, it'll cost hundreds of millions to replace, repair or rebuild damaged elements. It's no secret the goal of Afghan rebels is to bankrupt us, just like they did to the Russians in the eighties. And, just one silo, after it arrives from Oregon, takes two days to truck from Valdez."

"Nothing can delay this project," Ghirrard said. "We've set an aggressive schedule to meet the president's ongoing mandate. There's cutting-edge technology in the first six interceptors, and we're looking at up to forty missiles in the arsenal by the end of this term. Even the slightest delay in production will threaten our timeline and security."

"None of us wants to be a sitting duck." Weatherton ceded the colonel's point, but he knew his crew. "We've come in on time and under budget in every aspect of this project, working through winter in fifteen hundred feet of leaky cement tubing the dimensions of a prison cell. It's over a hundred degrees in there, crammed with pipes and conduit, and still the trades are putting out, full bore. I'm confident we can minimize down time."

"But can we trust you?" Orez matched Weatherton's scorn with a reminder of the local element. "The accomplice, the Secord woman. It's practically impossible to place a large force in range undetected, and that's where a single operative has the advantage. Or a small team of insurgents. Are others helping her?"

Weatherton had had enough. "How can I know? Each silo interface that connects the missiles to the launch equipment is in a sixty-four-ton vault. It'll take forever to untangle what she's done in the whole installation. Her foreman said she's been all over the project."

"Track her down," Colonel Lewis interjected. "We've got to determine the full extent of her involvement. Maybe she'll introduce us to her boyfriend."

"I'll talk to the foremen," Weatherton said. "All of them, on every shift. Our workers keep a pretty close eye on each other, mostly to combat depression," he added. "It shouldn't be hard to find out who she hangs out with, off post."

Yukon Flats' own security experts had entrenched extra monitoring measures immediately. "Security has been told to detain Ms. Secord on sight," Kalupik said. "We're checking all traffic and running snowmobile patrols outside the perimeter, flushing the bush trails. No one's sniffing glue around a campfire out there anymore," he said. "She may try to infiltrate maintenance, or support staff to gain access, so we'll be making spot identity checks. And we've sent casuals home until the threat is under control."

"Make sure no one gets sick, Mr. Kalupik," Colonel Lewis said.

"Yes, Colonel," he said. "There is one more thing. Our staff is alert to report abnormalities. You know, little things out of place. But if the staff on shift is denied access, they won't be able to perform their duties. Is that going to be a problem?"

"Not at all," Colonel Ghirrard and the garrison commander said in unison.

"Faith in our joint venture with Yukon Flats is implicit," Colonel Lewis assured the facilities manager. "For onsite surveillance you're a valuable partner. And it seems you're in complete readiness."

The colonel put her pencil down and picked up the yellow pad. "These are the following assignments. Colonel Ghirrard and I will direct a sweep of all installations, with special attention to those we've discussed. I'll contact Alyeska Pipeline security and request a sweep of all the Trans-Alaska pump stations. The colonel will contact ports and air. We will also review our response plans, especially a rebuilding schedule." She faced the lieutenant colonel and confirmed he would increase patrols on post, and double sentries at risk values, such as the fuel depot. She continued. "Master Sergeant, ask local law enforcement to canvas all traffic, continue your liaison with law enforcement in Canada and, concurrently, work with Mr. Weatherton to locate Ms. Secord."

Orez would have his hands full tracking Annabeth, and casting a net over Omar Ahmed.

"Have we overlooked anything?" Colonel Lewis asked. Each man looked to the next. "Good. We'll reconvene at twenty-one hundred to discuss progress. They must not reach the GMD." She stood, heels together, and closed the meeting. "Rule out nothing before this is contained. That's our priority: containment. Dismissed."

THIRTEEN

Cutting over to the Taylor Highway, the travelled part of the trail felt as smooth as an expressway after last night's slash and bash. Fanger arrived at Little Gold as the day's light departed, and parked with the motor near the cookshack stove.

The snowmobile's roar had brought Marty, sleepy-headed, out of the kitchen tent. "Hey, Marty, this looks great," Fanger said. "You've been busy." He'd been gone thirty hours, during which time Marty had torn down camp.

"I got bored." Marty yawned and stretched. "I'll show you around."

They shuffled to the barrels filled with leftover food, leaning cock-eyed against the dismantled stoves crammed full of unused kitchenware. He toed a tightly sealed bucket beside him. "The honey pot. I've taken down the outhouse and stowed it over there." He pointed to the panels, and Fanger noticed the tent frame poles were also stashed away, vertically, in the trees. Out of sight they blended in with the spruce branches, protected from becoming fuel, and kept off the ground to prevent rot.

"I've kept some water and coffee aside for us, and the last of the stew for you," Marty said.

"Great. I'm starved. So no one turned back after I left?"

"No. Except for an ermine, I've been enjoying my own company."

Fanger followed Marty into the tent. In contrast to the overcrowded accommodation of the day before yesterday, the dwelling felt as desolate as an empty barn with the wind tearing the door off its hinges. Other than their mats and sleeping bags, the only thing beside the stove was a stump table. On it sat a coffee and a stack of paper the texture of linen.

"It's all sorted," Marty said, handing the bundle to Fanger. He flipped through the reconstituted carbonless copies, in order of date and duplicate.

"You must have been really bored," Fanger said. "This looked like a gob of wet toilet paper when I left."

"I know," Marty said. "It took a while to dry roast it into individual sheets. What is it anyway?"

"Scheiss Papierkram," Fanger said. "Forms for Donny's community service. I'm supposed to hand them in to the probation officer."

"Well, it's illegible now," Marty said.

"It was just made-up bullshit anyway. But thanks. I'll sure relish the look on Janice's face when she sees this," he said, placing the stack with his race documents.

"Glad to see you haven't lost your sense of humour along with your voice," Marty said to Fanger, who was in the middle of gulping down a litre of water. "How's your throat feel?"

"Aah. Better now." He traded the empty water bottle for a full cup of coffee. Marty also gave him a bowl of stew. Fanger hadn't eaten much since yesterday, and fell to his food.

"So what did you find out there?" Marty asked, wide awake and hungry for news after a day in isolation.

"Donny's sled run off the trail and planted like a Popsicle stick in the snow. I tried to start it but the motor's seized up. I'll bet the fuel mixture was pretty lean, since Donny had the warm weather jets in."

"Yeah, the temperature dropped like a rock when that northwind blew in," Marty said. "My thermometer read below forty-five when I packed it this morning. Have you told Donny about his sled?"

Fanger blushed. "I left that to Felix. The State Troopers have probably towed it to their station by now." At least he'd get no hassle picking it up later. "The sergeant said Donny's been helping them round up volunteers for an overland search. I guess Erik's kept him busy at the race centre, too."

"Pity we couldn't get spotters in the air, especially after you built that landing zone over there." Marty waved in the direction of the cleared area the checkers had staked such a short time ago. "If they could even see in this weather," he admitted. Blowing snow clouded the sky. "The wind's been just flattening the trees around here." Canvas on the weather side of the tent whipped against its lashings. "I'm not surprised you lost Ahmed in this. I hope he's just as lost."

Marty's expression, a mixture of sadness and guilt, was becoming familiar to Fanger. He ate the last of the stew and threw the paper bowl in the stove.

"Even at the race start, he had the nerve to ask me about Marie's custody. Again." Marty emphasized the frequency.

"What's custody of Marie have to do with him?" Fanger naturally aligned himself with Marty, the wronged man, indignant and distrustful.

"You know, ever since Annabeth went to Alaska,

Ahmed's been a self-appointed advocate for her. At Christmas I took Marie shopping and he found me. Right in the middle of the store, in front of Marie and God and everyone, he let into me, preaching about how a child needs its mother."

Fanger now had a context for the confrontation he'd witnessed at the pre-race meeting. "Do you think Marie would go with him? Would Annabeth take her across the border?"

"Maybe. She tried it once," Marty said.

"What?" Fanger had heard nothing of a kidnapping.

"It started in August. We were already split up and Annabeth had agreed to work for the devil."

Did Marty mean the military or Ahmed? Fanger concentrated on the story.

"Marie was staying with her mother then, and it broke my heart, even though we talked every day on the phone. Then, out of the blue, I get a call at work from Port Alcan." Marty read Fanger's puzzled look. "You know, the US side of Beaver Creek, half hour further on." Fanger nodded understanding. "Anyway, they wanted to know — did I approve travel for my daughter into the United States? 'Like hell I do,' I said. Apparently Ahmed had picked up Marie on her way home from school and brought her to Annabeth on the day she left for Delta Junction. She just assumed Marie was going with her. Never told me a thing, just up and left."

"Thank God border patrol called," Fanger said. "What did you do next?"

"I made certain the officer knew I did not approve Marie's travel out of country. They held her, an eight-year-old girl, until I could get there to pick her up. I've never driven so fast in my life."

Both Canada and the US struggled to halt child smuggling, and required both parents to approve cross-border travel, but Fanger had never known someone who had so clearly benefited from the controls.

"When I got there Annabeth begged me to give her written permission to take Marie to Alaska, but I couldn't. I knew I'd never see Marie again if I did. We were in the parking lot where they do the vehicle searches, Marie crying, Annabeth shouting, me doing both. The border guards were inside watching all this. Finally, I had enough and just said, 'No!' Then I got Marie, kicking and screaming, into the car and took her home. All the way, five hours, she howled in the back seat. I felt like a monster, a childsnatcher, tearing my baby from the bosom of her mother. It was awful."

"Where is she now?" Fanger asked.

"With Sid Crawford and his wife."

"Crawford? The reporter?"

Marty nodded. "Now that Ahmed's urged Annabeth to leave, he's on me to give Marie over. Imagine convincing a mother to leave her own child, and then making me out to be the bad guy. I have no idea what he's told Annabeth, probably some rubbish about wealth and paradise and a better future than she could imagine for her daughter. He's like a snake charmer, you know." Defeated, Marty dropped his head into his hands and sighed.

Regular magi, Fanger thought. He excused himself and went out to phone Dawson.

Whirlwinds kicked up snow ghosts that howled over

the camp. Fanger cowered to listen. Sergeant Felix answered, relieved to hear from Fanger. "Welcome to Canada," he said.

"Glad to be back." Fanger shouted to make himself heard. "Any news about Ahmed?"

"The Americans are working on it. They'd like to speak to you and your friend, Bock. He'll be here tomorrow."

"What *here*? Dawson?" Fanger had been out of touch.

"Whitehorse. He's arriving on the five o'clock flight. Avery's going to meet him if we're not back."

"What's the corporal doing tomorrow? I mean, is he fully assigned?"

Felix gave a short laugh. "He's in his element. Headquarters sent his colleagues from Integrated Border Enforcement. They flew in from Ottawa yesterday and Avery's taken them under his wing. They're working on the big picture."

"Well, I don't want to overlook the small details." Fanger meant no nonsense. He laid out the points of Marty's confession and forwarded his own theory. "Ahmed meets Annabeth Secord, an Alaskan in Canada, discovers she's an electrician, and turns her head. He convinces her to leave her husband and daughter for a job over there."

Felix ran with the story. "He hits Boreal and gives her the leg wire, which she smuggles in to prep the site."

"Initially he probably played her along with promises of getting custody of Marie. At that point she'd do anything he asked and, later if she balks, he blackmails her with her own child."

"If she's as gullible as he is unscrupulous," Felix said.

"We've both seen abusive husbands pull the same stunt

in the sweetest tones. And I've seen the women accept it, when it seems to be the only way to protect their children," Fanger said.

Felix knew he was right. He'd get Avery to contact the child's network of responsible adults. "Where is Marie now?" he asked.

"With Sid Crawford," he replied.

"So much for keeping this out of the press. I better get our media liaison working on a statement."

"Or better yet, get Border Enforcement to write it. They're tight lipped," Fanger said. "It might buy us some time."

"Perhaps." Felix didn't sound convinced. He perked up when Fanger said he'd be at the Gambler's Den by noon the next day.

"I'll crash here first." Fanger pressed the end button and replaced the phone in its case. When he entered the kitchen tent, Marty was already cocooned in his sleeping bag. Fanger closed the damper on the stove and crawled into his own bed.

Ten hours later he awoke fully rested in the chill, dark morning. He shuffled out of the covers and into his clothes. He placed the last wood over the handful of coals in the bottom of the stove and opened the flue wide. While he waited for it to catch, he put on his headlamp and set the coffee pot on the camping stove. By then Marty was out of bed and painting a snowbank yellow. After a hasty breakfast, they broke down the tent and packed the trailboggans. For an hour and a half they rode in the dark with a thin band of grey that widened into daylight on the horizon ahead.

The marathon finish was a scarred patch of earth when they buzzed through the checkpoint. By lunchtime they'd pulled up in front of race central. Clusters of athletes gathered in the lobby. Another pair left the banquet room as Fanger and Marty entered. Directly inside the door, they were greeted by a uniformed officer Fanger did not recognize. "A member will be available shortly," the stranger instructed them. He had assumed they were race competitors, and in the hubbub of the call centre, Fanger could see why.

Partitions blocked off the phone bank, with all systems—land, radio and satellite—ringing off the hook. The units were staffed by runners Fanger had served at the checkpoint. A few more strangers with folders and clipboards buzzed between the callers and kept information flowing.

On the back wall, lineups formed before a quartet of officers, two scheduling appointments for interviews and a pair providing directions to detachment. Fanger looked for LaRouge but found not a sign. At that moment, Sergeant Felix came toward them, flanked by Donjek and Erik.

Fanger had wanted to shake Donjek's hand and publicly commend his rescuer, but the hand he reached for was wrapped in gauze that held thick burn dressings in place. It appalled him to see the extent of Ahmed's attack and how hard Donjek had had to fight to save both their skins.

"Thanks for finding my sled, man," Donjek said. "One less thing to think about." It was a short reunion before they were interrupted by a volunteer tapping the youth's shoulder. "It's great to see you, Fanger, but …" He shrugged as he was given a phone, handed a map and directed else-where.

"Any place in your organization for us?" Fanger asked. "This looks pretty intense."

"Right this way," Erik said, leading them to the strategy table at the back of two dozen chairs placed in rows of six before a podium, white board and projector screen. "We have our briefings here." He showed Fanger to a seat at a table full of maps and papers. Erik and Felix remained standing. Marty sat across from the trio.

The sergeant gave Fanger a quick tour. "That's Dawson detachment's intake. They're making appointments with each competitor." He pointed to a tête-à-tête at the head of the line.

"I haven't seen LaRouge anywhere," Fanger said. He looked forward to comparing notes.

"He's up the Clinton Creek Road, but we're expecting him back soon."

"I saw tracks on the way in. Looks like a pretty big crew travelled up there." He asked after the racers. "What about the ones who were underway?"

Erik answered. "Initially we brought everyone into the nearest checkpoint with individual escorts, took down their times and closed the course. We gave the racers an option to take a three-day — maximum — layover, when, we hope, the trail will be safe again. The Troopers are doing the same for the three hundreds in Alaska between Little Gold and Tok."

"The rest are cooling their heels?" Marty's quip failed to add levity.

"If Ahmed's captured, we'll finish the three hundred

and credit those continuing with the lost hours. If not, we'll call the race as it stands and shuttle everyone out. The Alaskan sweepers are pitching in at the checkpoints, for added protection."

"Over there" — Felix indicated an opening in the extended folding wall — "is the switchboard. We're expecting the detachment to put through a call from the Americans any moment."

As if on cue, a runner came out with a cordless. "Master Sergeant Orez for you, sir." She put the phone in his hand and trotted away.

"Orez?" Felix said as he walked several paces away with the receiver to his ear. "I hope you're calling with good news, like you've captured the thief."

"Not yet, although we are grateful for your swift response and prompt notification. Alaska command has met and we're closing off his opportunities."

"Well, we can help you with that over here," Felix said. He brought Fanger's multi-faceted family cube into the rubric. "We've informed Marie's teachers, parents of her friends, coaches and neighbours to keep a close eye on her. Ahmed's lost his own son and I doubt he's the soul of compassion. He might rob another parent of their child."

"Possibly." Orez's skepticism inferred myriad alternate motives. "Secord could also be a willing participant. We have an APB out on both of them." His gratitude for the Mounties' cooperation was genuine.

"Really the credit goes to one of our auxiliaries and a young offender. They were on the front line, as it were," Felix said.

"Sergeant, you said the checkers would return today. Is one of them available to come to the phone?"

Felix returned to the briefing table and gave the phone to Fanger, introducing Orez as he did.

"Markus Fanger speaking. How can I help you, Master Sergeant?"

"You have the intelligence from German federal police, is that right, Mr. Fanger?"

"Not exactly. A former colleague of mine is the one you want to talk to. We'll come in, but I'm sure the officer is going to want to remain anonymous. He has a career to protect."

"Understood," Orez agreed. Annabeth Secord would corroborate any evidence when they brought her in. "We'd like to interview both you and your assistant."

"You'll have to arrange that with my sergeant. Here he is." Felix took the phone and reminded the master sergeant of Donjek's delinquencies.

"We'll expedite that," Orez assured him. "Our staff will be on hand at the border to aid them in clearing customs."

"I appreciate that you'll let him enter. I'll work on his exit," Felix said. He'd ask Ruth to contact the sentencing judge and youth probation officer.

Annabeth wasn't on shift until tomorrow, for the commissioning, and she had to sleep before then. Her LeBaron crawled along the same stretch of highway she'd been scouring for hours. She'd been in position at exactly the prescribed moment, and Omar had stood her up. That was four hours ago. Since then she'd racked up nearly a hundred miles on the twelve-mile stretch between their rendezvous point and Tetlin Junction.

Afraid to be spotted in the waxing daylight, she was on her last pass. If he didn't show up, she'd go to Evy's.

Between the Cold War and the Gulf War, Evy had supported the state senator when he'd floated the idea of turning the deactivated base into a prison. Nowadays, the rumour mill derided her for saying, "I'd be safer in my home with convicts in the backyard than rockets." The small-town citizens had responded by taking their business to Fairbanks, a hundred miles away. But Evy didn't care where they shopped. She gave the peaceniks ten per-cent off and took Canadian money at par. And at Hallow-een, Annabeth helped scrape off a lot of the IGA's egg stock that landed as frozen splats on the Bull's Eye.

On the Tanana River bridge, a blur swirled in the bliz-zard. Wind buffeted her car on black ice. She mounted the curb and ricocheted into a head-spinning curlicue the length of the bridge deck. Her nerves blew apart. A dark smudge flickered into view and revolved into life-size as the LeBaron bore down, intent on the guardrail. Annabeth flinched and her wheels unlocked, gripped and held. She braked and slowed, stopped, at last, a hair's breadth from certain death. The figure collapsed against her fender.

Annabeth bolted from the car, but her body slipped and skid on unsteady legs to the side of the huddled form — a man, her man. She pulled him to her. "You were not to wait." Omar reprimanded her. Annabeth got him into the car. She cranked the heat to full and tucked blankets around him. "I am glad you did," he added, in a staccato chatter. She shut the passenger door and located his pulk a few feet away. The weight was a challenge for her, but she stowed it in the back seat and got behind the wheel.

A coughing fit wracked Omar's freezer-burned bronchi. He opened the window and cleared blood-flecked phlegm. His spit froze before it hit the ground.

FOURTEEN

Omar wheezed, then passed out cold beside Annabeth. She gave his face a soft caress; he stole the warmth of her touch. It was a marvel—she'd rescued her lover in the nick of time, and had nearly killed him in the process. It was obvious his plan had gone sideways, and she could only assume they were fugitives now.

She closed Omar's window and left the Tanana River behind her, accelerating as fast as she dared on the empty road to Tok and, a hundred miles beyond that, Delta Junction. A burn area surrounded them—ten years into its creeping reforestation, evergreens were still nevergreens, charred matchsticks grafted over the landscape.

Inside Tok community limits, the sleepy town seemed deserted, but Annabeth took the precaution of turning off the highway before reaching the State Troopers' compound up ahead. Had she not skirted the law, she would have been devoured by the growing posse—a pandemonium of on- and off-road vehicles revved to a frenzied pitch. Harnessed dog gangs howled in noisy contest with high-performance machines. Lunging against the snow hooks holding them back, they sensed purpose to their training run. The Race of Champions, the final leg of sledding's triple crown, was set for next month, and the search for Annabeth and Omar was fast becoming a prelim. As it was, on Sanford, every dog left behind sent up the alarm. Mortified the law would respond, Annabeth cringed along the edge of the sled dog capital of Alaska to Midnight Sun Drive, which would bring her out of this town where dogs outnumbered people.

She slowed a dozen car lengths from four teams and drivers who raced over the road and dropped into the ditch. Annabeth spotted them on Omar's side, weaving away in the trees. She had circumvented Tok undetected and, at the stop sign, she watched a trooper a block away at the intersection of "Mainstreet Alaska," absorbed in his job of unloading a pickup full of wooden barricades. They weren't looking for drunk drivers, she was certain. While his back was turned, she pulled onto the Alaska Highway.

They would be caught for sure at the next roadblock to Delta, and she had to come up with a plan. The Alaska Range loomed into view, but she had her head down and her eyes on the gas gauge — nearly empty. Her thoughts were a jumble on the rough drive ahead — stop for gas, tend to Omar, dodge roadblocks. By the time they reached Dot Lake Lodge, Omar had not woken and, on fumes, she rolled to a stop.

After she had refuelled, she parked her gas-guzzling LeBaron in front of the coffee shop. Omar could not be roused and, in his condition, she was wary of shaking him. She pinched the muscle at his shoulder, putting pressure on his trapezius until he flinched and raised his lolling head. "We're sixty miles from Delta and I'm going in to pay for gas," she said. "I'll be right back."

The fill-up entitled her to complimentary coffee, and she ordered two breakfast specials to go with it. When she returned to the car, Omar, awake now, was in the throes of a wracking cough.

The suffocating congestion inside his chest was plain to hear, and Annabeth uncapped her coffee to hold it near his mouth and nose. "Breathe in the steam," she said. "This worked last summer when Marie got asthma from wildfire smoke." Omar's spasms eased enough that he could take the cup from her hand and douse his raw throat.

Food reoriented him, as did Annabeth's announcement: "We've got a problem." About the roadblocks she said, "They'll draw a noose around our necks if we don't act fast."

"Drive then," he ordered.

She pushed the speed limit and Omar's lucid moments were lost in dozy consciousness.

"Down!" Annabeth ordered as they met a convoy of army transport trucks approaching in the oncoming lane. She threw her heavy jacket over him, which knocked the wind out of him. At a safe speed, she passed the carriers without incident.

Eighteen miles from Delta, a few log structures at the Silverfox Roadhouse sat under the snow like mushrooms waiting to sprout. Annabeth proceeded with caution. There weren't enough troopers to cover every intersection, but they'd be where the Alaska Highway met the Richardson.

This close to town there should have been a stream of local traffic, but Delta's thirty-two hundred residents were eerily absent. A radio tower blinked above Allen Airfield where not a bird flew. Annabeth approached the heart of locked down silence, unmindful of the erratic effect her lookout had on her steering.

Red, white and blue bloomed in the sky above a distant nest of official vehicles. On her left, a quiet street branched off and, with driving test precision, she turned onto Fifth. She took Bear to Puma and, where the track ended at a barn, she camouflaged her sedan among a handful of gutted parts cars.

She held Omar's face and slapped him with great follow through. He moaned in response. "Wake up," she demanded. "We have to walk." She released him and got into the back seat. She dealt with the pulk, making short work of slashing the tarp and nets away. Only the dynamite and detonators, and Omar's pistol remained. "Where's your stuff, honey?" No response. "Come on! Wake up. Speak to me."

"Dumped it," he mumbled. She lined the empty toboggan with blankets, sleeping bags and afghans, and rewrapped the package as she would a toddler. It took as much effort to get the two-hundred-pound baby out as it did to get the one-hundred-seventy-pound father on his feet. She clipped the harness around her waist, took Omar by the hand and feigned a casual pace as they tottered over the snow-covered fallow. The charade reminded her of similar walks she and Marty had made with their own child snuggled in a toboggan. She tugged on Omar's hand and hurried away from the idea.

In contrast to the Alcan, the Richardson, which they paralleled now, bustled with traffic, all army being deployed from Anchorage in the south and Fairbanks in the west. The convoy she'd seen outside Tok must have been the first line of defense, but they'd been able to sneak past, all the way to Evy's sports store — a haven fifty yards away.

At the moment, a dumpster obscured them from view, and they kept covered when a Trooper's half-ton rolled by. As soon as he was out of sight, Annabeth sprinted to the back door with the pulk wobbling behind her and Omar dragging her down. She shoved him into the storm porch and took Evy's key from the last boot on the rack.

She raced up to a landing, opened the door and ran back for Omar, who proved to be an awkward mannequin to get onto Evy's sofa. She made another trip packing the load upstairs, and then went down a separate flight that ended beside Evy's desk in the storeroom. About to step out from behind the ice fishing lures, Annabeth heard her name mentioned in an enchanting southern accent.

"A tin-basher on post reckons you see Ms. Secord quite regular, Evy." Trooper Ray Lacroix drawled over job site gossip. "You say she has not come around this fine mornin'?"

"No, nor any other fine morning this week." A typical acid answer from Evy.

"Well, if she should honour you with a visit, you be sure to invite me. Here's my card."

Paper tore. "I know your number, Ray."

"I'll be going then." His felt Stetson tipped above a rack of hunting vests, and the door chimed when he left.

With the coast clear, Annabeth came forward. She knocked the display rack of fish hooks. Rubber ice worms jumped on their pegs.

"Who's there?" Evy whirled around and looked up at a convex security mirror. Her mouth made an oversized O in the reflection. Annabeth froze, exposed.

"My God, girlfriend! Are you okay?" Evy nearly leaped the counter to embrace her.

"Yes, I'm fine, but I'm not alone." She confessed her secret affair — which, it turned out, was no secret. She outlined Omar's condition as she found him on the Ultra trail. Evy had what they needed: hot packs, electrolyte crystals, first-aid supplies and, most importantly, her help.

"Well, you won't get any from anyone else," she retorted. "The place is hopping with cops and your trailer is under armed guard."

"You're not going to tell them we're here?" Annabeth's question was more an expression of disbelief than concern.

"Not in the shape you're in. You look awful. We'll talk about what to do later. Let me flip the sign around." Evy closed the shop for an hour, the sign indicating she would re-open at three. They went upstairs with supplies for Omar.

"He's frozen to death!" Evy exclaimed.

"No, look," Annabeth said. She folded back the blanket to reveal a slight blush, a vivid contrast to the ashen skin of the man she'd found in the cold. "He's got colour in his cheeks again."

"Help me get him up," Evy said. "Put him in my bed."

Omar followed Annabeth's instructions to stand, but his gait was a clumsy stumble. "Annabeth, Muharran. Salat," he mumbled. The women took an arm each and shared the chore of dragging him to the bedroom. He murmured garbled verses on the way.

"Reminds me of putting the ol' man to bed after a binge," Evy said. "Thought all that was behind me, Annabeth." The short chorus line spun on its axis to shuffle through the door, made another quarter turn and, in unison, sat on the unmade bed.

"I'll fill a hot water bottle. You get him undressed," Evy said as she got up, propping him against Annabeth, who manipulated his flopping limbs out of his reeking clothes and bundled him in the thick top cover.

"Salat, Anna, salat." She removed the slashed plastic binding from his foot but decided against redressing the wound until he woke. She wrapped a light towel around the injury and put hot packs at his neck before taking his rotting outfit to the bathroom.

Evy was plugging in a space heater at the foot of the bed when Annabeth returned. "I straightened the sheets some." In fact, she'd changed the linens and tucked Omar in like a hospital patient. He snored in peaceful rest.

"I gotta get back downstairs." Evy looked at her watch. "The store's open until nine. Get some rest."

Annabeth was speechless. Evy's only question had been about her well-being. True friends, to the bitter end. The door clicked shut.

Too exhausted to cry, Annabeth undressed and wrapped herself around her lover's body. She used to complain about her husband's cold feet, but that was nothing like what she felt now. Goose flesh plucked her thighs. It chilled the water in her bowels and set her teeth on edge. In this position, she'd wind up as frozen as Omar. She got up to pee and, back in bed, slipped an extra blanket between her and Omar. The layer of insulation tempered her sleep.

Annabeth woke when Omar turned to face her. Her leg was draped across him and he lifted her thigh to rest high on his hip. Raw heat from his vitals diffused into her groin and, from his soul, into her breasts. Her breath was a gulf stream against his neck.

"It's dark," he said, cradling her in his arms. Adonis sculpted from ice would not have felt this cold, she thought. She opened her eyes.

Dim shapes shifted into a feminine jumble spilling out of a steamer trunk, and on the dresser stood a varied assortment of archery trophies. No light shone under the door and, from the jingle of the cash register below, she knew they'd be undisturbed.

Sensation invaded as Omar stimulated the contours of her body. Deep-seated cold vaporized in hot passion.

"Ahlia," he whispered, with manifest solemnity.

Annabeth stroked his hair and brushed the damp curls from his face. "What does that mean? Ahlia. You say it nearly every time we make love."

"Ahlia is my wife," he said.

She propped herself up on one elbow. "You mean *me*— your wife? Me, you and Marie?"

"If you want, yes." Her honey-gold hair spread a tear across her cheek, as his wife's black-gold hair had when he'd last seen her. They had been at home, in a distant part of the city. On the patio was their son, pushing a toy tank over marble flagstones. The memory of cumin from the lamb, fresh roasted and sizzling, warmed and fed him. She'd taken her chair, cushioned to hold her and their unnamed child, and served first the father, then the brother.

Ahlia spoke the family blessing. "Thank Allah for our good health. We wish you the very best for this, your thirty-ninth birthday, husband." And before her *salaam*, the explosion blew their life apart.

To the woman in the bed, he said, "Mohammed teaches that for every union of husband and wife there is a reward in heaven." Ahlia had received hers too soon. He had found his expectant wife with no innards, his bright boy with no brain. Overhead, tracer bullets and flak filled the sky. He had aged more than a year on that night and, without looking back, reported for duty with a new brand of anger.

"I guess we'll reap plenty of reward then," Annabeth teased.

"When you have died, Kleine. Only then," he said. "And then we will learn how good you have been at relieving the unendurable sexual frustration of a single man." He pinned her down and repaid America's barbarity.

Well spent, he released her, flicked the covers over her head and went into the bathroom. When he returned, she was dressed and rooting through Evy's red lacquered trunk. "Try these on." She gave him a pair of jeans and a plain white blouse.

They fit, but she shook her head in disappointment. "You look like a fag. Put this on." She handed him a wool sweater she recognized as Black Watch plaid.

He scowled at her. "Do not insult me."

"What?" She gave him a suede safari jacket that lent an air of masculinity to his ensemble.

"Homosexuality goes against the Qur'an. It states very clear, not like the confusion of the Bible or Torah, that to live like *that* is unacceptable."

"Against the faith, against the law." Annabeth thought about special interests. "There's no diversity? No room for debate?"

"What is stated in the Qur'an is outside human criticism. It is treason to criticize God."

"No wonder you hate democracy."

"It is what makes the West weak." He put his hand around the back of her neck and squeezed. "You will learn." He forgave her with a kiss and then pushed her away.

Many think it makes us strong. Annabeth's unspoken rebuttal was shushed by Evy's footsteps climbing the storeroom stairs. They quickly left the bedroom.

"My God. What a day," Evy said and went straight for the scotch, a thick-fingered double. "I've been jumpy as a cat since you got here, and everyone in town's asking about you. Let's see if you made the news." She flicked on the living room television and listened from the kitchen, where she prepared a quick meal.

"American forces were spared losses in today's desert attack, which left seventeen civilian casualties and two hundred eighty-seven wounded." A line of Muslim youth with hands behind their heads reached to the regions off-screen. "Several demonstrators were detained for questioning." Marine-clad boys herded them at gunpoint into waiting buses.

"They can't all be terrorists," Annabeth said.

"Not a one, I am sure," Omar confirmed. "Not yet. But

by the time they are released they will be." His chair rocked with rage.

"This just breeds hatred," Annabeth said. "Same as it did in Southeast Asia."

"History repeats itself," Evy commented, setting their plates before them.

"Yes, and as before the underdog gains sympathy," Omar said. "They do not report that eighty-five percent of Indonesians are against the US and half the Saudis support al-Qaeda."

"No, they think it's a hundred percent." Evy said.

The newscasters broke for commercial, and when they returned, led the local report with photos of "these two suspects" — Evy's guests' faces shared a split-screen — "wanted in connection with a bomb threat received yesterday."

Annabeth imagined herself in line for the bus.

Evy let her fork fall to her plate. "You're in a jam, girlfriend." She held Annabeth, whose tears fell in silence. "What are you going to do?" Omar looked away.

Annabeth withdrew and wiped her eyes. "I don't know. It's all a misunderstanding, Evy. But we can't stay here. You'll be in danger."

"I've been in danger since this afternoon. If they haven't figured out by now that you're here, it's unlikely they will."

"We should turn ourselves in," Annabeth announced. Omar gave her a wide, blank stare. "But safely," she added. "Evy, you still have your taxi on the road?"

"The minivan?" Evy had the blank stare now. "Yeah, but it's been parked all winter."

Omar sensed the opportunity and admired Annabeth's quick thinking.

"Please? I really need your help," she said. A puppy in the rain could not have seemed more abject. "If we just show up on post, we'll be shot first, no questions asked. Probably at the first roadblock. But, if we slip past and go to someone reasonable — my foreman would be our best bet — we can explain."

Annabeth paused for effect, a forlorn supplicant. She should be in recruiting, Omar thought, impressed by her natural talent.

"Will he listen?" Evy accepted this as the best option so far.

Annabeth laid the play book open and the team took their positions — hers shovelling the driveway to the road, while Evy plugged in the battery charger and checked the fluids.

Omar stayed indoors and dug into the first-aid kit. He couldn't risk going outside and being identified, not even down the short path to Evy's garage. Also, he felt he had done enough shovelling for a lifetime. He used the time alone to gather up the few of his items that Annabeth had salvaged and put them in her carryall.

When the women returned Omar was in the shower. He heard their voices as he stepped out.

"Omar," Annabeth called to him in the bathroom. "While your hair's still wet, come and sit down at the table." He did and she draped his shoulders in a towel. Another she rubbed through his hair. She fished scissors out of her bag and started cutting.

Fine curls darkened the *Fairbanks Daily News-Miner* spread over the floor. Finished with the scissors, Annabeth folded up a dropped lock in a corner of the front page. She picked up an electric trimmer and, when she was done, a fresh brush cut bristled from Omar's white scalp. She stood before him and appraised her efforts. "Not bad. What do you think?" She gave him a hand mirror and looked up to see the live form of the image he saw in reflection: Evy, wearing bright orange gloves, stood in the doorway of the bathroom with a bottle of hair dye in one hand and a stick of PowerPro in the other.

"I found this in my bathroom closet." Her voice did not quite match the movement of her lips, a poor translation of her horrible awareness.

Omar lowered the mirror into Annabeth's bag. Then he brought up a nine-millimetre and held it with both hands. "Annabeth." He did not waiver. "Bring me those things."

"A handgun? In my house?" Evy turned on her. "Are you crazy? How could you! I've got the only hunting store in Alaska with no gun shop. No guns on my grounds. Ever!" She threw the dye bottle at her best friend, and the tirade worsened until a cloud of plaster dust exploded out of the wall behind her.

"Quiet," Omar ordered, in calm control.

"I thought I was helping you get on post to turn yourselves in, not to carry out your mission."

"It is a pity you do not think that now. But you will get us on the post." Omar had put his hand on Annabeth's shoulder and drew her close. "Are you afraid to die, Evy?"

She nodded, speech caught on her trembling lips.

"Do not be." He pulled Annabeth tight against him. "If you disobey me, *she* will pay the price." The muzzle of the nine-mil pressed into his fiancée's left cheek. He kissed her on the right. "Paradise awaits my love after her demise. Nothing awaits you. I think a lifetime of guilt will be more effective." The safety jumped to red.

"No! No! Don't do it." Evy rushed toward them. Omar released Annabeth, who took a step back. She wore a look of ugly surety.

"You will not interfere with us."

Evy nodded agreement to Omar's command.

"Good. I cannot hold a gun on you all night and, I can tell you, it is painful to be tied up for hours."

He kept the gun, and Evy, while Annabeth squirted bottled blonde over his stubble and dabbed a touch on his eyebrows. As it set, he shaved off his moustache. In short order he became Phil Sikopolis, a supplier whose visitor's pass Annabeth had copied. She took a couple of Polaroids of Omar in front of the powder blue shower curtain, and switched the mug shot. The second snap she cut and pasted onto Phil's Oregon driver's licence. The skill she used on the forgery showed she was no novice.

Evy had sat cast in stone during their preparations and now, in the early hours, she fought sleep on her lumpy kitchen chair. Omar kicked the aluminum leg, startling her and scraping the floor. "Show me where you found the dynamite." He took their drowsy accomplice by the arm and led her into the bathroom.

"There." She pointed to a collection of beauty products and unwashed towels in the bottom of the closet. Annabeth pushed the laundry away from the stash.

"Where is the rest?" Omar asked.

"Downstairs," Annabeth replied. "I hid it under the

office stairs, behind the desk." Together they marched to the cubbyhole stacked with blocks of orange explosive.

"Both of you, bring what is upstairs down here. I will make my tool caddy ready." Evy made a weak protest. "Get to work." Omar put Annabeth in charge.

Alone behind Evy's closed bedroom door, he tossed her wardrobe on the bed and pulled the drawers and shelves out of the steamer trunk. He fitted the space for size and replaced one divider on each side. Satisfied, he flung open the door and called the women. They stood agape at the scene of plunder within. "Take this crate downstairs and put in the dynamite," he said. He pushed Evy, who moved in stunned obedience.

A new man, with tools packed and a forged work order for commissioning tucked in his breast pocket, Ahmed was ready for shift change.

From the minivan's passenger seat, Ahmed kept his gun trained on his driver. Annabeth was tucked in the back with the goods. Rotating lights grew brighter at Sixth and Richardson as they approached a pylon-sided path. "Slow down," Ahmed said, jamming his weapon against Evy's side. "I am going to conceal this"—he pressed the cold metal into her ribs—"but be certain, I am ready to use it. Stay calm and answer only what you are asked." He slipped his hand with the gun in his outer pocket. "Put your seatbelt on."

They were safely buckled in when Trooper Ray Lacroix waved them to the side. "Surprised to see this thing on the road," he said when Evy lowered her window.

"Special occasion." She offered him her licence and registration.

"Won't need that today, Evy." Lacroix bent down to look inside and said, "Howdy." He stood up. "Who's that you got with you?"

"A fare," she said, then turned and asked, "Tell me your name, again, Mister…?"

"Sikopolis. I pressed her into service, officer, when my car, it would not start this morning." Ahmed made a worried laugh. "Is this going to take long? I am a bit late, and they are waiting for me to start commissioning." He produced the work order.

Ray's eyes slewed over the form. "Identification, sir."

Ahmed gave him Phil's licence and inched closer to Evy, who was starting to squirm. She stiffened when he laid a hand on her to reach out for the documents the Trooper returned.

"What's in the back?"

"Calibration instruments," was Ahmed's ready reply.

"Uh-huh. All right then. I'll announce you to the guards, and you can be on your way." Lacroix spoke into the radio mic clipped on his lapel. "They'll be expectin' you. Drive safely, Evy."

"Goodbye, Ray," she said.

Ray looked up. Was that tenderness he heard from her? Her window was already raised and her tail lights receded. He radioed for a recap of the suspects' descriptions.

The dull black semi-automatic was out of Ahmed's pocket. "Well done. Yes, a good practice for the next control," which came much too soon for Evy's liking.

An armed guard stepped out of the gatehouse when they halted at a placard—VISITORS WILL STOP AND REPORT—fixed above the post entrance.

The guard lowered his firearm. "Sikopolis?" he asked. Evy nodded, dumb, and gripped the wheel with both hands. Ahmed proffered his documents to the guard who read every word and checked the photo. "Turn your head, sir." The guard detected no deformity in Ahmed's replacement photo. "Wait here, please. Do not exit the vehicle."

Inside the hut, the guard made a brief phone call and returned. "The foreman is on his way from the inner gate. You must wait here. Pull in there." He pointed to secure parking.

Ahmed pocketed the orderly paperwork and asked, "Do you have a dolly I may use? The instruments are delicate."

"Affirmative."

While the guard was occupied, Ahmed slid close to Evy. "You have saved the life of your friend and I congratulate you. Make no mistake, however. If you alert anyone, both of you will die."

She quaked with anger and shot him a defiant glare. "I will do anything to get away from you."

Ahmed unloaded the chest, during which time the foreman arrived. "I've told the sentry we'll be in the mechanical-electrical room on the new post," he informed the guard. Evy didn't wait for them to finish the hand over and made good on her getaway.

The foreman drove like a maniac, and Ahmed watched the toolbox with Annabeth inside riding out the curves. He ignored the shifting thunk he heard as they rolled over a bump and hoped the foreman did, too. At a mandoor and loading bay enclosed in corrugated metal, they parked, unloaded and entered. A ramp dipped to a congested tunnel they followed single file. "These are our utilidors," the fore-man explained. "We work in them all winter."

Ladder trays full of wiring hung from the ceiling, which barely cleared their heads, and they brushed against weeping pipes. At an intersection a sentry stopped them because Ahmed had failed to display his pass. Clipped on his jacket, it got him into the electrical room without a hitch.

"Here she is," the foreman said with pride. He stood before a row of metal clad units with indicators flashing from floor to ceiling.

"May I see your copy of the specifications, please?" Ahmed asked his empty-handed escort.

"Of course. They're in my office. Follow me." The foreman took a step in the lead, but it was his last as Ahmed's arm closed around his throat and his hand pressed the nape of his neck.

The phalanges of the vertebrae snapped first — c3, 4 and 5. The torque on the spinal cord exceeded tensile strength and severed. His victim stopped breathing and slumped to the ground.

Ahmed dumped the deceased behind an air handling unit and flicked open the latches on the red lacquered trunk.

FIFTEEN

Corporal LaRouge and Edwin Stoneman entered the call centre together. They'd returned when it was obvious the extraction crew would need hours to free the explosives magazine. The officer went straight to Fanger and accepted a Yukon handshake — fresh coffee put into his hand.

Edwin found Donjek and brought him into the crowd. "I want to take my son home now. So you sign off on his hours, okay?"

"Gladly." Sergeant Felix jotted "level-headed in a crisis" in the space for notes before putting his signature on the community service report. Donjek held it between his bandaged fingers, and Fanger walked him to the door.

"We'll meet at breakfast," Fanger said.

"What if something comes up?" Donjek didn't want to miss out.

"I'll come and get you myself," Fanger said, but not before a meal and a long sleep, and a shower. "Get some rest. It's not over yet," he said. Edwin caught up to them. Donjek nodded and helped his father out the door. Marty was in the care of Erik and Jenn, who had returned from Tok as the fastest woman in the Yukon.

At Felix's suggestion that they escape the racket of the race centre, they gathered in the bar at the Gambler's Den. Seventies-era naugahyde chairs sat empty around aged Formica tables under dim lighting filtered through rows of liquor bottles on shelves behind the bar. Fanger hitched up onto a stool in the best-lit part of the room and lifted his feet to the rail below.

He asked the underworked bartender for "two Chilkoot and something like breakfast right away." The beers and a glass were set before him. The glass remained dry as Fanger drank the first lager like water. The second he nursed over a hot Denver and fries. He had no idea that, while he ate to kill starvation, Felix and LaRouge were propping him up.

Before he could pass out in his chair, he was poured

into his bed, and a DO NOT DISTURB sign was placed on his door. When he returned to the race centre hours later, the bustling atmosphere was replaced by a pall of tired wakefulness from the few volunteers left staffing the phone bank. Fanger poured himself a lukewarm coffee.

The mayor poked his head into the room and brought in the rest of his bulk when he spotted the auxiliary. "How long you staying, Fanger?" he asked.

"Don't know; I just got up. Why?"

"Oh, nothing. I'll just add your room to the RCMP's tab." The mayor put his hand in his pocket, checking that it was well lined, Fanger figured, and took out his keys. "Night," he said, and left.

"Good night," Fanger responded to the swinging door. Was that a dream? he wondered. No, more like a nightmare. He shuffled down the hall to the bar where the now overworked barman tallied up an order and nodded in Fanger's direction. "Last call for off sales."

"Six Hi-Test." A lively crowd heckled a TV behind the bar.

"Fanger!" LaRouge called from the dark end of the room and waved him over to a table he shared with Felix and Erik near a large screen. Canadian and American networks had picked up the feed from local stations and were reporting the story before all the facts were in. On a third set at the end of the counter an all-news channel aired the hardline demanding the border to Canada be sealed.

The roaring boos and popcorn bombarding the screen were quelled by the appearance of a towering stranger who rushed Fanger and lifted him from his seat in a crushing bear hug. Only one person had the strength, and the nerve, to do that — Fanger's long-time friend, Hannes Bock.

"Halt! Halt." Fanger gasped for air. "Meine Guete," he coughed and Bock put him down. The two RCMP officers stared in mute astonishment until Fanger explained. "Some friends are allowed to take liberties. Besides, I've known Bock so long, I couldn't stop him. Ein echter Kumpel." He looked at his solid friend warmly and asked, "When did you get here?"

"Before, for one hour. Here, on the streets is no traffic." Bock's foreign grammar gave his sentences an odd structure, except when he waved the waitress over and ordered. "A beer and a Glenfiddich, quickly." He put a twenty on her tray and winked. "And a beer for me, also." She smiled at the suave hiss in his English.

They sat in the swivel chairs on either side of the sergeant, who said to Fanger, "We didn't expect you until morning."

"I woke up restless. I thought I'd come down for a coffee and a smoke." Fanger took a roughed-up pack of Drum out of his jeans. Bock took it out of his hand.

"That stuff will kill you. Smoke this," he said in brusque German. A blue and black pack of Schwarzer Krauser landed in Fanger's lap. "There's a six-pack of Flens upstairs for you, too. And ten or twelve bars of Aldi Schokolade."

Fanger opened the pouch and breathed in the moist flavour of new tobacco. He tucked a healthy pinch into a crisp paper and wrapped it up. The first drag was like a drink for a parched man. He savoured the aftertaste in a swirl of neat scotch.

"Cheers," he replied to Bock's *Prost* and the glass tapped the bottle. "So other than beer and chocolate, what have you brought for me to work on?" Fanger asked in English.

Bock indicated the sergeant and corporal. "Your Kollegen asked me the same thing. I was waiting for you, for help. Also, schnell auf Deutsch."

Fanger listened carefully, since the split-brain exercise of translating after each pause in Bock's report fell to him. "Well, the overall situation will be familiar," the auxiliary said to the Canadians, and added, "Especially to you, Erik." The race director nodded; he'd read the headlines in Germany. "But the set up is new.

"In Europe there are about twelve and a half million Muslims, most of who are busy living peaceful lives. But an echelon maintains Muslim law." In the face of LaRouge and Felix's perplexed looks, Fanger clarified. "Visa holders, students, exchange workers, refugees — they are easy targets. Most have family in the Middle East. They're bullied into co-operating, performing small tasks — carry a message or meet a stranger."

LaRouge grasped the idea first. "We want you to be a suicide bomber and if you don't we'll torture your family until you agree."

"Do it for Allah." Felix understood. "With violence to enforce decisions."

"Omar Ahmed is that violence," Fanger said.

Bock confirmed it. Fanger continued the explanation of an active network of cells following orders from a fluid leadership.

"The Syrian community is particularly oppressed, kept in fear with constant beatings and rapes. Staatsschutz,

Germany's inland security, had been working for over a year to make a case that will hold."

"Lining up witnesses who would testify," LaRouge said. To Bock, he asked, "Is this the case you were talking about on the phone? The one that ran to ground?"

Bock nodded. Fanger cited those on the victim list. "Wives, the elderly and children, and the doctors who treat them." Fanger paused. "It's hard to speak up when your house is burning down. From what Bock says, the BKA did succeed in gathering enough evidence to convince the justice ministry to issue warrants for arrests."

Fanger caught his breath, but before he could lift his beer for the last sip, Bock urged him on with a curt "mach weiter."

"Things were looking good to crack the cell," Fanger continued, "and maybe get further up in their organization when, a few days before the case was to open, the ST was told the government would not proceed with the trial. But now the jig was up; it was public record. Family and friends of the witnesses knew who the traitors were."

"Over a year of work, pfiff—weg. Nothing," Bock said.

"My God. What happened to them?" Erik's imagination of the worst was confirmed by the look between Fanger and Bock.

"That night the emergency wards of local hospitals were very busy," Bock said. "So was Mordkommission."

"Homicide," Fanger said. All who listened squirmed. "The BKA could not protect everyone. At their mosque in Hamburg, the imam used the incident to encourage resistance. He meant against Ahmed and his sort, but the message was received as a call to arms. Bock and the rest of the BKA are certain the cells harvested a new unit."

Bock added, "With your information the ST can question again the known offenders and many new ones. Sorry, one more time, please," he said, and launched into another lengthy explanation to Fanger, who scribbled notes on a coaster.

"Okay, schnell auf Englisch," Fanger said, and translated for the Mounties. "What they were able to confirm was Ahmed's active membership in a cell known to the BKA. After the ST's case was dropped, they lost contact with him, nearly ten months ago."

Felix counted months on his fingers, then looked at Fanger. "That would fit with his early June arrival in the Yukon."

"Also, when Ahmed heard about the Arctic Ultra," Fanger continued, "he presented the idea as a possible infiltration method, figuring it would be easy to enter Alaska from the Yukon. He was financed as the man on point, to check it out, set it up and if possible make a trial run."

"This is no trial," LaRouge said. "It's his revenge mission."

"It's impossible to comprehend," Erik commented in a low voice.

"Ahmed's motivations are not yours and mine," La-Rouge replied.

Bock added another fact. "Two days vor I come here, the ST had a new lead from Ahmed's cellmate. He had supported Ahmed to the others and, it is not hundert pro, but he might have helped Ahmed make a private small-arms sale with family living in Vancouver."

"Avery will know what to do about that," LaRouge said. Fanger groaned. "What? Border Enforcement's his old unit. Also, he doesn't think much of you either," the corporal said. The whole detachment knew Fanger had ruffled Avery's feathers in an earlier case.

"What happened next?" LaRouge looked from Fanger to Bock.

Bock looked from LaRouge to Fanger. "Ende. Schluss. Eine von unseren Kolleginnen hat mich informiert."

"Right, one of our *female* colleagues told you." Fanger laughed at his friend's embarrassment and told the others how much the women of the BKA loved Hannes Bock. He returned their affection happily, when it opened dialogue between the departments. "Bouquets are probably still growing on desks all over headquarters in Wiesbaden." Fanger had no doubt a few were seen blooming in Berlin's Abteilung Staatsschutz, too.

"Come on, Corporal." Felix rose when the laughter quieted. "These two probably want to catch up on cases."

"Bed's calling," LaRouge agreed. The officers said good night. Erik returned to the call centre.

When they'd left, Fanger suggested, "Let's go up to the bar in my room. This one's closing." He tucked his fingers between the cans in the six pack from off sales and carried it upstairs. "Here." Fanger stopped Bock at the second door on the left and put the key in the lock.

"Give me your key, I'll bring the bottle of Obstler I smuggled in," Bock said.

"You didn't," Fanger admonished, and tossed him the fob. When Bock returned, the bathroom door was shut and steam and light were pouring out the crack at the floor.

He took one of Fanger's Hi-Test, but in his too powerful hands, the pull-tab snapped off. He found a Leatherman on the dresser and stabbed the can to open it. At that moment Fanger cracked the bathroom door and called out, "Do you have a beer for me?"

Bock brought one to Fanger who, with a towel wrapped around his waist, was standing on his dirty jeans and combing his hair. Through the hot fog, Bock reached for a glass on the vanity and emptied his can into it. "You're really awake now, aren't you?"

"Yeah, my time's all messed up."

"Good. Then I can tell you everything that's happened, in one language."

"Please. Translating is pretty demanding."

Bock took his drink to the dresser and sat by the drapes drawn over the window. He checked his watch and wondered how long it would take Fanger to ask after Inge, the woman Fanger had met on a case over five years ago in Germany. Without fail, whenever they spoke, Inge was a topic of conversation.

Reflected in the bathroom mirror, Fanger could see Bock deciphering the beer can. Now would be a good time to ask. "Inge?" Had Bock looked out for the woman Fanger had nearly called wife?

Bock glanced at his watch; less than five minutes. "She's fine, still running the hotel," he said.

"Is she seeing anyone?" To his mirror image Fanger shook his head. Inge had given him plenty of good reasons why she felt compelled to stay in Germany, but not one of them was "to hook up with another guy."

"Doesn't seem so. We don't have her under surveillance."

Bock couldn't understand the couple's stubbornness, so melodramatic, letting ideals keep them apart.

Fanger opened his duffel on the bed. "Did housekeeping bring up my clothes?" He remembered how he'd abandoned his sled on the street, but not how his clothes got there.

Bock nodded. "You're changing the subject."

"No, I'm changing my clothes." Fanger pulled a work shirt on over his T-shirt and a clean pair of jeans over his Stanfields.

Bock wouldn't get any further on the topic of Inge. Fanger was obviously sorry he'd brought it up. They killed their beers over political affairs.

"Did I tell you what happened after the talking stick was returned?" Fanger asked.

"No. I thought the case was over with the handler's arrest." Bock passed a Flens to Fanger. The cap popped off with a satisfying *floop*.

Fanger told him about Donjek's circle sentencing and the part the talking stick played in their present case. He emphasized how Donjek had impressed him with his reaction to the days' events.

"Respect, Fanger," Bock said. "You've earned it from the Ureinwohnern, and the younger generation."

Had he? Fanger considered if he'd won the elders' respect. He could only hope he had Donjek's.

"Fanger, you awake?" LaRouge called from the hall.

He opened the door. "Yeah, come in."

"No time." LaRouge took the beer from Fanger's hand. "Detachment called. The military's on the phone downstairs."

Across the hall, Marty came out in his pyjamas and terry robe. Dishevelled and disoriented, he shuffled beside Sergeant Felix. "Is it Annabeth?"

"No," Felix snapped, and then softened his tone. "It's Master Sergeant Orez. They're putting him through now." He turned to LaRouge. "Where're the others? Ted? Rick?"

"Gone back to Whitehorse. Rendezvous." Felix rolled his eyes and muttered an incoherent complaint. At the end of the hall, he thrust open the call centre doors. Erik buzzed around the room that hummed along with the fluorescent lights overhead.

They took their seats at the strategy table and Erik connected to speakerphone.

"We're here, Master Sergeant," Felix said.

"I apologize for the hour; you're my last call tonight. We've been in conference since nine o'clock and I wanted to update you. Based on your intelligence we've loaded our firefighters with retardant to douse small nitro explosions and, if they've rigged a big bang, we'll fall back to muster points outside the blast zone. For now, all is quiet."

"Perhaps they've seen reason and called it off?" Felix suggested, half-heartedly.

"Nobody's turned themselves in," Orez said. "A friend of Ms. Secord's is being questioned, but she's maintaining they haven't seen each other."

The sergeant put the soldier on hold. "Marty. Shall I ask him?"

Marty, his features tortured, nodded. Puffy red sorrow rimmed his eyes; Fanger doubted he'd been able to rest at all.

"Ms. Secord's husband is here. Is there anything you can tell us?"

"We are proceeding with the protocols against terrorism. When we capture them, they will be prosecuted to the full extent of the law."

The PATRIOT Act. Marty choked off a single sob. "Please find her. Just end this."

Erik led him out of earshot and remained to comfort him.

Felix lowered the volume and asked about the terrorists. "Is there indication Ahmed is progressing with his plan?" Out of respect for Marty's distress, he avoided mentioning Annabeth, although she was clearly implicated.

"On post? Slim." Orez's reply had a hint of bravado. "Hey, what the…?"

"Master Sergeant, is everything all right?" Felix asked.

No response. "Master Sergeant," he said louder, and louder still, "Master Sergeant!"

Seconds ticked. Each looked to the other and jumped when the master sergeant issued orders to the call centre. "Monitor this line; it may be the last one open. I'm going to investigate." Orez's communication with the Canadians ended with the slide and slam of the phone being tossed into a desk drawer in Alaska.

The blank space of an abandoned conversation filled the room. Fanger whispered, "Have they succeeded?"

"We won't know until Orez returns, or we see it on the news," Felix said. LaRouge was already rolling a television trolley closer.

SIXTEEN

"**Alone at last**," Ahmed said to the blinking panels in the empty mechanical-electrical room. He'd reached his destination at Fort Greely and, with Annabeth at his side, penetrated the underground heart of the GMD. He took Annabeth's hand and helped her step out of the cramped caddy.

Fumes from the dynamite had turned her green at the gills. She massaged the aches earned tumbling around in transport. He kissed a bruise that darkened her face. "A small wound," he said. "Hurry. We have much to do." Annabeth turned to the wall for support. She'd endure any abuse to be reunited with Marie.

Confident at having thwarted the Canadians, who possessed the most knowledge, and the Americans, on the alert for they knew not what, Ahmed worked his plan. It would take all day for the finishing touches.

Annabeth groaned and rubbed her back. "I sure got bashed around in that jeep." She went to her toolbox at the panel wall, spun the combination and dropped the locking rod. Inside was a lanyard with a pass she'd ripped off a labourer. She hung her altered identity around her neck. "It didn't do much for my nerves, either."

She took an insulation tester to a panel that didn't appear on any specs because, supposedly, it wasn't hooked up. "A dummy unit for testing," she'd said whenever asked. Inside were all the controls for the network she'd linked from the communication vault on each missile silo to its breaker in the three-hundred-square-foot brain.

She worked on the panel, with her back to Ahmed.

He removed a package of PowerPro from the trunk and wheeled the dolly to a recessed corner. This close to success, he avoided testing Annabeth's loyalty with a display of the foreman's lifeless remains. He stripped the murdered man and folded the arms and legs over the torso. The body filled the trunk where Annabeth had been jostled black and blue. Ahmed squeezed in the clothes and forced the latches shut.

"Omar." Annabeth was ready for him. She stood where the turquoise legwires sprouted from the circuitry. He pushed one, then another of the probes, not unlike meat thermometers, into the bars of explosive gelatine. The sticks he packed into a tight compartment Annabeth had installed. The enclosure would increase the pressure of the blast.

Beside him, Annabeth, on her knees, twisted off marrettes capping the leads she'd fanned through the new post to all six targets. She linked the legwires to her panel and stood, supporting the small of her back.

"Okay," she said. A device equal in size and weight to a model airplane remote was in her hands. "This is my Megger, a resistance tester. Although it's meant to gauge the grounding of high voltage, we're going to use it as our arming device." She traced the wires from the dynamite to a breaker. "These nine sticks are spliced in here." She pointed to another cable. "That's our main power source. It comes in from the loading bay, and it's wired to run through these six terminals to the silos before looping back here to fire this room. Everything's in parallel, which requires the least power to ignite the caps." Annabeth twisted the single dial on the face of her Megger and watched the readout reset.

"This little box creates a thousand-volt charge, but more importantly, it gives us the one amp per silo we need for the firing current."

She packed up the rubber-coated tester and strapped on her tool belt. "All that's left is to rig the vaults." Annabeth opened the door a crack. The passageway was clear, and Ahmed pushed the dolly carrying its gruesome cargo into the utilidor. Annabeth kept her head down. Seven hundred and fifty construction workers were contracted to this site; only one had to recognize her to ruin everything.

Twists and offshoots in the warren of tunnels confused Ahmed. The grimy walls pressed in and obscured his view. He, a man never at the mercy of another, was at Annabeth's.

She whispered, "Freeze." Ahead, two guardsmen crossed a disc of light thrown into an intersection by a single bulb overhead.

"Who are they?" Ahmed demanded when they disappeared into the darkness.

"Battalion. Some specialty outfit, but if that's as close as they come, that's fine. I don't need a closer look."

"We will make it," Ahmed said. "Go." He ordered her to lead him along ductwork, around communication exchanges and past waterworks branching left and right. Initials, numbers and arrows stencilled on the walls pointed in every direction under the missile bed until the signs thinned and the only code remaining was siv, silo interface vaults. Annabeth made a sharp right to a niche in the tunnel.

"It's busy up there. Look like you belong." She charged

forward with the stressed-out stride of her co-workers and halted at the door.

An MP with a pair of fully automatic helpers came forward and asked her business. "Commissioning." Annabeth stood behind her filched pass and kept her eyes on the name over the soldier's breast pocket. Thank God it was no one she knew.

Ahmed produced his work order and turned Sikopolis' visitor's pass face up. The soldier's weapon swung like a hammock while he read the documents. "You're cleared. Stay within the zones designated on your order." They forward marched.

"I saw him earlier," Annabeth said.

"Reinforcements," Ahmed replied. "Still they cannot find us, and we are right under their noses."

"Yeah, well now's not the time to get cocky."

They reached the first vault, pulled the probes and wired in without incident. Annabeth ran a systems check on the completed circuit and noted the time. Forty minutes to wire one silo and there were five more missiles on the field. But it wasn't simply a matter of a few more hours of work. The risk was navigating the utilidors.

Between the first and second vaults they were plain lucky. Annabeth knew the plumber from her shift who approached them, but she slipped past unnoticed when he entered the men's room. They quick-marched to the third; Annabeth shut the door on an officer who, at that second, exited from the door opposite. The officer thought nothing of civilian trades going into the silo vault. On the way to the fourth, Annabeth intentionally invited conversation with a couple of technicians who were strangers to her. She charmed them into giving such detailed directions to the loading bay that she could have walked there and back in the time it took to explain. Ahmed slipped into the vault and waited impatiently.

The far end of the corridor seemed uninhabited, and they jogged to the fifth silo. But, when they tried it again to reach the final panel, a lone guard blocked their path and demanded they halt.

It was the other half of the dynamic duo Annabeth had spotted earlier, but the "state your business" he uttered came from the back end of an all-too-familiar weapon. Ahmed prodded her to answer. She approached with their passes and paperwork held like a talisman.

"That's close enough." The soldier shifted the weight of his rifle to one arm and held up a flashlight with the other. A yellow halo passed over the work order, then clicked off.

Annabeth pushed their luck. "I haven't seen your unit here before. What'd they call you in for?"

"Secure the missiles. There's been a threat. Surprised you haven't heard about it."

"Uh, no," she said and tucked the documents into her coveralls. "Been focused on my work, getting this thing up and running," she said, pointing at the missile silo. "Just in the nick of time it seems." She hoped it masked her nervous tremors.

"Yes, ma'am. But until this is over be careful where you tread. I might have killed you, you know." He returned to his post. "Carry on."

And they did. Like rats in an alley they dodged staff and sentries by a whisker.

Eight charges per silo left them with a dozen sticks for cover. "Let's get out of this maze," Annabeth said, closing the door on the last vault.

She could have beaten Omar in a race out the door, but she kept to his purposeful gait past all the checkpoints, to their coats in the electrical room and through the utilidors to the loading bay door. Outside, she steered him mere steps to a blind corner she'd discovered in the army's video surveillance. She removed the cover from a junction box exposing her renegade power service.

"Here's where we hook in." She attached the alligator clips from her ground tester. "On, off, push here—the whole place goes bang before your very eyes."

"Are you sure it will work?" Ahmed asked.

Annabeth's voice tingled. "It did when I tested a cap in the bush on New Year's Eve. Let's go try it out on the old post."

It had been dark when they'd arrived in the morning and it was dark again. Ahmed opened Evy's trunk and took out the foreman's clothes. "Put these on and stuff your jacket under his."

"What?" Annabeth's question sounded distinctly untrusting. "Omar, what have you done?"

"Nothing, Annabeth." He cajoled her, as he would have Marie. "Do not worry. I took these from his office when I tied him up. You were locked in this box, yes." Ahmed dropped the clothes and loaded the trunk in the jeep that the foreman had parked by the bay doors that morning.

Annabeth picked up the pants, skeptical about the fit, and used them to hold her parka against her belly. With her hair under his toque and the hood up on his snow goose, she would pass the thirty-mile-an-hour test.

"You drive." Ahmed got in the passenger seat. Annabeth peeled along the edge of the missile bed, a mile of spoiled boreal pockmarked by silo caps — festering blisters of destruction. There was one last hurdle — the control gate between the field and old post. Usually she was waved through, but usually she wasn't in disguise.

"Remember," Ahmed said. "You are the foreman. Drive like the boss."

During her reckless approach to the booth, she assessed the atmosphere: slack. The barrier was up, and the guard looked bored. She breezed by his window, concealing her face in an acknowledging wave and couldn't believe it when she got one in return. Apparently, the military felt more threatened from the outside than within. Or they've underestimated us, she thought.

She cut the jeep's lights. The old post, built to accommodate fifteen hundred residents, had a weird emptiness. Wind shushed the kids' gym equipment jutting from a sheer ice playground, where a slide, without the daily polishing of children's behinds, rusted. The drive through desolation was as depressing as Annabeth had ever seen it.

Well behind them was the post administration building where terrorism topped the agenda of an energetic meeting.

Master Sergeant Orez and Deputy Commander Thurlow, with the Canadians' help, had compiled Annabeth Secord's full biography, from her high school report cards to her last performance evaluation.

"'Does not play well with others' seems to be the over-all impression Ms. Secord makes," Orez said to Colonel Lewis, who chaired the meeting.

"Specifics, Master Sergeant?" She uncapped her pen.

"Expulsions and juvenile charges for fighting while in school. Complaints of disturbing the peace in Canada. She resisted arrest at an anti-American demonstration. It all stopped when she married. She settled into a quiet church-going lifestyle, had a daughter and supported her family on a journeyman's wage."

"Until now," Thurlow broke in. "We've got a tough kid who grew into an angry young woman and has developed into a crazy mommy. It's obvious she blames Defense for her horrible childhood, and the Syrian fostered her desire for revenge until it equalled his own. To neutralize that threat we need to eliminate it, on sight."

Orez kept his opinion to himself, but it was seconded when Colonel Lewis said, "No. Pruning the branches is not enough. To root this out we need to see how deep it goes. Then everyone will pay the consequences."

Thurlow, apparently satisfied with the promise of harsh justice, conceded with a single nod.

"And regarding Ms. Secord's current work and social life, what have you discovered?" Lewis directed this question to Yukon Flats' manager, Clive Kalupik, and the project manager, Jeff Weatherton.

"She kept to herself," Weatherton said. "A few of the fellows were quite sour about her. Seems she'd shut them down pretty hard when they showed a personal interest."

The facilities manager spoke next. "We've identified Evy Simpson, Ms. Secord's only contact in the community.

Ms. Simpson owns the Bull's Eye, the bow hunting outlet on Route Four, and she runs Delta's taxi. Yesterday she denied all knowledge of Annabeth's whereabouts when State Troopers questioned her, but our security team did report her arrival at Fort Greely this morning."

"I was not notified." Exasperated, the colonel threw down her pen. "This constitutes a gross breach of security."

"Ms. Simpson's business was legitimate," Kalupik said, attempting a defense. "And her access was minimal. Both the road block police and the post guard verified the fare's documents."

"What do we know about her fare?" Colonel Lewis snapped, on her feet now, pacing.

Weatherton answered. "Phil Sikopolis, from Last Frontier Systems Controls. He was scheduled to commission the installation of their components."

"Do we know where he is?"

"At home in Oregon. He was under the impression the commissioning was postponed."

"I can't imagine how he got that impression," Colonel Lewis said. "Okay, so the terrorists used Sikopolis' identity to gain access to the base. Who was their escort?"

"The shift foreman," Orez said.

"And has anyone seem him?"

The men braced in sheepish gloom for the colonel's growing storm.

"No, ma'am, we have not," the master sergeant replied. "But shortly after Ms. Simpson cleared the police control on the Richardson, State Troopers contacted us for a description of the suspects."

Colonel Lewis sat and put her hand to her head, a

gesture that seemed an attempt to squeeze logic out of what she heard.

"Are they holding Ms. Simpson?"

"Yes, ma'am. She's right outside."

"Hallelujah. Bring her in." The colonel stacked her reports and placed them face down. Orez opened the door to a trooper who sat beside a bedraggled woman. They stepped forward and Orez presented Raymond Lacroix. Ray led Evy to a seat at the foot of the table, a plank of ash separating her from Colonel Lewis. Lacroix placed a manila folder in front of the colonel and took a seat near the civilians.

"Ms. Simpson, you dropped off a man named Phil Sikopolis at Fort Greely at ten minutes before eight o'clock this morning. Is that correct?"

"Yes ma'am."

"Did he discuss the purpose of his business with you?"

"No." Evy used a well-wrung tissue to wipe her mascara-smeared eyes. The colonel coaxed out a distraught version of the lie Ahmed had given Lacroix at the roadblock.

"Ms. Simpson, it seems suspicious that after having your taxi parked for the past five months you chose to take your vehicle out of cold storage for this fare." The colonel passed the file to Thurlow who held it so he and Orez could skim the pages. "Describe your passenger for us."

Evy made a tearful description of a clean-shaven blonde man.

Thurlow cleared his throat and sat forward. "You're very popular in the local peace movement, Ms. Simpson. The media have often captured your low opinion of American defense policy, especially during your divorce from the general. Irreconcilable differences. Was that why you left him?"

"My husband left me — for the bottle."

Evy's bitterness spurred Thurlow's antagonism. "In these court documents, he states you left him. For another woman no less. What can you tell us about Annabeth Secord?"

Enraged, Evy declared, "She's the best woman I know."

Thurlow badgered her. "Did she leave you for another man?"

"Who I fuck is none of your business, asshole," Evy spat back. "And who Annabeth fucks is none of mine."

"Why didn't you come forward sooner, as soon as she contacted you? Why did we have to come looking for you?"

"What option did I have? They showed up nearly dead. Later, Ahmed said he'd kill her if I talked." Evy collapsed into sobbing incoherence.

"Show Ms. Simpson out," Colonel Lewis ordered, annoyed. To Lacroix she suggested Evy be kept in custody. "If she's been in contact with our suspects, she's in danger," she whispered to the trooper. Lacroix nodded and closed the door behind him.

The colonel recalled the meeting to order.

"So Sikopolis is not our terrorist," Kalupik said. "He's got dark hair and Ms. Simpson's passenger was blonde."

"Colour is a minor matter taken care of by an appointment with Miss Clairol," Lewis replied. "Orez, phone the installations to alert them of Ahmed's altered description. I'll inform security on the new post myself. Mr. Kalupik, Mr. Weatherton, come with me. Thurlow, double the guard here."

"It's been done, ma'am." Thurlow snapped to attention.

"Then sweep the grounds." Lewis marched out of the room and down the hall.

Annabeth brought the foreman's jeep to a stop at a run-down bunker, where Fort Greely's independent power supply was controlled by the original mechanical-electrical system. Inside, it was obvious the equipment was well maintained, but it was seedier than the reactivated site. The mechanics were oilier, shabby and worn, and the panels were scuffed, but neatly marked in felt pen where warning plates had long ago lost their gum.

Annabeth fished the legwires out of the works and concentrated on the path of least resistance. Ahmed opened the foreman's coffin for the last of the PowerPro.

"Is this enough?" she asked.

"Yes." He shut the lid; a closed casket would be preferable to a public viewing. "The charge will divert them and add confusion to our cover."

Annabeth proved their system, and then stuffed her screwdriver in her pouch. "I think I did a good job." The junk panel mounted on the wall bore her signature. "Pity it'll be shattered in the blast."

"Yes." Ahmed zipped up his coat and put the tester in his pocket.

Outside they lurked under a thieves' moon, tricks of fleeting light. Annabeth's deft fingers rigged the feed in minutes. "There won't be any panic for a moment while everyone waits for the back up generator to kick in," she explained. "But, when I bypassed the system fault indicator, I disabled the automatic switching so the generators will fail because there's no start-up signal. By the time someone comes to manually reset, which will be impossible due to the rubble, we'll be blasting the silos." She flicked on her treasured possession: the arming device. "It's live."

Rather than pass the controls to Ahmed on her left, Annabeth held on to the rubber box. She had the jitters, eager to see the culmination of her efforts. "Can I do it?" she asked.

"Do you want to?"

"You bet," she said, proud of her invention.

"The final act," Ahmed replied and rested his hand on her shoulder. He stroked the thick hair that escaped her toque and spilled down her back. A weight from his sleeve fell into his palm. The simple device trembled in her hands. The one in his was sure. His touch never left her skin at the base of her tender neck. His strength took hold, her resolve likewise.

Enraptured, he pressed his lips against hers, filled her mouth with his tongue, felt her sharp bite when his blade pierced her skull.

"When you get to Paradise, tell Ahlia I love her," he said as he laid down her life for Islam.

The Megger bounced from her grasp and he picked up the sturdy instrument. He jumped into the jeep and sped toward the new post. Life barely moved. Annabeth had been right. Only when he was out of range did he see the first soldiers approach the bunker.

Orez was among the first to reach the blast, the only bright light on the old post. He had mustered a squad on the spot. "You and you. Fall in," he said. The stink of seizing motors and flaming copper mixed with poisonous gases and boiling coolant seeped from the cracks of the concrete boiler room. For now the closed doors contained the healthy panel fire, until an eager recruit ploughed past. "No!" Orez shouted. The mechanical-electrical building shot skyward with the hot-headed hero pinned to the door, and the squad was flung to the edges of the blast zone.

Orez landed beside the fixed stare of a woman in perfect surprise. Her head lolled and Orez recognized Annabeth. The black mass in her sticky hair revealed her vitals, and he closed her eyes before searching her pockets. He found a lock of hair, wrapped in yesterday's newspaper. The pair had been here the whole time.

Soldiers stirred and Orez assessed the aftermath. Motion highlighted a jeep hurtling away from the toxic blaze and toward the new post. An approaching fire attack team aimed to collide broadside at the guardhouse.

Orez hijacked a vehicle idling nearby. He put on the set of night goggles that lay on the passenger seat and screeched to a halt to glass over the adjacent compound. From the sidelines, he cheered the spectacle of chicken; Ahmed was head-on to the fence, the pumper trucks belted alongside it. The crash was imminent.

A scrawny private abandoned his post in the instant the high beams lit the silhouette of a jeep on the guardhouse wall. Ahmed's wheels climbed the curb, and he drove straight at an awning. Clearance dropped to zero, the roof shattered behind him. The fire attack team, undaunted by their duty, came howling down on Orez, who cranked the key and stomped on the gas, desperate to get off the road. He hopped the curb in front of administration and bailed to sprint up the stairs to his office.

Could he get a message to the missile unit? He'd dropped the phone in his haste; he'd never hung up. Flinging open the office door, he yanked out his desk drawer and grabbed the phone. "Canada! Do you read me?"

"Loud and clear," Fanger replied from race command. The RCMP had left him to monitor the connection when the recovery team had called. They had the explosives magazine at the detachment. Erik was on the phone with Donjek at Fanger's request.

Orez spoke. "Power's been cut. Call Missile Defense. Secord's dead. Ahmed's heading for the silos." Silence met his report. "Confirm."

Fanger found his tongue and responded. "Yes. Yes, sir. Call the GMD. The name and number?" The digits came at rapid fire.

"They should initiate lockdown, mobilize all units and sweep the post. I'm in pursuit." Metal clacked in the background. "Stand by on this line. Oh, and Canada?"

"Yes?"

"We owe you one."

"You can buy me a beer when this is all over," Fanger replied.

SEVENTEEN

Orez secured the phone and, from his gun locker, selected a rifle. He felt the same charge he did before every skirmish, face down in Mississippi mud, his drill sergeant in his ear. *The weapon in your hands is not just a weapon.*

Under Asian artillery, *it is your bride.* In Honduran hostilities, *love and care for her.* Preventing Saudi suicides, *and she will defend you.* And now, in an arctic ambush, *to the end of time.*

He grabbed his bride and loaded her breech. With his rifle riding shotgun, Orez drove double-time.

In Dawson, Fanger relayed Orez's request to Felix at the detachment. "I'm on my way over," the sergeant said. "Don't wait for me. Make the call."

Fanger dialled Alaska. "Pick up, pick up!" The line buzzed unanswered, and he realized whoever did pick up had better believe him; Orez wasn't around to confirm the wild orders he was charged to deliver.

Upstairs was Marty Secord, grieving for his wife, unaware she was dead. Fanger had been true to his word and, in the middle of the night, Edwin and Shirley had crossed the river with their son. On arrival, they had found Marty weeping. Erik explained the exhausted racer's story to Donjek, who helped his parents take the distraught man to Fanger's room. The elderly couple had seen their share of grief, and they stayed to console the runner. To break the news of Annabeth's murder, Fanger would need their help—later. The phone was answered.

"Security."

"My name is Markus Fanger. I'm assisting the Royal Canadian Mounted Police. Master Sergeant Orez instructed me to call you. The GMD is under attack. Put me through to Colonel Lewis." Seconds ticked by in the ages it took for a reply.

"Who is this? How'd you get this number?"

"You are in peril." How much slower can this guy be?

The grunt's tried patience became open hostility. "Why wouldn't the master sergeant call us himself? Where is he?"

"On his way to you. The power went out when we were on the phone and the other lines may have failed."

"America's defense is threatened, and you get the call, in Canada?"

"Yes. A terrorist strike is at hand." Fanger gripped the phone so hard veins sprung along his carpal bones. "Instructions are to lock down, mobilize all units and sweep the post."

"We don't take orders from civilians, sir. There's a chain of command and this is not it."

Fanger didn't have time for a "safety of the free world" speech. "May I speak to Colonel Lewis? Donna Lewis."

"The colonel is not available at the moment."

Fanger tried the hero approach. "You can avert disaster. Respond before it's too late."

"You could be causing a diversion to distract us."

"Distract you?" Fanger had never witnessed such plodding logic. Felix arrived at the moment Fanger growled, "What's your protocol for today?"

"To report anything unusual," was the quiet reply.

"Isn't this unusual? Me, talking to you, on a secure line at Missile Defense?" Fanger vented steam.

"Yes," he agreed timidly.

"Then report it."

The Canadian force assembled and Fanger muffled the extension. He held it out for the sergeant to take over, but Felix declined.

"This is Colonel Donna Lewis of the United States Army in Alaska. Identify yourself, please."

Fanger's name was immediately familiar to the colonel. He reported Orez's instructions.

"Mr. Fanger, I'm standing in front of our video surveillance monitors as we speak and all is as it should be, at the moment."

"Are any cameras oriented toward the administration building?"

"Yes, several units show the old post in the background. One moment."

Fanger needed the colonel's eyes to make an assessment. "Is the power still out?" he asked.

"Yes, what's happened?"

"Omar Ahmed caused a blackout while Master Sergeant Orez and I were speaking. He fears the phones have been tampered with as well."

"It seems you've kept communication open." The colonel sounded pleased.

"Ahmed's using the darkness and confusion as his cover. Both men are heading in your direction."

"Just a minute, Mr. Fanger, I've picked up something on our monitors." Fanger strained to interpret the ambient sounds. "It's Master Sergeant Orez, on foot at loading bay eighteen. He's advancing along the wall, stalking, but there's no target. No, wait." Fanger heard her switch the orders. "He's dropped from view."

Thick emptiness from Alaska sounded like the end of the world. "Colonel Lewis?" No response. "Colonel? Can you hear me? Do you see Orez?"

"Yes," came back, countermanded by, "No. It's the

strangest thing. There seems to have been no shots fired, but Orez has gone down." The outlook was grim, as was the colonel's assessment.

"I'm sorry, Colonel. Is there any sign of Ahmed? Or what he's doing?"

For a second, nothing. Then, "No. The video is holding on the loading bay doors." Lewis sounded stressed. "Hang on, what's that? Orez! He's signalling, three repetitions. That can only mean distress." A squad of booted feet marched on her command.

"Mr. Fanger, we can chalk up any victory we achieve to you," Colonel Lewis said. She cleared the line and left the Canadian hanging.

Orez had wasted no time putting the Cold Regions Test Center behind him and had raced along the runway lights, blue beacons of electricity signalling that it wasn't too late — yet. The saboteur had not struck and, in the final lap over the defoliated missile field, he'd shortened the gap between them. Ahead, rows of silo caps studded the ground like a lethal blister pack.

A jeep idled in the distance at a loading bay door; Orez tucked into the shadows and continued his reconnaissance on foot. He'd tried the mandoor — locked — and crouched under a wall of overhead doors until he reached the far corner. Where were the battle-ready troops to defend them?

Ahmed, with his back to the world, had his fingers in an open junction box mounted on the bay wall. He kept watch on the GMD security centre and worked a spray of wires with a pair of strippers while mumbling to himself. "One, two more moments, Allah, to witness my victory."

A low whir diverted Orez when a video camera turned toward him. It reached the end of its arc and still Orez had not come under its eye. We're invisible, he realized, and slid into view. The camera fixed on his new location and transmitted the motion of three controlled sweeps he made with his arm extended. He prayed the signal was heeded, and repeated it twice.

Ahmed's position remained unchanged but for a length of wire that unravelled into the snow at his feet and the pair of alligator clips he'd attached to the stripped leads.

Orez swung his bride into position and snugged her butt into his shoulder. He followed a wedge of dark shadow until he was near enough to read the labels on a device in Ahmed's hand. And hear a toggle switch snap on.

Orez's rifle covered the target and led out of the dark. "Disarm or I will disarm you."

Ahmed reeled, the detonator in his dominant left, a nine-millimetre in his right. He protected the panel connections at his back. Orez put his finger through the trigger guard.

Ahmed laughed and put his thumb over the controls. "You, the destroyer of families, are the terrorists who will fail, yes."

Ahmed teased with the arming device, just out of sight. He led to the left. Orez followed, calculating angles through his enemy and the detonator. Ahmed blocked Orez's advance with one of his own.

Orez cross-stepped forward. "And Annabeth Secord?"

"She was a true and loyal believer in the Muslim struggle for freedom." Ahmed trained his pistol to the right.

Orez rolled aside on the balls of his feet. "She was violent, smart and driven."

Ahmed, equally spry, parried with, "She was very resourceful, yes, and proved all her skills to Allah."

"Including piggybacking her agenda on yours. You get revenge for losing your family and she gets revenge for losing her childhood." Orez gained a toe-hold.

"No. She died for the glory of Islam." Ahmed realized his misstep.

"By your hand," Orez twisted.

"It saddens me but, yes, I could not risk capture. By my hand is Annabeth in Paradise."

"Or Purgatory. Annabeth's sole friend in Delta Junction was Evy Simpson, your taxi driver. Ms. Simpson left her husband for another woman. Did that woman leave her for you?"

Ahmed balked. Had he heard correctly? It could not be possible that Annabeth had tricked him so. The very basis of his beliefs, defiled by a woman? And now the suggestion that his betrayer was a lesbian? Ahmed physically withdrew from the idea, but he clearly recalled the intimacy when the women embraced, Evy's compassion and her hysteria when she found herself also betrayed.

It sickened him, as much as the truths that he would never see his son again, never see his wife again, never see Paradise at all. He trembled and events whirled; his reputation was smeared before Allah. Annabeth Secord had reduced his pains and exertions to a crime punishable by death, and death is what Allah would have.

Ahmed gazed at the gun in one hand and the detonator in the other. One zealous gesture would right the wrong, annihilate the unbelievers and prove his loyalty. "With my success Allah will welcome me with open arms and Paradise shall be mine."

He raised the arming device, his thumb over the push-button ignition, ready to shock the world with high voltage. Orez, in position for a point-blank shot, shattered Ahmed's ideals. An angry flash escaped his rifle. A jagged war cry of hatred and revenge shattered the frigid standoff.

The shot blew Ahmed's wrist apart and flung him backwards against the loading bay wall. The dismembered handful of destruction ricocheted in a trajectory that arced toward Orez.

Still hot, the amputated wrist seared into the snow. Could he scoop up the Megger and keep the shot? No matter how Orez positioned himself, left or right, for a split second the terrorist would be uncovered. In every part of a second Omar gained advantage. One-two, Orez dropped with his rifle. He rolled with it and landed within reach of the hand.

Crystal ice cauterized the stump. Orez thumbed the toggle off.

From Ahmed's right, a burning thunderclap stung Orez's temple. Orez's rifle screamed vengeance and tore a strip off the fanatic from neck to knees.

Out of the night, a company of rifles surrounded them and kept the perforated corpse at gunpoint. Orez lowered his weapon and yanked the wires out of the circuit. Pain and wrong-handedness had impaired Ahmed's shot.

Nonetheless, blood flowed freely past Orez's eye, as freely as adrenalin flowed from his brain.

A medic arrived and placed a compress in Orez's hand. In the middle of being guided to staunch the bleeding, Orez dropped to one knee. His medic followed him to the ground and called a second attendant. They wrapped the deep graze; Orez heard vague discussion.

"That'll do."

"Let's get him to the health clinic." He was led to a waiting jeep and heard the click of the passenger seatbelt buckle around him. He flinched from the oncoming lights of army investigators swarming the scene.

At the administration building Orez whispered, "Stop the vehicle." The command was obeyed, although the master sergeant couldn't know his drivers expected him to start concussion-induced vomiting. Instead, Orez, fully conscious, darted from the vehicle, across the road and up the stairs to his office. The startled attendant caught up with the medical curiosity as Orez reached a desk and bellowed into a telephone.

"Canada!"

Fanger answered with deafening clarity. "Master Sergeant? What happened? Were we in time?"

The Canadian's questions had a dampened cottonball quality, even with the phone to his good ear. "The installation is secure. The threat has been terminated." Overhead, the lights sputtered to life. Orez released the receiver as he crumpled. Arms caught him and lowered him onto the floor and the phone on its cradle.

A dial tone hummed into the banquet room in Dawson,

and Felix disconnected the call. The auxiliary had managed the communication seamlessly. A roomful of taut nerves eased in an audible sigh, broken when Donjek, who had quietly returned with Erik, pointed to the television. "Check this out."

On screen, media camped in the Crawford's living room. Marie and Sid were the centre of a ring of radio, TV and print reporters. Behind them ranged boom mics and cameras from stations recording every detail for viewers Outside and in the Lower Forty-eight.

Donjek adjusted the set so everyone in the call centre had a clear view. He turned up the volume just as Sid, completely comfortable surrounded by his own kind, started speaking. "It's been difficult for Marie. Even more so when the attention started."

"That would account for why she's up at this hour," Felix commented as the overtired child hammed it up for the cameras. The picture jumped to viewers from coast to coast, declaring what a brave little girl she'd been, and how sad it was about her parents.

"Let's put this case to bed," Felix said, dialling the Crawford house in Whitehorse.

The sergeant heard the phone ring on TV and watched Sid answer it. At the sound of Felix's voice, Sid put his hand up to quiet the pack of newshounds.

"The Americans stopped him, Sid. Marie's safe," Felix said.

"Oh, thank God." Flashbulbs and spotlights lit Sid's jubilant face. He kneeled to hug Marie. "We're out of trouble, sweetie. Daddy's coming home soon."

Media squeezed the heart-felt moment for all it was

worth, camera crews shot close ups of tears rolling down Marie's cheeks and her guardian enveloping her in a strong, safe embrace. Playing on emotions, some reporters crouched down for Marie's perspective. "My daddy's a hero and a really fast runner and he stopped mommy's boyfriend, so now mommy can come home and live with us."

A dozen sad smiles betrayed the discomfort of the adults who realized this little girl would need a lot of therapy. Sid's wife pushed through the throng and ushered the child offscreen.

Journalists shot rapid-fire questions at Sid. "How were they stopped? Were there any casualties? Injuries? Is the girl's mother under arrest? Will the embassy get involved?" Too emotional to speak, Sid shouted into the phone. "Thanks for the news, Sergeant. I'll call you when the circus has left town." The media swarmed around him. Both men, on and offscreen, hung up.

"I don't envy Marty having to break the news to Marie," Felix said to the solemn faces around him.

"And I don't envy whoever tells Marty," Erik replied.

"That's right," Donjek said. "He's been with my parents all this time."

"I'll tell him." Fanger volunteered for the grim duty.

"I'll come with you," Donjek offered. "Tell my folks. They'll help us." Erik, the Mounties and Bock stayed behind.

Upstairs, Fanger tapped on the door to his room, which was opened by Edwin. "How's he doing?" Fanger asked the elder.

"Shirley's praying with him right now. Come in, we'll

make tea." They followed Edwin and filled the hotel room. Donjek's mother sat beside Marty on the bed, hands clasped over his, asking for God's help and guidance.

Donjek filled a carafe with water, and when he brought it to his father for the tea, he whispered for Edwin to join him in the hall. Outside, he explained the latest events. Inside, Fanger searched for the words to convey the unspeakable. He faltered until Shirley laid her hand on his shoulder and nodded.

"The Americans have stopped Omar Ahmed," Fanger said. "He failed, and died trying."

"Annabeth?" Flat hopelessness filled Marty's voice.

Fanger glanced down and shook his head.

Rather than responding with an outburst, Marty stared with expressionless, bland grief. Saturated with torment the others could only imagine, he buckled under the overload. Shirley held him and Fanger turned away.

Edwin and Donjek returned, and the youth poured three sugars into a cup of fresh, hot tea. Fanger stirred and held it out to Marty.

In a flat, lifeless voice, Marty asked, "When will they release her body?"

"There'll have to be an investigation, and then, I guess, Annabeth can be released." Fanger would endeavour to make his guess a fact.

"Yes," Marty said. "They should find out how he killed her and tell me she died quickly." Marty put his face in his hands; sobs poured through his fingers.

Edwin, wise and sure, uttered no words of comfort, but held the man and his burden. Shirley stood and beckoned her son and Fanger to follow. At the door she said, "He's not alone." The men nodded and she closed the door behind them.

Downstairs, from every corner of the conference room, victory was telegraphed.

Erik was on the speakerphone to racers and volunteers in Alaska, who were cheering the news that they could proceed. When that died down, a perky team member repeated the formula Erik had devised to adjust the racers' overall times.

"That should make up for the hours lost waiting at the checkpoints," he said. The checker agreed and commenced reckoning in a low murmur, which Erik interrupted. "You can tell the athletes I'll meet them at the finish line."

At the phone bank, Felix, speaking to Sid Crawford again, discussed Marty Secord's reunion with his daughter. "He'll drive down with me or LaRouge. I estimate our time of arrival to be mid-afternoon, depending on Marty's condition." Undoubtedly, the sergeant had told Sid of Annabeth's demise. The reporter could be trusted to keep it to himself until the news was broken to the child.

On a third extension, Hannes Bock was talking to Germany. Fanger listened in. "It's ten minutes before half four, here," Bock said looking at his watch. "Tell Tina, or anyone in her sector at Staatsschutz, that I'll phone again at sixteen hundred." Fanger calculated the time change; it would be seven in the morning here, only a few hours away.

Fatigued, Fanger definitely wanted to spend those hours and several more in a bed. Bock, who hung up first, offered him the spare double in his room. And Donjek, who was on his last legs, could stay in Erik's unassigned room, Bock suggested.

Events replayed through Fanger's whirling dreams — black pistols held by mutilated men shooting flaming brands from the cover of wind-whipped glades on a ghost-white landscape. Irregular explosions woke him often, until he gave up and got up.

Rumpled sheets lay across Bock's empty bed. Fanger flicked on the television. The time and temperature posted on the rolling ads said it was cold and late, almost too late for breakfast. He washed and dressed and rushed downstairs to the hotel restaurant. He met the Stoneman elders as they were departing for home; race command was in the dining room.

There, Donjek held court, telling Bock and Erik about *Muharran*. "Seems the thing about death by year's end for missing New Year's prayers is no hoax."

"Well, thank God Allah was on our side this time," Erik said.

"No," Donjek emphasized his point. "According to Ahmed himself, the whole plan was not Allah's bidding. If it was, it would have worked. Obviously Allah did not want Ahmed to blow up the GMD."

Fanger ordered an omelette, then joined them, his chair in the aisle between tables.

"Allah also did not want Ahmed to try anything else," Bock said, followed by "Morgen," to Fanger; he continued in English. "The BKA called and with the new arrests we have cut out one cell of this cancer. You broke a network that was unbroken from Syria, to Germany, to Canada." Specifically to Donjek, he said, "It is not with Allah, our success. It is with you and Fanger. You should be very proud of that."

Sergeant Felix arrived. To Donjek, he said, "In light of your enormous contribution to the terrorist's capture, Donny, we can escort you into Alaska. You can get your sled. I've got here a fax copy of a letter signed by your judge and probation officer."

"Janice?" Donjek ran his fingers across her signature at the bottom of the letter, which he read a second time. "I never thought she'd trust me."

"Why not? You're a trustworthy guy," Fanger said.

"Well, I wasn't a week ago." Donjek looked him in the eye — acknowledgement that much had changed.

"That was a lifetime ago," Fanger said. He felt equally rewarded by Donjek's pride and confidence as he was by the fulfillment of a long-held debt.

He finished eating while Felix delivered more news. "I just got off the phone with Alaska. Master Sergeant Orez awaits your arrival, to congratulate you, both, personally."

"In that case," Erik piped up. "What are we waiting for? We've got a race to run." He stood up and threw his parka around his shoulders. "To the finish."

EIGHTEEN

A parade of heroes in detachment vehicles rolled out of Dawson heading south toward the Alaska Highway. In the lead, Felix drove a white Suburban with the RCMP buffalo head on the door, bracketed by the force initials in English and French. For fun he let Erik, in the passenger seat, switch on the full array of flashing lights.

LaRouge and Marty, in the second vehicle of the fleet, followed, although their wagon's festive exterior was not matched by the dour silence inside.

Next in the convoy were Fanger and Donjek in Fanger's Datsun, pulling a snowmobile on a trailer. Bock, in the rental that followed, towed his own machine. Behind him, Donjek's parents were tailed by a string of Whitehorse members returning home to M Division headquarters.

They crossed the Klondike River bridge and the caravan wove through a crazy maze of overburden, ribbons of rock chewed out of the district by hungry gold dredges.

Donjek made himself comfortable — travel mug in a cupholder, tunes playing, smoke lit. "Now that everything's over, can I ask you something?" He cracked his window open and exhaled.

"Sure," Fanger said.

"Out there, you didn't have any choice but to trust me, which I appreciate, but why'd you take me out there in the first place?"

"I told you. I needed a checker and your experience."

"Uh-uh." Donjek shook his head and waved away that response. "You could have got anyone from around here for that — my dad, Uncle Jake, local cops, anyone. But you went out of your way to get me. What was that about?"

Fanger collected his thoughts in the business of shifting and coffee drinking. "To be honest, my motivation was selfish, in that it didn't have much to do with you personally. You just provided the opportunity."

"Opportunity for what?"

"To keep a promise, I suppose. It's a bit awkward,"

Fanger explained. "When I was a kid, an old cop used to organize activities for us in the forest. Or what passes for forest in Germany. Nothing like this." Fanger looked out the window. Pure sun, the colour of raw ore, washed over the gold fields. "By the time we were your age, we were busy throwing bricks, drunk and disorderly, wreaking havoc at demos, B and Es."

"Break and enter?" Donjek gaped at Fanger. "What were you after? Cars and liquor?"

"Not quite. Cash and valuables. That's what we took when we knocked over the cop's house. We knew he'd be in the *Wald* with the kids for the rest of the day."

"What did you do with the money?"

Fanger paused before answering; now came the hard part. "My share of the bounty went into my best friend's veins." Donjek shivered at the absolute truth. "I knew he was smacked all the time, but it didn't occur to me I had a part in it."

Donjek didn't let him stop in mid-confession. "How'd you find out?"

"I found him on the floor of a public toilet in the train station. Or over it rather; his seizures were lifting him off the tiles." In reality, Fanger'd found him with foam coming out of his mouth, his fixings under him, and a pool of blood where he'd smashed his head against the ceramic.

"Did he die?"

"Nearly. I sent one of our pals to phone one-one-two — I mean EMS — and in the meantime, Christian's seizures stopped. I was holding him, wiping out his mouth and crying to him to wake up, when, suddenly, he comes to, alert but nowhere near oriented. In his hallucination he was ranting about 'blue sky Saturdays' and the Wachtmeister, the guy whose house I'd just ripped off to feed this habit."

Fanger clammed up. Donjek puzzled over his frankness for a minute, then asked about the promise he'd mentioned earlier.

"That came later. Those memories from our childhood kept Christian conscious until the ambulance arrived. Subconsciously, I guess, I vowed if Christian lived, I'd repay the Wachtmeister."

"And you got your chance with me. How did you know it would work out this way?"

"I didn't. I couldn't know that we'd be chasing terrorists through the bush."

Donjek laughed. "I guess not. So what happened to your friend? Is he okay?"

"After a fashion. He's comfortable in this new sanatorium."

Donjek's immediate thought was of his own friend. Not dead, but not well. "And the Wach-guy, the old cop?"

"He passed away years ago. It took me some time to come to terms with that, since I had this feeling of unfinished business with him. But you know, watching you and thinking about how things have worked out, I think the marker is settled."

Fanger spoke no more, and Donjek sunk into contemplation. They stopped for a quick lunch in Carmacks, and on the rest of the drive to Whitehorse Donjek propped up the Datsun's owner's manual to support a paper on which he wrote at length.

As the convoy rode into Whitehorse, Donjek capped his pen and tucked the paper into his jacket. He patted the bulge it made in his breast pocket.

At the lights, LaRouge and Marty fanned off toward the river. The rest of the vehicles maintained formation to the detachment and parked.

Donjek and his folks were staying overnight with Peter Stoneman and were first to take their leave. But before they did, Donjek showed his parents the writing he'd kept close. It was the long-awaited letter of apology; at last he could face his friend's mother. Shirley hugged her son, and Edwin beamed.

The rest of the force trooped inside to the bullpen. Noisy camaraderie bubbled out of them, bringing Ruth in full Rendezvous dress from her desk at reception.

"Prisoners! Report!" she commanded. She emphasized herself as "Madam Matron" by slapping a truncheon into her opposite hand. The sudden warping of time to a hundred years back that took place in Whitehorse every February caught them off guard. The bustling group halted.

"Prisoner Fanger, step forward." Ruth pointed the tip of her staff at a spot front and centre, marking her impatience with taps of her baton against her palm. Her soft chin wobbled in a giggle as the offender edged forward and then jiggled in a rollicking laugh when the truant auxiliary stood before her, the centre of attention. "For exemplary service in the commission of untold acts of bravery, you are hereby pardoned of all your crimes."

"Free at last," he crowed in jubilation and planted a noisy kiss on each side of Ruth's smiling face, eliciting hoots and catcalls from the rest of the force. Fanger, both hands on the receptionist's shoulders, held her at arm's length. "You look great." He admired the detail of her costume, from her tightly laced, pointy-toed shoes under the spread of her heavy black skirt, to where her figure gathered into an hourglass at her raw wool shirt. A smooth black tie led to the high collar under her tightly knotted auburn hair and steel blue eyes that held Hannes Bock, at Fanger's side, captive before her. Fanger twirled her around to read "Matron" stencilled above "Whitehorse Women's Prison" across her back.

"Rick talked me into being a Keystone Kop this year and I got carried away with my uniform." Ruth about-faced, flung a caped topcoat over her shoulders, holstered her nightstick and clapped a flat black hat on her head. "It makes people a lot more eager to get arrested," she said, referring to the iron prison cell on wheels where weekend revellers were held for mock offences against the spirit of Rendezvous. "We'll raise way more bail that way," she said. Prisoners were released when their friends paid the guards a suitable bribe to unlock the cage. The graft was then funnelled to local charities.

Bock's elbow poked Fanger in the ribs, and reminded him of his manners. "Ruth, this is Hannes Bock, a friend of mine from Germany. Did you get to meet before he went up to Dawson?" The couple shook their heads. Ruth held out her hand for the stranger to take, which he did; and did he just click his heels and bow? Fanger had never seen such formality from Bock.

"We spoke on the phone," Ruth said. "Nice to meet you, Herr Bock. You fellows ought to come by the Cap tonight, around seven. I'll be done being Madam Matron then, and we can catch the floorshow.

"Yes. I would like that," Bock murmured. He stood transfixed and watched her sail from the room.

Fanger tapped him on the shoulder. "Alles in Ordnung?" he asked. Bock snapped out of his trance and nodded; he felt fine. More than fine.

Erik invited the Germans to join him for dinner at his hotel, and all three took the opportunity to get cleaned up before their meal. By the time they pushed back, full, from the table and made their way downtown, the bars were overflowing with locals curing cabin fever. They wedged themselves in and found a table in the boozy throng.

Turn-of-the-century gamblers and prospectors, painted ladies and society wives in fancy dress mixed with the real thing on the dance floor. The band finished their set and in the midst of the shuffling patrons stood Bock's Rendezvous queen, an Amazon in silk and lace, an empress. Attired in a madam's corset, her wanton femininity embodied his every desire. It was neither the hefty nugget nestled in the cleft of her breast, nor the gold-studded garter around her ample thigh that attracted him, but the grace of her tailored figure under a full-length fur.

She moved like a cat, an Angora, toward him and purred in his ear, but her words were lost in the band's request for the crowd to put their hands together for the Kapital Kickers. The opening *ba-boom* of "Patricia the Stripper" blasted from the sound system, and a string of long-haired and bearded miners in red long johns and pink tutus shook their booty in a straggly parody of the cancan. "Remember, all you Rendezvous party animals, with a little encouragement, they kick higher and dance better."

Along with everyone else, Fanger and Erik clapped and stomped. Bock whistled and, beside him Ruth let rip with a whoop to Jerry, the last Kicker in the chorus line. Jerry sweated it out to the last note and then worked the room collecting very charitable donations; fives and tens in his garter, loons and toons in the trapdoor behind. When he neared, Bock put a five in Ruth's hand and took her picture as she folded the bill into the bulging band. When Jerry got fresh with his thanks, Bock reached forward and pulled Ruth's regal form toward him and onto his lap in the nearest chair.

"Oh, Herr Bock, you swept me off my feet." Ruth rocked, but Bock steadied her.

"Hannes. That is the idea, no?" He laughed and gave her his drink. Fanger and Erik, innocent bystanders, looked on, shrugged and put their hearts into making the real cancan girls kick the ceiling. They didn't see Bock again until morning.

Now Bock sat in the passenger seat of Fanger's truck, and Donjek slept in the jump seat. It wasn't a smooth ride as they rolled and bounced over frost heaves. Ahead a grader ploughed the highway at ninety kilometres an hour. A plume of gravel studded snow spewed into the ditch.

Bock sat with his hand holding his chin, as he had for most of the drive, not dozing or talking, but rather thinking and dreaming. Fanger wasn't going to pry, but he was busting a gut to know what had happened last night. The boarded-up service station at Otter Falls flit past, and even when they stopped for lunch in Haines Junction, Bock had said little. It wasn't until they were on the far side of Destruction Bay, beside the frozen shores of Kluane Lake, that Bock put his hands on his knees, glanced at Donjek spread out in the back and turned to Fanger.

In quiet German he said, "While the boy's asleep, I want to ask you something." He reconsidered and started again. "Do you know Ruth's children? Is she a good mother?"

Fanger delayed his answer. More was coming.

"She reads Dashiell Hammett and dresses like the Thin Man's wife."

"The girl for you, eh?" Fanger teased.

"Do you think I would be a good father?"

Fanger swerved and never answered, because just then Donjek woke up, bleary eyed and kinked. "What's up? Where are we?"

"Past Beaver Creek. That's White River on the right." Long, shallow channels braided in a mesh of half-pipes in the snow-flooded plain, except where the main current ran fastest and rarely froze. "We're almost at the border. Do you have your passport handy?"

They crossed into no-man's land at Snag, near the 141st meridian, the geographical international border. The agent at the Port Alcan stop line waved them through. Even Donjek's trump card, his letter of dispensation, was barely glanced at.

There was plenty of road to travel before they would reach their destination. All slowed at a billboard pegging this year's roadside moose kill at over three hundred, and followed the advice to "Give Moose a Brake," but after a few miles resumed speed until they reached a temporary archway on the right.

A skewed archway constructed of a vinyl banner slung on thumb-thick cord belled in the sway of the charred pines holding it taut. Four feet lower, a twice-knotted ribbon of orange survey tape fluttered in anticipation of the home stretch, and of snapping apart again on the chest of the final runner.

Flags waving in the stiff crosswind added to the fanfare at the crossroads of the Taylor and Alaska Highways. The cavalcade joined the spectacle at the official finish of the Yukon Arctic Ultra.

Erik lit the wick of a red kerosene lantern and held it aloft. The single flame, when extinguished, would end the vigil maintained until the last runner on the trail was home.

Erik separated himself from the others to speak with the checkpoint volunteers. The rest of the Canadian contingent yawned and stretched to shake off the drive. A woman in fatigues with a silver eagle on her parka joined the cluster and extended her hand to Fanger. "Welcome to Alaska, sir. US Army garrison commander Carla Lewis. It's an honour to make your acquaintance."

"Markus Fanger." He placed her then, and said, "You were my eyes when I called the missile silo. A pleasure to meet you."

"We owe you a debt of gratitude," she said. "Both of you." She shook Donjek's hand and presented him to Greely's commanding officer.

"You were the one who got word out, affirmative?" Axton asked the young man before him. "A brave warrior."

Praise from the lieutenant colonel, his hand upon Donjek's shoulder, translated into respectful awe, and a faint blush on Donjek's part.

Last in the informal receiving line was Master Sergeant Orez who, with both hands, gave Fanger a vigorous handshake. "There's a man who's earned a beer."

Greely's top brass mingled with Canada's finest until Erik hung up his satellite phone and swung the red lantern. The last runner was spotted about a half mile out. "He should be here at any moment." Fanger and everyone else strained and heard measured steps tamping down the crusty trail and into the flickering brightness at the end of the three-hundred-kilometre route. A moment in the kerosene limelight was the finisher's reward.

"It is with appreciation for the accomplishments of all of you that I am able to present this red lantern to runner number 314, Lorenzo Abruzzi of Italy, in honour of his safe arrival at the finish line and the successful completion of this, the third running of the Yukon Arctic Ultra. I declare this race officially closed." Erik blew out the flame and passed the red lantern to the last-place finisher.

Mittened applause, whistles and whoops nearly drowned out the racer's halting acceptance speech. "Tired. I am very tired. It was hard." Erik uttered a few words of Italian to congratulate the exhausted runner and took charge of caring for the last man in.

The lantern was quickly relit by Fanger, muttering, "Can't stand on ceremony forever. It's dark out." In the meantime, everyone—Bock, Donjek, the Mounties and military—swapped stories for the Stoneman parents, and pieced together a complete picture of how each one's actions affected the other. They were spellbound by Orez's account of the bomb detonation.

"It took some false logic on my part, but I cast a moment of doubt in Ahmed's mind. That was all I needed to line up the shot and disarm him. I was amazed, really," he admitted. "I couldn't do it again if my life depended on it."

"Luckily, you only had to do it once," Fanger said.

"I heard you had your close calls, too," Orez said and turned to Donjek. "So what next, hero?"

Donjek laughed. "Well, maybe something peaceful and quiet, like finishing high school. But then?" He shrugged.

"The military?" Orez asked. "You'd have a future in the armed forces." The crowd of friends and family listened closely.

"I thought about that, but after working with you" — he nodded to Fanger and the pair in Red Serge — "I was leaning more toward the academy, in Regina." The soft, tanned faces of his parents nodded to him. "Keep the family name in the RCMP," he added. Fanger's beard creased in a broad grin.

Their hosts reminded them of tonight's dinner in their honour and Colonel Lewis had her staff car lead the convoy directly to the PX on the old post. On the way, Donjek asked Fanger about his community service. "Did those reports ever get to Janice?"

"Oh, sure," Fanger assured him. "They were sort of a thick crumpled bundle when I handed them in, and I told her they were incomplete, but if she wants to know what happened, she can buy a newspaper."

ACKNOWLEDGEMENTS

The people I'd like to thank fall into two categories: those who were a source of information and those who were a source of encouragement. Then there are Yukoners and the Yukon Arctic Ultra athletes, race director Robert Pollhammer, and all of the volunteers and organizers who are a source of both.

To the people who were sources of invaluable information, thank you for the open and generous answers you provided to my endless questions. Diane and Fred Sullivan shared their experiences at Fort Greely, the Yukon Powderhounds and Sled Porn stars fuelled the chase scene, Yukon Explosives provided a crash course in blasting, Chuck Morgan and Eric Meyer entertained me with their backcountry snowmobiling escapades, and Jorg Hofer lent his trapping expertise, all contributed to this book. Former M Division media liaison Brigitte Parker and Gabrielle Noll of Staatsschutz Meckenheim (now headquartered in Berlin) were my sources on the inside. Your input brought *rom Ice to Ashes* to life and any inaccuracies you detect are purely my fault.

Yukon writers contributed substantially to *From Ice to Ashes* in all its forms, providing guidance and nurturing through careful and thorough critiques. Special acknowledgement goes to Marcelle Dubé, Claire Eamer, Eleanor Millard and the Round Table Writers. Outside the territory, I received early encouragement from Joan Clark, Edna Alford and the September 2004 Writing with Style participants at the Banff Centre for the Arts. Over the border, Gabrielle Herkert held my hand when I made my first foray into the world of publication, for which I shall be forever grateful. Freelance editor Lynn Vannucci also provided invaluable feedback as the story unfolded.

The local media, especially Tanya Blakeney from CKRW and *What's Up Yukon,* helped with marketing and publicity. Monika Broeckx assisted with German publicity. Thanks also to ultramarathon athletes Shelley Gellatly, Keith Thaxter and Tammy Reis for sharing their Ultra experiences with my readers.

Special thanks also to the Alaska Sisters in Crime, who hosted Bouchercon 2007 where I found enthusiastic support from established authors Simon Wood, Kelli Stanley, Vicki Delany and Rita Lakin.

And, of course, to my ever-patient husband, Mike Simon. I assure you the writer aliens have almost completed their experiments on me and I'll be home any day now.

Writing is a solitary task that can rarely be accomplished alone. Thank you for giving me a story that stems from all of us.

Jessica Simon has called the Yukon home for over twenty years. Currently a literary arts columnist for *What's Up Yukon,* Simon has contributed articles to *San Francisco Chronicle Magazine, Outdoor Edge, Yukon News* and *Yukon, North of Ordinary.* Before devoting her life to the written word, she worked as a typesetter, first-aid instructor and guide for a wilderness tourism company for German-speaking visitors to the Yukon, which she co-founded with her husband. She lives near Whitehorse.